I0597864

I didn't know what they wanted, but I wasn't waiting around to find out…

I brushed cobwebs from my brain and analyzed what had woken me. Heard the deck's French doors rattling. *Again?* Found my baseball bat and tiptoed into the living room to investigate. Turned on the light and stared into an unshaven face on the other side of the glass. An angry young man's face!

"Nate! Tracy! There's a babe in here!"

I didn't wait for Nate and Tracy. Didn't bother asking the young man's name either. He didn't look like date material. I headed for the garage, hearing the door's glass break behind me, thoughts of gang rape and that drugstore girl's spread-leg mutilated body giving wings to my feet.

There were more of them outside. I gunned the motor and backed over two with satisfying thumps and crunches—who needs a gun?—and continued backing onto the road. Threw the big SUV into drive and flattened another dude just as he shot twice, peppering me with safety glass shards and leaving me weaving like I was a drunk riding a wounded hippo. Fought for control and then tore off down the road, one jerk firing at me.

The PCH never looked so good! I turned south toward LA. Took Sunset inland and pulled into a strip mall where I sat shaking, knowing I'd avoided rape and death, as well as an accident along the way, dodging both human and vehicle corpses. *The world's going mad!*

The apocalypse kills billions—numbers so large that most survivors' minds snap shut. Foes of the US have attacked with a bioengineered contagion that spreads around the world. One of only a few survivors, Penny Castro, ex-USN diver and LA County Sheriff's Deputy, reacts differently. She fights back and creates a life for herself where death is the common denominator. On a forensic dive, she is interrupted. When she surfaces, she finds all her colleagues dead, so she has to battle starvation, thirst, and gangs of feral humans until she ends up in a USAF refugee camp. A post-apocalyptic thriller for our times, Penny's adventures will entertain and shock you into asking, "Could this really happen?"

KUDOS for *The Last Humans*

"If Dr. Asimov had written a post-apocalyptic novel, it might read something like *The Last Humans* by Steven M. Moore. It is packed with action scenes, and at the same time is thoughtful and introspective. Readers will find themselves caring deeply about Penny Castro and the members of the family that she creates from the wreckage of society after a biological attack devastates the world." ~ Scott Dyson, author of *The Inn*

"Shocking and intense, this chilling tale will keep you glued to your seat, turning pages as fast as you can. You won't be able to put it down." ~ Taylor Jones, The Review Team of Taylor Jones & Regan Murphy

"*The Last Humans* is a chilling account of the best and worst of humankind in a world where law and order is a distant memory. Combining marvelous characters with nail-biting suspense, Moore has created a poignant and intense tale that you won't soon forget." ~ Regan Murphy, The Review Team of Taylor Jones & Regan Murphy

THE LAST HUMANS

STEVEN M. MOORE

A Black Opal Books Publication

Lied 3

As products of pleasure and perhaps pain,
We are brought into this world of tears.
We yearn to return to the womb again,
Yet we cling to life, hiding our fears

That death is somehow a terrible thing,
A world of darkness, a world filled
With black angels who will sing
As they fight for our bodies that are grilled…

By the long summers of good friend Death.
How wrong we are, for death is a return
To the state before our first breath.
It is human nature to never learn…

That the waters of our lives fall to Earth
To flow where we dwelled before our birth.

~ from *The Poems of Benjamin Thomas*

PART 1

Survivor

"We are living on the brink of the apocalypse,
but the world is asleep."
~ Joel C. Rosenberg

CHAPTER 1

The steel cable attached to the metal cage containing the body was no longer taut. I'd just removed some construction blocks that had kept the body on the ocean's floor—snip, snip, with my wire cutters to free the body—and rolled it into the cage. Took pics of the "crime scene" before that, of course. Not hard to do. Instead of a spear gun for fishing, I carried an underwater camera mounted on a selfie stick on my back, the whole kit fitting into a slim holster nestled between my air tanks. Even had a light—didn't need it on that dive. Also had to perform a few other CSI tasks too—not many, though, because forensics underwater was always limited.

I had tugged on that cable to tell the guys above me to haul up our victim. It should have resisted my tug, but it seemed to be broken. Sure 'nough. Could see the end floating down from its own weight toward me. *What the hell?* I thought. Wasn't easy to shake your head underwater with a mask and mouthpiece, but I would have done so on land. *Penny Castro, you're seeing something new on this dive.*

I'd felt something new too. A couple of muffled booms like a few USN destroyers doing target practice above me by firing salvos at a Channel Island, and the sea floor shaking enough to feel it in my finned feet. That was all before seeing the falling cable. *Cause and effect? Had our little dive boat exploded above me?* Sheriff's personnel were targeted just like other cops, but targeting a department's boat would be a first. Didn't see anything else floating down, though.

George had picked me up at my apartment. My deputy friend gave me a wink as I tossed my duffel on the old patrol SUV's backseat and then climbed into the passenger side. I was dressed modestly in a beach cover-up with my deputy's badge pinned to it, but I'd left it open, revealing a skimpy bikini. No way would I wear a wetsuit all the way to the dive. His wife would understand. He knew that, so the wink was just him being a Latino.

I would have made a play for him, of course, if he weren't a married man. Generally good-natured with a full head of hair and enough gray around the ears to be interesting, he had treated me well from day one when I joined the department. Old gruff Sheriff Hancock, not so much, but I'd come to respect him too. In general, all guys at the substation, wary at first to have a woman join their ranks—saw that in the navy too—came around as I earned my stripes. Helped that I could do things they couldn't do. Also helped that what I did had only a peripheral nexus to their own work.

George took one call from Marge, our dispatcher. Her voice sounded like everyone's sweet old grandmother, even with the com unit's distortion. She'd been a deputy for years, but she had wanted to spend more time with her kids, so she became one of the huge department's official voices on the airwaves, a job not without its own stress but with more regular hours. She'd grown up in Fresno but found employment in SoCal after receiving her degree in criminal justice. I loved the old Okie almost as much as I loved George. She was my West Coast mother.

My East Coast birth mother was in a New Jersey facility for Alzheimer's patients.

After talking to Marge, George was quiet as we drove along PCH toward Leo Carrillo State Park. I eyed him. Sure, the highway was busy and motorists were avoiding us like we carried a contagion—flashers on the top of a sheriff's patrol vehicle and sirens were responsible—but his focus on the road after that wink was a bit suspicious.

You tried to help people who were your friends. "Anything wrong?" I said.

"Angela and me. We had a bit of a verbal battle. I left her crying."

Knew his wife was expecting her third. *Men! Sometimes they just don't get it.* "Want to talk about it?"

"She's moody lately. She wanted a normal morning where we could snuggle and cuddle. I was willing until Marge called. Angela took maternity leave too soon, so she's bored. And I have a job to do."

"Cut her some slack, asshole. She's the mother of your kids, and she loves you."

He nodded. "I love her too. If I were rich, neither of us would work, and we'd both stay home and enjoy raising our kids together."

"Aren't rich, won't be, so get beyond it. Buy her a bouquet on the way home tonight to patch things up." I turned my attention toward the traffic too. "Marge didn't tell me much, and she only confirmed the crime scene just now. What's the story?"

"Fisherman reported seeing a body below his boat and informed the LA Sheriff's Department. He'll be waiting for us. Paul and Zeke are on the way too. We'll question the fisherman there while waiting for Baldy and the boat."

The dive boat, *Wave Queen III*, was my launch platform for ocean dives. In rivers, ponds, and lakes we used smaller crafts the SUVs could tow. The *Queen* could also launch a speedboat to go after perps who tried to escape. The US Coast Guard often helped in the latter or took over when circumstances called for it—mostly newsworthy chases for drug interdiction, gun running, and terrorist activity. Like the ATF or FBI, DHS agents didn't receive too much love at the LA County Sheriff's Department. I didn't consider them publicity seekers, but some deputies did. I thought we just worked at different levels.

'Course, I might be prejudiced. Knew the prevailing opinion in the department, likely shared by the police, was a twist on Tip O'Neill's quote—yeah, I'd studied US history— all real law enforcement was local. I understood the sentiment, but I was ex-navy, so I thought the feds had their place. Especially coast guard guys, who did so much and did it well.

❧❧

I'd been under for twenty-plus minutes and had discovered the body almost at my 180-foot limit. Half-covered with sand and silt, the ocean had already begun its job of returning the vic's body to its evolutionary home. Some fish had recovered from having an intruder in their midst, and those bold fellows swam around me, trying to figure things out too. *Maybe they were around when the body was dumped?*

Hadn't believed much of the fisherman's story when George and I arrived and we spoke to our "witness." Guy looked a bit like an old rocker. *Had he been smoking and communicating with Jerry Garcia?* We watched moments later as he paced a bit and muttered to himself. Voice had been shaky. The fisherman seemed fishy.

Okay, he'd just seen a dead man. Okay, the water was clear enough and the bottom almost white sand. But seeing a body at that depth seemed a bit of a stretch—you're looking where your cast goes, after all, not beneath your boat—but some light filters down even to about 600 feet. Not my business to distrust him, but I mentioned these doubts to George before the *Queen* arrived and we went out, and he had agreed to have others keep an eye on our "witness" while I did my shtick.

I had sat on the diving platform as the boat moved away from shore. Could see some of those water desalination plants north of our path, huge man-made Channel Islands, some still under construction, part of an expensive solution to the area's drought problems. They lost some priority in the monsoons and good snow cover in the mountains for a few years, but they were coming back, hence the plants' construction. Government becoming proactive for a change. The previous long drought had taught everyone a few lessons.

I wondered during my dive: *Do functioning desalination platforms increase water clarity?* I'd have thought what they discharged likely made it worse. Probably an eco-discussion somewhere online I should read. The state was crawling with eco-activists. More power to them as long as they kept out of my way. My support stopped when they became eco-terrorists, though. Putting spikes in trees so chainsaws would recoil and kill and maim loggers was unconscionable.

Understood enough of the new technology to think desalination plants might do some good, but also thought the jury was still out, especially when it came to the ocean environment. Sucking in salt water and using tech magic to remove the salt and produce fresh water seemed okay, but discharging super salty water back into the sea might have unforeseen consequences. *Yeah, I understand: the Pacific has a lot of water. Still...*

Solar and wind were supposed to solve the energy

problem too—energy experts had been saying that for years—but usage just increased faster than power production. Water consumption was similar. The state was between a rock and a hard place. I thought the overall solution might be moving a lot of people somewhere else—maybe Alaska. If they paid me a lot, I might go. Would encourage Angela and George to do the same. Must be hard to provide for a large family these days—the economy was like a roller coaster.

The victim on the sea bottom didn't care about any of that, of course. And now I was faced with a problem. Decisions, decisions. *Penny, you're alone on a dive just doing your job, stuck with a broken cable and a wrinkled, gray, and water-logged stiff, and there's no one around to tell you what to do.* I made up my mind without over-thinking it, though. Left the body there on the bottom—figured that in the cage he wasn't going anywhere—and headed for the surface. Passed the descending cable on the way up. Its end looked shredded like it had snapped. Metal strands trailed behind it.

☙❧

Our dive boat had drifted away from my dive point. Or, maybe I swam sidewise a bit? Fifty yards was nothing for me, even in full scuba gear. If Olympic swimmers had fins, they'd halve their times. I took peeks to see if I could figure out why the cable had snapped. Couldn't see anything obvious or anyone standing on the boat who looked baffled—no one standing, period. I swam to it and swung onto the diving platform.

"Baldy?" I called out after removing my mask and mouthpiece. "George?"

Baldy was the deputy who piloted *Wave Queen III* when we had to go into the Pacific, which was often enough to keep me employed and him with a sizeable gut because the secret beer compartment was usually well stocked. We also teamed up on dives in inland waterways—those dives were often more difficult because of the terrain and dirty, weed-clogged water. I found it amazing how many murderers think weighing a body in deep water or tossing a murder weapon there will hide their nefarious deeds. *Not if Penny can help it!*

George was more friend now than coworker; Angela and he had invited me to some family functions. Their kids called me *Tia* Penny. I wasn't anybody's real aunt. My SOB brother Roberto had never married as far as I knew. Didn't think he had any kids either, but I knew he fooled around.

I shed my tanks, fins, and mask, slipped out of the wet suit, and went exploring. Found the two deputies soon enough. They were both dead. Stunned for a moment, I stared into the distance at the islands and desalination platforms, tears in my eyes. Wiped them away with the back of my hand, just putting more salt into my eyes, and began examining bodies.

Their bloated red faces looked like they'd stuck their heads in a blast furnace—too red for an hour's exposure to sun and sea breeze. They had already sported nice tans and wore Dodgers caps too. *California's the Golden State for many reasons.*

Their tongues were swollen. Did they suffocate from that? Nostrils were pinched and the pupils in staring eyes dilated. I thought of allergies. What'd they have for lunch and where? Couldn't have been the same place. Weird if they had the same allergies too. Maybe food poisoning? The pupils in their staring eyes were dilated like they'd just visited the ophthalmologist, but whites were red-veined. I closed the eyes. If the ship's deck was a crime scene, I'd already mucked it up anyway.

I decided further examination was a job for the ME and not the CSU. Climbed stairs to the wheelhouse. Handled the *Queen* before, so I'd have to take her in.

"Well, shit!" I said to a few gulls circling in the sky. "Fuck the body. Fuck the dive. Fuck this job. I'm heading for shore."

By the time I arrived there, I didn't have any answers to my questions. And there were more questions on the way.

CHAPTER 2

The situation onshore proved that something strange was going on. The two other deputies, Paul and Zeke, were also dead and exhibited the same physical signs as Baldy and George. So did the fisherman who had seen the body underwater. His boat was still beached on the sand, parked next to the dinghy used to go back and forth to the *Queen*.

I fought back vomit and then went to George's SUV.

"Hiya, Marge, Deputy Penny Castro here," I said into the com unit. A bit of frying static, but no response.

Found my cellphone in my duffel bag. Our substation was on speed-dial. Again no answer. Malibu wasn't far. I couldn't be out-of-range. Looked at bars. Yep, lots of signal strength. In LA you could go into canyons or behind mountains and lose it, but not on the beach.

I looked around. It was October, so you wouldn't expect to see a lot of beachgoers, but waves were coming in high because of a storm far offshore, so you'd expect to see a few surfers. *Nada. Nadie.*

I sat cross-legged on the sand. *What now? Did the world just end while I was underwater?* Thought of George and his family. An ominous and prescient image of the family's bodies made a chill travel along my spine.

Lower lip trembled. *Bummer!* Hugged myself and rocked a bit, staring at the crashing surf. *Am I the last human on Earth?*

Didn't want to be that person. Considered walking into the Pacific to drown myself. Doing that without my wetsuit in the cold water would wake me up if I was just having a bad dream. Reconsidered. *I can drown if it isn't a bad dream!* As much time as I spent in and under the water, drowning in it wasn't on my bucket list. Probably not on anyone's! Davy Jones was just the Grim Reaper in disguise. I didn't want to meet him in any form.

I wasn't too religious. I'd observed there was a lot of evil in the world, but human beings create it. I saw God as some super-engineer who set up this whole experiment and was now watching it unfold. I'd never seen an ET, but was pretty sure they were out there, so we were just one small section of the whole experiment. No, my anti-suicidal beliefs stemmed from the idea that we're given one chance at making a go of it, so we better play along with the experiment and be happy we have that chance. Call it a defeatist/optimistic attitude: we're born, we live, and then we die, so make the most of the living part.

I pinched myself instead. Cried, not because it hurt, but because, by doing so, I knew my friends were really dead. *This sucks!* Here I'd been in a comfortable time of my life and the world decided to put me through the wringer yet again. *What did I do to deserve this? Yeah, okay, section of the experiment! I'm beginning to feel like a rat in a maze.*

You might say I was being a bit theatrical, but the primordial silence—just pounding surf and seagulls' laments—was unnerving. I wasn't much of a social animal since I lost Ned, my navy SEAL boyfriend, but it was nice to have some human beings around all the same. Marge had been like a mother. George's family had been my surrogate family. I had a good job and a roof over my head.

I stood up, dusted myself off, and returned to the SUVs. Realized George's fob was likely still in his pants, but his body was on the boat. No way would I use the dinghy and go back for it. Found the fob for the newer SUV in the pants of one of the dead deputies.

I started it up. Everything seemed fine. Turned on the AM/FM radio. Static there across both AM and FM bands. Same for police bands. Not a good sign.

At that time, survival instincts kicked in. Okay, maybe a bit of panic too. Had six-packs of bottles of fresh water but no food. Decided to drive to a McDonald's nearby. *Was I deserting my job? Not paying proper respects to my dead colleagues?* Didn't much care. And they weren't going anywhere. I needed a Big Mac and fries before I could make any serious decisions.

⅌⅌

When I drove into the parking lot, I saw the long line of cars at the drive-thru window and groaned. Too many people wanting unhealthy food. Or was the rush caused by yet another "new healthy menu"? *Who the hell wants a salad when you can have a Big Mac with fries?*

I then noticed the cars were either still running or out of gas, which I confirmed by leaning into drivers' windows, already opened so they could give their orders. They all seemed to be taking a nap. Bloated red-faced, swollen-tongued, pupil-dilated drivers and their passengers taking permanent *siestas*.

I went inside. Eat-in customers and staff were dead too. Had spilled food all around because diners had collapsed, pushing food off the tables. I started to back out the door, stopped, and shrugged. Fought down puke.

C'mon, old girl, you've seen dead bodies before. Not that many all at once, of course.

Went to the case where heat lamps were still on and found Big Macs with cheese and fries. Stole a paper cup and filled it with ice and coke. Normally, they'd charge an extra dime if you wanted ice—water was becoming scarce and expensive again and electricity less scarce, but even more expensive. Found an empty table and sat to eat my free unhappy meal and think. File that under contemplating my mortality. *Is this my last meal?*

I had a good imagination. Things like an ET invasion, huge solar storm, Second Coming in the *Book of Revelations*, scientific experiments gone awry, biological warfare, and others—all went through my mind as I finished my McDonald's feast. Seeing no obvious evidence for any of those—*but why am I still alive?*—and not receiving any divine inspiration from those Golden Arches, symbol of religious bliss for fast-food-niks everywhere, I policed my table and returned to the sheriff department's SUV. Time to drive to any substation.

LA County, like many California counties, was huge. There were bigger ones, like those Sierra-foothill counties in the Big Valley. But LA County was the most populated county in the US, not just the state—or was. Everyone seemed to be dead now. I had to swerve around dead bodies and vehicles, some still running at a standstill with no driver's foot on the gas pedal, others probably out of gas, and a good number in clumps of damaged vehicles, with some pileups with flames still flickering after cars had smashed against each other. PCH was always a busy road, but the highway was one huge obstacle course back to the substation.

Substations were sprinkled around the county, forming something like NYC's precincts because of the dense population. I'd applied for a diving job with the NYPD—

they wanted me to go to cop school first. My home base, Malibu/Lost Hills, was a smaller one in Agoura, although it was newer than most. Found a space in the parking lot and went inside.

Lovely old Marge was dead at her dispatcher's console. Grumpy old Sheriff Hancock just happened to be there, dead at his desk with his face half-buried in a piece of cherry pie. Other staff were dead too, including the captain. Even Tod, the bleached-blond mail boy who had tried to convince me to go surfing a couple of times—I can swim and dive, but I don't surf.

All those people had the same symptoms. I went into the ladies' restroom and heaved up my McDonald's meal. Nothing wrong with the fast food. Just that without AC, the stench of death was increasing, making the place smell worse than a cow barn on a hundred-degree day.

No AC? I flicked a light switch on and off. *No electricity.* Not a general phenomenon, considering the McDonald's I'd visited, but right there at my place of work it meant no computers and no communications. No connections to the outside world. *Is there an outside world?*

Those thoughts led me to wonder about all the nuclear power reactors in the world. Most modern ones could be shut down. The key issue became the coolant pumps because the pile kept running for a while. I remembered that on the navy's nuclear-powered aircraft carriers, they had onboard emergency backup with generators and batteries, but maybe those old reactors, many as bad as Chernobyl had been, might not have backup electric power for those pumps. I thought that I might not want to be near any nuclear reactors for a while!

I supposed similar questions could be asked about hydroelectric and solar power. Maybe those dams just kept pumping out power even if no one used it. I couldn't say

I understood the national power grid—I was just like everyone else, taking everything for granted. Originally those desalination platforms used solar to power their equipment. What was going to happen when the panels started failing?

I washed my face and cleaned my hands and then went and closed a lot of staring eyes of people I'd known, some for years. Marge, the harridan with the sweet voice and heart of gold. The gruff old dog who was sheriff, a man who was a fair but strict taskmaster with a bark worse than his bite. Eyed the sheriff's badge. Decided I didn't want his job. Captain's either. Figured there was no one left to pay me even if I did. I was on my own.

I sat shaking in the SUV a bit and thought about where to go. Decided to return to my apartment.

CHAPTER 3

y townhouse complex wasn't far from Angela and George's house, so I stopped there first. Shouldn't have. The quiet and peaceful neighborhood of ranch homes and rental dwellings was filled with death. Under the unforgiving sun, the stench was becoming as unbearable as the meats' at McDonald's. Men, women, children—dead kids made me want to dry-heave all over again. The red, bloated faces were mostly peaceful though. Maybe they hardly knew anything was wrong? Who could do this?

The world had always been a violent place, but World War One had begun a trend where war became not so up front and personal. Sure, there were boots on the ground, but aerial combat and bombing missions could inflict major casualties and destruction that armed forces couldn't see until the advent of recon sats. With cruise missiles and ICBMs, war ops at a distance were possible, making consequences of an attack something detached and remote. Chemical and biological weapons could focus on killing people and leaving infrastructure intact.

Ned, my boyfriend in the navy, and I had talked about this a lot. Human beings' ability to maim and kill other human beings was out of control. But we slogged on, deciding that anything we could do to limit fanatical and paranoid psychotic leaders' abilities to do harm was a positive contribution.

Everyone, including Ned and I, had been worried about nukes from North Korea or terrorists getting hold of nuclear weapons, but whatever had been launched at us was just as lethal even though less violent. Didn't know what it was. I'd concluded it didn't much matter. Saw the results. Friends and colleagues were dead. Innocent people I hadn't known were dead. Why was I alive?

Decided to bury Angela and the two kids in the backyard in the shade between two small trees George had planted—three kids if you counted the one inside her.

That was tough and took some time. I didn't know if I achieved the prescribed six feet. Environmentalists encouraged cremation now. Damned if I was going to look for a drive-thru mortuary that performed them. Probably no longer functioning. I fudged a bit by creating mounds. Found some scrap wood in the garage and made crude crosses. Remembered some holy words from my upbringing, said them, and then felt guilty about wondering why any loving God would do this to this perfect family. Or anyone else? *Maybe because George is really Jorge Maldonado?* I just called him George. Angela had kept her maiden name out of convenience for work—she was Angela Bautista. Maldonado plus Bautista should have been neutral. Kids were Mary Jo and Joey, for the ubiquitous Maria Jose and Jose Maria. Crazy thoughts about names. They were just labels for human beings, but my internal dialogue showed how bummed I was.

But maybe God the Engineer's love for everyone in the Universe was spread too thin? The Universe was big, and maybe one purpose of the experiment was to see what shit His creatures could do to each other? If I was supposed to have some revelation about the meaning of it all, it wasn't happening. My Id, Ego, and Super-Ego weren't even talking to each other, let alone listening for divine inspiration. And don't ask me what that meant—I was a bit overwhelmed then.

After the holy words, I sat on the lawn and cried. Made Angela a promise to return to the dive site and give George a burial at sea. I thought he'd like that. Baldy too. Didn't think they were going anywhere, so I wanted to go home and take a shower and change clothes. That plan went up in smoke. Not literally, but I couldn't bear the stench of more ripening bodies when I arrived.

Some neighbors were retired old codgers. Their bodies were baking in the sun by the pool. Frank, my immediate next-door neighbor, one of those nice, interesting gay men a woman just wishes wasn't gay—I thought he was a bank manager somewhere, but wasn't sure—hung over his balcony attracting flies. *Wouldn't you know moscas survived!*

In some sense, these people were family too—not close, but a lot closer than strangers. More names I'd want to remember if only to honor them in my thoughts.

I changed, emptied my diving duffel, and packed it with clothes and personal necessities as if I were sailing on an aircraft carrier from San Diego that evening, and tore out of there back to the PCH, Malibu, and beyond. There was only so much death you could take at one time. And I knew I didn't have the energy left in me to bury all the bodies.

On the drive, I thought of nights I'd spent playing chess with my neighbor Frank and discussing the problems of the world. I'd known another gay guy well…

❧❧❧

Joey Archer, one cook on our carrier, was as WASPy

as they come, except for being gay. The don't-say-don't-tell period had long passed, but macho seamen still harassed gay ones, albeit not as openly. A bunch of us, Joey and Ned included, were playing poker one night when one jerk crashed our jovial party in drag, using an old mop as a wig and sporting outrageous scarlet lipstick.

"Hey, pal Joey, want to fuck little ol' me? We can screw each other in the ass until the rooster crows."

I glanced at Ned who just looked embarrassed. I stood up and faced the SOB with my hands on my hips. "You want to try to screw someone, go find a goat, you bigoted bastard. That's your speed!"

The goat idea had just come to me. It got his goat. Saw the drunk's right haymaker coming my way, stepped inside it, and gave mop-head a tap to the chin. He went down. I waited. He stood up and went for me, but Ned stepped between us, punched the SOB in the gut, taking the wind from his sails.

"Sober up, asshole. And develop some human decency, or you'll never fly a Tomcat again."

I smiled. The Tomcat was an F-14, the navy pilots' old standby. Knew that punch had hurt. My SEAL, Ned, was tough. Stuck out my tongue at my attacker. He avoided Ned and me for a long time.

The peculiar thing about that incident was that I was responsible later for saving the asshole's ass when the cable broke as the tailhook latched on. He had come in too fast. Landing on a carrier wasn't an easy task. This pilot had done it many times, but it only took one little loss of concentration—or a cable that suffered metal fatigue. That landing deck was huge but still not a landing strip on land. He and his F-14 landed in the drink.

A rescue at sea off a carrier wasn't easy. A rescue-squad teammate saved the wingman. I went after the asshole. At sea in this case meant high sea state—five-foot waves in stormy conditions. No chance of launching a chopper. No rain. That squall had already hit us and left. At sea also meant a lot of swimming and motorboats to catch up with the carrier afterward. The big ship couldn't slow down at the snap of fingers, although I was sure the XO on the bridge wanted to save his pilot and wingman.

That pilot wasn't a big hunk—fighter pilots generally weren't, which explained why I'd been able to make him kiss the floor. *Think of Tom Cruise in Top Gun, if you can remember such old movies.* Typical pint-size pilot. My size, except for muscle mass.

But the dude fought me. I was trained for that. You approached from behind, wrapped one arm around the person's neck without choking him, and swam with the other and your finned feet. If he didn't settle down, you applied some pressure with your wrapped-around arm, in this case enough to make him unconscious. I'd put him on his back, of course, so he wouldn't drink or breathe the ocean. Hard to do in that sea state, but I did it. I still felt like drowning the bastard, but that wasn't my job.

I wasn't gentle by any means. Funny thing: we became best of friends, and he eventually apologized to Joey. Knew Joey didn't care much, but it was a good moment for everyone. Life's nice little moments sometimes follow bad ones…or vice versa. *Does it even out? Probably not, considering my present situation.*

Why did I survive?

❦

I saw the *Wave Queen III* still anchored and the dinghy and fisherman's boat still beached. Piled the two deputies and the fisherman into the dinghy and headed for the *Queen.*

Once on board, I went almost as far out as I'd been for

the dive and dumped the five bodies. George was the last.

"Don't know if you can hear me, *amigo mio*, but I gave Angela and the kids a decent burial in your back-yard. Wish you could tell me what's going on. I feel so alone. Everybody's dead but me, George, if that's any consolation. Isn't that a big cosmic joke? Maybe the last person on Earth who should be alive is the last person on Earth that is. I hope I awake tomorrow and this is all just some horrendous nightmare."

I remembered the words I said over Angela and said them for George, and then I consigned him to the water too. Thinking of the irony that George and the rest had just joined the original victim we'd come to ID, I was pretty sure that crime would never be solved.

I sat cross-legged on the deck for a while, fighting off mental anguish. Almost decided again to dive overboard to drown myself but then realized I didn't want to go back into the deep for a long time, if ever. Also realized I'd been through that internal discussion before. Wasn't thinking straight.

I left the *Queen* anchored near shore and rode the din-ghy back to the beach. Wasn't about to return to my apartment, but I had a lot of other choices. Laughed as I imagined all the "for rent" and "for sale" signs that should be in SoCal right then. Talk about busting the housing bubble! Definitely a buyers' market because there were no sellers and maybe I was the only buyer.

Decided to visit Malibu, home of the rich and famous.

CHAPTER 4

Malibu Beach had been the epitome of California's hedonistic lifestyle for several decades. Buying a place there was beyond the means of any average person making an average salary. Malibu was *Elysium* and I was Matt Damon heading toward it, a person denied it all these years, but now on a house-hunting mission. You never saw the movie? Better-than-the-average sci-fi thriller. But I was in my own fight for survival in a post-apocalyptic nightmare not of my making. Guess Damon's character didn't make his either. The movie was a bit fuzzy in my mind.

One-percenters owned all those rich digs. Maybe zero-point-one-percenters? The only poor there were in the service industry—butlers, maids, cleaning people, pool cleaners, delivery people, and so forth, and their jobs were taking care of the beautiful people. I figured class distinctions didn't mean much now. That many service workers were green card holders didn't either. Far as I knew, I was unique and one of the privileged now—the last human being on the planet. Sort of squashed the savory realization of vicarious dreams anyone could have about living there.

I cased several beachfront properties of the rich and

famous. I should have felt guilty about not feeling guilty, but I didn't know these dead people. They could have been great people and innocent victims of Lady Luck's caprice for all I knew, or they could have been SOBs. I was wise enough to know that riches didn't correlate much with behavior toward your fellow human beings. Was stupid enough to envy their lifestyle, though.

Maybe some had survived and gone elsewhere in panic? The rich were subject to panic attacks too. Maybe more so than normal people because they had more to lose? I supposed they did, but Death was the grand equalizer.

Hadn't seen any survivors, rich or not, so it didn't matter. Questionable whether I was better off as a survivor. I enjoyed my private moments, but I also liked people for the most part. My situation was ridiculous. Felt more akin to the Will Smith character in *I Am Legend* than Matt Damon's in *Elysium*, come to think of it. Again it was a fuzzy flick in my mind. Ned and I had watched both old movies on the carrier.

I didn't much care about the fancy cars on driveways and in garages. Had my sheriff's department SUV, so the only thought about them was whether they had gas I could siphon or parts I could use. Didn't much care for fancy clothes in walk-in closets either. Some women would have put Imelda Marcos to shame. Remember her, the Filipina VIP with the shoe fetish? My shoe preferences were always simple: two pairs of flats, two pairs of sandals, and sneakers, unless you counted my diving flippers and sand shoes, which I'd left in my apartment along with my underwater camera and scuba tanks.

Finally chose the house, simpler than most, that had the most food supplies—a full pantry and refrigerator plus a freezer full of steaks and chops and goodies for parties, from pigs-in-a-blanket to frozen shrimp. The electricity was on too, so nothing had spoiled except the old Hollywood stars' cadavers—they had old still shots from their movies plastered all over one wall, so I wasn't guessing about that. They had owned the beachfront house or paid an exorbitant rent—couldn't ask them which one, of course.

I put that pair into garbage cans. Couldn't find any lime around—they likely had a landscaping crew that made more money than I did, or used to—but the cans had lids. I still had two cans left for my garbage. *What luxury! My own cans and not the big bins in my complex.*

Found some yoghurt in the fridge to calm my gut. Checked out their music list and was impressed. Put on some Bizet suites. *How did that French guy write such good Spanish-sounding music?* Lounged in a comfy chair and considered my future. *Do I have one? Will I get sick too?* Knew people often had bucket lists, but my bucket so far only contained one item: survival. And chances for doing that seemed slim. *And do I even want to survive?*

The panic had dulled. The sorrow over my friends' deaths was still with me but was vanishing with the thought that they might be the lucky ones. The memory of Angela and her baby who'd never be born was still raw, but the first thought continued: *Who would want a kid to be born into this hell?*

I was tempted to take a nap to see again if the whole experience was a nightmare—I was exhausted from dealing with dead and stinking bodies—but cold logic told me I should be planning some future for myself beyond role-playing as some Hollywood starlet living in Malibu. But unanswered questions kept interrupting that logical process.

My first thought had become an echo in my mind: *Why am I alive?* My second thought: *Am I dying, but just more slowly than everyone else?* That leitmotif also kept repeating in my chaotic symphony of thoughts. Not a great start for a long train of logical ones. Knew I couldn't stay long where I was, though. The food would last a few weeks at best. Electricity could fail too. *Here and elsewhere.*

I returned to my guilty feelings. I'd become a looter or scavenger—whatever you want to call me. And I was getting lonely. Turned on the TV and found a test pattern. When Bizet finished his shtick, I thought about Berlioz's "March to the Gallows," but I put on some Albeniz. Not even those cable music channels run by computers were working, Of course not. Computers were probably off-line. So the old couple's canned music was the only game in town.

Ned had called me a geek. Typical sailor's tastes in music ran from rap and hip-hop to heavy rock and country. I liked it all, could play some at one time, and was always selective, depending on my personal opinions about quality, even with Disney—liked Phil Collins'song from *Tarzan* better than that overplayed dreck from *Frozen*, for example. Liked classics because I could hear them over and over again without getting bored. Only so many riffs you can make on the electric guitar, after all.

The music cheered me up. Became cheerier when I found all the liquor hidden away in under-the-bookcase cabinets. Broke a few locks doing it. The old couple likely hadn't trusted the housekeeper. I smiled as I thought she might be someone like me. The couple might have been Hispanics like George, but they would be white Hispanics, not black like me…and they were card-carrying members of the club of "beautiful people."

⁊ꙮꙅ

I discovered too much cognac gave you a killer hangover no matter how expensive it was—the tag had said $215. Maybe a bargain at your local Malibu package store? I'd spent the night in an overstuffed recliner. Awoke with Albeniz still repeating on the stereo. Shut it off, peeled off my clothes, and headed for the shower.

In the bathroom mirror, I checked my tongue for swelling, pinched my wide nostrils, and then stared into my eyes. Some dark-faced stranger with frizzy black hair and bags under her eyes broke out laughing. *Penny, you can't lose it now!*

Thought came that going crazy might cause me to be suicidal. *What makes someone go off the deep end?* Seeing my reflection in the mirror seemed like a close approximation. It was like looking at another person, one who no longer existed—a time traveler from the past arriving in my present to haunt me. Stuck out my tongue at the reflection and felt better.

The warm shower felt good. I'd splashed my face a bit at my apartment and a bit more on *Wave Queen III* after my brief duties as mortician-at-sea, but there was still salt on my dark brown skin, making it feel itchy. I was going to take a long shower. Figured California water consumption had diminished a lot if what I'd seen was generalizable to all of LA County, but the water went off in the middle of a good shampoo, so I had to rinse off the suds using the seltzer dispenser from the bar. Navy taught me to be resourceful.

I thought about those desalination plants again. With electricity gone in some areas, would pumping stations stop? Probably. In my ignorance, I didn't even know whether our water depended on those plants. Knew the political battle a few years back to finance them had been long and heated, like most political battles in the Golden State—or in Washington, for that matter. Guess some environmental nuts in California had figured we didn't need artificial islands off the coast doing more damage to the maritime environment. *Likely not a worry for them now.*

The plants were even approved after that first long drought came to an end. Like many other things, national politics had forced California to follow its own path. Because the rest of the country depended on a lot of local products, there wasn't much the rest of the country could do. That "California Republic" on the state flag had more than historical meaning. The state led the country in a lot of issues and fashions, and pretty much showed Washington DC the middle finger when push came to shove. Except for having too many people, I liked living here.

My electricity was still on, but something or someone had shut off the water. No one was consuming electricity either, so somewhere pumping machinery that ran on electricity had to be going offline. And here I'd been just getting used to the fancy shower with heads on both ends of the stall, one with that hose contraption you could use to spray the private parts.

Decided to have steak and eggs for breakfast. Made the mistake of thinking about bad things after eating, though—funeral services for George and his family and the multitude of cadavers, including the old couple's cadavers in the trash cans waiting like jumping jacks ready to pop up and accuse me of being a home invader. Left my vomit in the kitchen sink. The garbage disposal was working, but I didn't think that using it without water would be good for it. Not that the old couple would care now.

Used the seltzer dispenser again to rinse my mouth, and what I spit out to rinse the sink. Needed to find a drugstore for some essentials—comb, toothbrush, toothpaste, feminine hygiene products, bottled water, and maybe some Snickers bars. I was low on margarine and eggs too, but drugstores had everything nowadays. It occurred to me that some of those necessities might be in the house somewhere. Maybe not feminine hygiene products—the woman had been old and wrinkled and long past menopause. And I didn't need Depends—at least not yet.

Continued my scheming about how to make the Malibu shack Penny's own. Who'd have ever thought that Penny Castro would end up living in such a ritzy place? Certainly not Mamacita, who always said I was stupid and a slut. Figured now I was the smartest person on the planet by default, and the slut moniker was a moot point.

☙❧

There was a Sav-On not far away. I figured prices were much higher than a Sav-On in East LA, but what the hell? The electricity was still on at the drugstore too—sliding doors kept thumping against two cadavers wedged in them and bouncing back—*for safety's sake, you know: you can't trap either live or dead people according to some state ordinance.* I moved the two bodies to the street, went inside, and cased the joint. Filled an entire shopping cart and felt weird going right through the checkout to the SUV. *Sheriff's Deputy Robs Sav-On*, the headline would say.

Only there would be no headlines. I hadn't found any news about what was going on. I'd learned nothing since I'd seen that frayed steel cable start to descend except that a lot of people were dead and rotting. In particular, I wanted to know if there were any other survivors. *Is the whole US affected? The whole world?*

Like everyone else less than eighty years old, I'd come to depend on my cellphone and other electronic gadgets for news. The internet had ramped up in the nineties long before I was born. No essential technological gadget worked now. Sometimes I could send a call through only to go to voicemail, but most of the time I'd just receive an "out of service" message or static. And that with all my bars filled. Radio, TV? Except for TV test patterns, *nada.*

On the drive back, I saw a few cats and dogs milling around, some dogs already in packs. When they ran out of food, mostly carrion unless they figured out how to catch cats or open dog food cans, I knew there would be problems for me and any other human who was alive. Wild dogs might as well be wolves. Gulls were still flying around too. *So, animals aren't affected?* Insects weren't affected either because flies and their maggots were still having a great old time. Whatever happened, it seemed to only affect humans. My mind turned to the *Book of Revelations* again. *Will I be the only witness to the Second Coming?* I laughed. My Catholic upbringing increased my paranoia. There might be four horses, but there wouldn't be four horsemen riding them in this apocalypse.

Yeah, I know the saying about paranoia. I returned to my Malibu hideaway and hit the liquor cabinet again after stowing away perishables.

CHAPTER 5

For the next Sav-On trip, I'd decided to break into drug storage cabinets. Wasn't looking for any hard stuff, but I was almost out of the happy pills I'd been taking since Ned's death.

I stopped at a gas station and topped off the tank. Hadn't been using much gas, but you never know. What tanker trucks would come around? And when the power went off completely, how would I be able to pump? Seemed like civilization might come to a grinding halt soon. As much as modernists believed in robotics, humans were still needed to keep basic things functioning, if only to throw switches and program gizmos.

I thought of the ice cream still in the drugstore's freezer department. That and my happy pills might make life a bit more bearable and keep me from becoming an alcoholic. Decided to find a short garden hose too in case the house didn't have another one. I'd cut up the only one for siphoning gas from neighbors' cars. When I saw the drugstore's state, though, I backed out. Looters had tossed the place…and more.

As I drove home, I considered the multiple implications of what I'd just seen. First conclusion: I wasn't the only survivor. There were others. Second: those survivors might be drug-crazed and violent loonies. I'd found the drug cabinets looted. I also found a young girl's dead, naked, and mutilated body inside the drugstore. Didn't have a rape kit, but the bloody spread of her bare legs was telling enough. Third: I might need a gun. Hated the things, but hated the idea of dying violently a lot more. Where would I obtain one? *Obvious, Penny.*

I took a long detour back to the substation. The bodies were a bit riper now, and the gun cases had been broken into. *Penny, you missed your chance.* I thought of George's SUV I'd left abandoned on the beach. Remembered it had contained a sawed-off pump action. Also put that out of mind because I knew that shotgun likely wouldn't be there any longer either. Knew there were plenty of guns around, even in the LA area where gun laws were strict, because the NRA and its acolytes had ensured that small arms would be available to almost anyone who wanted them, even though they might be criminals or crazy. *Don't qualify for a license? Go to a gun show!*

So there should be plenty of guns if only for road rage on California's freeways. *Of course, your car is a lethal weapon too.* Problem was bad guys had likely co-opted them, leaving us good guys without defenses. I decided that the NRA chairman wouldn't be applauding those empty gun cases, though. He was probably dead, just like most gun nuts and regular people.

I never liked guns, but thought I might need a few if I was going to survive. *Penny's one of the good guys!* Maybe a bit immodest, but that was my opinion, and there wasn't anyone around to contradict me.

Seeing the apocalyptic aftermath, including that rape victim, was enough for me to resurrect the NRA all by my lonesome—my own Second Amendment Lovers, or SALs. I'd have to be on the outlook for weapons, as much as I hated them. At that moment, I'd have to be creative, though.

By the time I returned to my Malibu hangout, my nerves were on edge. I was alone and unprotected.

You're probably thinking, "Big, strong ex-navy gal, whatcha have to be worried about, honey?" First of all, I'm not big or strong. That rape victim was bigger and likely stronger. I'd gone through basic training, but my sojourn singing "Anchors Aweigh" hadn't put me in danger. I was more search and rescue and working in the ship's galley. Ned—remember my boyfriend?—he and others had been more in harm's way. The most dangerous mission I ever had was to detach an underwater mine from a dock once. I abhorred violence. Wouldn't even let Ned be rough in the sack, but he could do gentle as well as create mayhem, so never was much of a problem.

The homeowner helped me out a bit. The old bat had a bat. I found some softball equipment in a closet and slept with a shiny aluminum bat from then on. Planned on doing some skull-crushing if anyone tried to rape me—a gang would eventually kill me, but I'd take some of them out. Although I longed for Ned's comforting arms, violent gang rape just wasn't my cup of tea. I'd go down fighting.

❦❦❦

The next evidence of human life on Earth besides me was more neutral than my drugstore experience. I'd driven to a neighbor's house to dump my trash—my cans were already full—when the cruiser's com came to life.

After lots of static and squeals, I heard, "Wolfpack One, head north to Oxnard. Three more refugees at Colonia Park on North Juanita."

"Roger that."

And then silence. The signal had been weak with lots of distortion. Lots of whump-whump noise like what came from a chopper. *Maybe dying batteries? Or just distance?* Oxnard was just up the road, though. *Where the hell is Wolfpack One? And where are they based?*

I checked the channel. Thought the Wolfpack might be military, of course. *Maybe they'd know what's happened?* Picked the mike up, but then had second thoughts. Those thoughts continued during the drive home.

If the voices belong to military types, they'll have guns, I mused as I keyed my garage door opener and stashed the sheriff's SUV.

Went inside and put new trash bags in my wastebaskets, fixed myself a single-malt on the rocks—the ice cubes probably an insult to expensive Scotch—and sat to think some more. *If someone is picking up refugees, is there a refugee camp?* As big as SoCal is, finding that would be next to impossible. Didn't much like the idea of being a refugee either, but thought I might be safer. And I might finally learn what had happened.

It then occurred to me that maybe the Pentagon was responsible for all this. Maybe not directly, but some sworn enemy of the good ol' US of A might have felt threatened by US military might. A few administrations had made both the country's allies and enemies nervous—sometimes it was hard to know the difference between them, of course.

Although I found my conjecture uncomfortable and unlikely, I liked it better than the ET invasion or Second Coming scenarios. I was ex-military after all, and, while they were good guys in general, that wasn't necessarily true for higher mucky-mucks or political hacks. *Sometimes the government doesn't want people to know about the shit they do.*

I drank myself into a stupor, hugged myself, and dreamed I was back with Ned.

~∘~∘~

At two-seventeen a.m. PDT, I sat bolt upright in my stuffed recliner. I remembered the exact time because I looked at the digital clock sitting on top of the music system cabinet. It was supposed to show weather data too—maybe even more, because it was hooked to the house's ISP service—but there were no functioning ISP companies now. I wondered how much the old couple had paid someone to set it up for their electronic bungalow. They had a sophisticated alarm system too, but I had soon realized that the callout was internet-based—all part of a "smart house" that had become stupid and irrelevant.

I brushed cobwebs from my brain and analyzed what had woken me. Heard the deck's French doors rattling. *Again?* Found my baseball bat and tiptoed into the living room to investigate. Turned on the light and stared into an unshaven face on the other side of the glass. An angry young man's face!

"Nate! Tracy! There's a babe in here!"

I didn't wait for Nate and Tracy. Didn't bother asking the young man's name either. He didn't look like date material. I headed for the garage, hearing the door's glass break behind me, thoughts of gang rape and that drugstore girl's spread-leg mutilated body giving wings to my feet.

There were more of them outside. I gunned the motor and backed over two with satisfying thumps and crunches—who needs a gun?—and continued backing onto the road. Threw the big SUV into drive and flattened another dude just as he shot twice, peppering me with safety glass shards and leaving me weaving like I was a drunk riding a wounded hippo. Fought for control and then tore off down the road, one jerk firing at me.

The PCH never looked so good! I turned south toward LA. Took Sunset inland and pulled into a strip mall where I sat shaking, knowing I'd avoided rape and death, as well as an accident along the way, dodging both human and vehicle corpses. *The world's going mad!*

After about twenty minutes of hyperventilating, I tried to start the SUV again. *No gas. What?* Got out. Saw the bullet hole in the car's side and smelled gasoline vapors. I'd have to find other transportation.

Checked some vehicles in the strip mall's lot. Skipped the van with the woman and five kids; she'd likely been waiting for a husband who would never return from the convenience store. After hotwiring five and not getting any results—their batteries were either dead or they had no gas—I became desperate.

But then I calmed down some. *Where will I go?* Not back to Malibu for sure. Imagined more bloodthirsty gangs of drugged, pubescent, and pimply teens searching for women to murder and rape. *Don't gangs have female members anymore?*

Take away that thin veneer of civilization and what do you have? Depends. My experience that early morning told me that there might not be much left. Crazed human beings wondering why their lives had come apart, becoming violent, and doing anything to survive or act out their drug-induced fantasies. I thought of that old show *The Walking Dead*—used to watch reruns on the carrier with Ned along with old movies. *But who needs zombies when crazed humans are scarier?*

I went inside another drugstore, this time a Rite-Aid, with no definite plan in mind except post-apocalyptic consumerism. *Gotta spread my purchasing power around. Where are my coupons?*

Not many bodies in this one, and the store was still intact. A late-night pharmacist had plugged someone looking for drugs between the eyes, though, apparently paying the price when the assailant's buddy knifed him in the gut. I'm no ME, but I was pretty sure the protruding knife there was the murder weapon and COD.

Knew I wouldn't find my happy pills there. Took two new kids' backpacks off the shelf and filled them with random supplies, though, including two flashlights and batteries, and headed for the street. At the corner, I stopped and looked up. There were apartments above the stores.

If first you don't succeed, try, try again? Would one be a safe haven for a few days?

I bashed in a door between the Rite-Aid and a bookstore and ascended narrow stairs. Another break-in introduced me to a comfy one-bedroom apartment. *Thank you, realtor. I'll take it.* I tossed the woman's dead body out the window—likely the renter and not a realtor, so I felt bad about it—and made myself at home.

CHAPTER 6

Next morning, out of curiosity, I turned on the TV. Usual test patterns, but I noticed the old DVR. It had been set to record some afternoon soaps the day I took my dive. The old woman must have been a fan. I decided to play them back.

Typical soap operas. I sat with a yoghurt to watch the millionth episode of *General Hospital*. No zombies there. About half-way through, an Emergency Alert System broadcast interrupted the show.

"This is not a drill! We are suffering a biological warfare attack! Seek shelter immediately! Repeat—"

I had taken high school English. The gerund form of the present tense indicated the announcer felt he was in the middle of a shit storm. Somehow authorities had put the word out that it was biological. Not hard to figure out when the first hits didn't produce mushroom clouds, I guessed, and after that, no one cared. And, because networks' HQs were on the East Coast, not the West, they'd still be broadcasting the warning even after the plague did its dirty deed in the west and the contagion began its inexorable trip east, riding on the prevailing winds across the continent.

But the network alert stopped with an abruptness that

took my breath away, silence ensued, and the test pattern came on, recorded for posterity—*c'est moi*—on the DVR. My spoon hung suspended in midair with a glop of yoghurt still on it.

Okay, Penny, you were underwater then. Is that why you survived? Dives are part of the forensic process and logged because judges and lawyers, both prosecutors and public defenders or other defense counsels, loved that kind of data.

But what about military transmissions? And the gang of kids? Why did they all survive? And why did the broadcast end? Technically it hadn't—TV programming had ended, but probably just locally. I could imagine a sterile computer voice. *Sorry. We're having technical difficulties. We apologize. All our staff members are dead.*

I wasn't enough of a techie to make sense of it all. But biological warfare could explain the symptoms I saw among the dead, including the woman's body I'd just thrown out the window. But how could it act so fast? Aren't you supposed to become ill and crawl into bed to die a horrible death in a week or so? What kind of lethal crap had fallen from the sky? How did it propagate so fast? Lots of questions, still no answers save one— biological warfare.

Put the spoonful of yoghurt into my mouth but couldn't swallow. Went to the sink and spit it out. Barfed what I'd already eaten. *Have I been contaminating myself all along?*

Came to my senses a bit. *Biological means non-chemical, right?* Some especially designed pathogen, a gift from evil geniuses. A bioengineered virus variant in aerosol form? *Maybe whoever attacked really wanted to kill everybody, but some of us were immune?*

I found the woman's bed, stripped, and pulled covers up to my chin without worrying much about the contagion. Fell asleep staring at the swirling patterns on the plaster ceiling. I was missing my liquor stash.

Never liked soap operas.

✂✂✂

I stayed in the dead woman's apartment for a week, only leaving it to scavenge in the strip mall's stores and beat a pack of starving dogs off the dead woman's body. Put her remains in an industrial trash bin that had a lid. Same with a few other bodies until back and front of the six-store strip mall was body-free.

The electricity was still on, so Rite-Aid provided provisions all that time. Didn't much worry about expiration dates for what I ate. I needed that week to plan, including my choice of primitive weapons. Settled on a small garden pitchfork, a collection of knives, big roll of duct tape, six small bottles of drain cleaner for throwing in zombie faces, four cans of bug spray with the same target in mind, and other items.

My plan wouldn't have satisfied strategists at the Pentagon or even the sheriff's department. I decided to go farther inland. Every place seemed dangerous, but I had a bad feeling about coastal living. Kind of sad that feeling because the ocean had played such an important role in my life. Water in general. Sailing on it, swimming in it, and diving beneath it. My work had put me into ponds, lakes, and ocean—a bit gruesome at times, but that silent water world had been comforting. Not anymore.

The lack of technological gizmos had my hands tied. Thought about finding a gas station and stealing a battery for one car in the parking lot, but no yellow pages and no internet to help me find the nearest service station. Same for auto parts stores—probably scarcer. Wasn't about to roam around on foot trying to find one. Decided to walk, but I needed a destination. Found some maps in a drawer—Hollywood, San Fernando Valley, downtown LA, a big map of SoCal, and Paris. *Paris?*

In the folds of the Paris map was a first-class roundtrip plane ticket from LAX to the City of Light. Had the old woman been planning her dream trip? Made me want to cry.

I liked Paris. Was tempted to try to fly there, but knew no commercial flights would be taking off from LAX. Not from anywhere. The ETA for Armageddon Airways had already come and gone.

Laid the large SoCal map upon the breakfast counter of the galley kitchen, closed my eyes, and then spun around until I was good and dizzy. Grabbed the edge of the counter with my left hand and jabbed at the map with my right index finger. San Fernando Valley. Found that map and put it on top of the SoCal map. *Okay, Penny, that's where you're heading.*

Packed backpacks and arranged them and my arsenal as best as I could on front and back while I sang "The Gypsy Rover" *a cappella* in my husky contralto voice—Ned had taught it to me with a few extra raunchy verses, and it seemed more appropriate now than in the Gulf of Oman. I looked at myself in the mirror and saw a cross between a homeless person and a large elf. The homeless adjective wasn't appropriate, of course. I had millions of homes to choose from. I'd just have to clean out some more dead bodies. The elf was sad—Santa wouldn't be coming this year to SoCal.

Dead bodies? They didn't worry me so much anymore. I worried more about living ones now.

～～

I continued inland on Sunset to where it met the 405,

AKA the infamous San Diego freeway, and then followed that north. Walking along that freeway was both exhilarating and depressing. Only a few days earlier I would have been taken out by a semi or caused a multicar collision. Checked for live cars, and, after a few miles in lane three, I found an old battered pickup with a weak battery and some gas. After the soap opera's emergency broadcast interruption, I was a bit more careful. I had a box of rubber gloves from the Rite-Aid and put a pair on before pushing the driver out. Thought it likely was a waste of time if the crap they hit us with was still around in the air and virulent, which it probably was, but you never know.

After a few miles, I gave up. Vehicles and their dead drivers, some having managed to open their doors, stagger out, and then collapse, made working around them just too tiring. Decided I'd make better time walking again. Patted the pickup on its hood, wished it luck, and continued north.

After about a hundred yards, though, I spotted a motorcycle. Ned was going to teach me how to ride one. We'd watched that old feel-good classic *An Officer and a Gentleman* and I had streamed *The Motorcycle Diaries* not long ago. Ned was a romantic and wanted to carry me off to a romantic tryst on a Harley, I supposed. Knew he had a scooter as a kid. Guess he wanted to move to the big time. Never did, but the two of us took one on a short road trip on leave in Greece. He let me drive a bit until he became nervous, so thought I knew the basics about handling one, but it wasn't easy for a small woman.

Ignoring the owner's body lying beside it, I tried to start the thing. I'd checked for gas but didn't have much hope after previous experiences. It would be easier but still dicey dodging through the obstacle course the 405 had become. There had been a multi-billion dollar project to "improve" that freeway for several miles as it wound through Sepulveda Pass. Would have worked too, but making a bigger parking lot during commuting hours didn't imply success. Thought maybe those who used alternate routes before decided to try their luck on the 405, making planners' calculations irrelevant. Maybe some of those idiots were still in their cars?

When the cycle awoke from the dead, I had the problem of getting my gear stashed. Cinched it the best I could in back of me—the duffel stuck out and hung a bit on both sides—and took off. Didn't worry about a helmet—no way was I putting a dead guy's helmet on—even though it seemed that surviving the end of the world didn't mean I was a lucky kitten with spare lives left.

Wobbled a bit at first, but practice makes perfect. On a whim, I pulled off on Mulholland and worked my way back to Santa Monica Boulevard via Coldwater Canyon, a nice little trek that took me through Beverly Hills. Everything looked peaceful, but I knew there were dead people in those posh estates. I saluted them with my middle finger. On Santa Monica, I found the Chicano Radio Network. I'd once tried dating a DJ from there. Hadn't worked from the start—Carlos worked at night and slept in the day, the opposite of me. But I knew CRN's location by memory.

Pulled around the back where employees parked—noted they'd resurfaced both front and rear parking lots recently—and broke into the station. I'd developed a purpose during my little joy ride.

If the transmitter is still working, can I broadcast a message to SoCal?

I knew a lot less about radio stations than diving, but more than about motorcycle riding, yet I'd decided it might be as easy as bringing a DJ's lair back to life. And I knew where Carlos had hung out when he was working.

He had thought a commercial break was long enough to bring me up to speed. *Men!*

I'd seen him do his gig. Tried to repeat it. When the "On Air" sign came on, I almost said "Eureka!" I then had a sobering thought. *Even if somebody is listening, what should my message be?*

CHAPTER 7

Okay, I was not the best and brightest of radio show producers, but I thought I did well enough with my adlib: "This is LA County Sheriff's Deputy Penelope Castro speaking to SoCal via the Chicano Radio Network. If you're authority and listening—sheriff's deputy, police officer, or military—I'd like to make contact. I'm on the move and won't say where I'll be, but please put the word out that I'm still alive and sure could use some help."

I repeated the message in Spanish, except that I didn't translate a section of it. No fucking way would any respectable Hispanic citizen from the county say, *"Diputado de la Oficina del Alguacil del Condado de Los Angeles."* Spanglish was *de rigueur* in such things, if you pardon my French.

Yeah, not great, especially the "if you're listening" part, which, in hindsight was absurd, but I'd wanted to be circumspect. Wasn't about to tell crazed people where I was and wasn't about to stay in one place where any crazies could find me.

I figured nobody would be listening, but...*what the hell?* Set the recorded message on repeat. It should keep repeating as long as the station's power lasted. Couldn't remember the broadcast area, but it was large enough. *Who knows? Maybe even Wolfpack will be listening!*

I went downstairs to the canteen and gorged on snacks and lukewarm coke—the soda machines had failed for some reason. Didn't feel guilty about vandalizing the vending machines to obtain my goodies. I was now vandal, squatter, looter, and scavenger. Sat and pondered my future. Put my head on the table for a bit and fell asleep.

A noise woke me, just like in Malibu. You know how it goes. You awake knowing you heard something, but you can't remember what it was. Maybe some primordial protective mechanism but often a false alarm? I downed the last bit of coke and went into the dark corridor lit only by emergency lights. Had someone shut off the electricity? Or was the lighting in the station on some kind of timer? The red glow made me think of blood—*mine!* And my arsenal was still stowed on the motorcycle.

I went back into the canteen and searched through drawers. Found some cutlery and wondered if a fork would stop a gang member. *A tine in time stops a crime?* Maybe only if I jabbed it into a carotid artery. Had a different idea. Yanked off the rubber hose that went from the coke tank to the dispenser. I now had a whip with two heavy metal ends. More lethal than a fork, at least.

Went back upstairs where the studios and entrance were. Heard people muttering in the studio where I'd made the recording. *Is it still transmitting? Has someone responded to it?*

"Look what we have here!" said a voice like a cement mixer.

I turned and used my whip. A man with a naked torso took it full in the face and went down. Not a man. Another teenager. And up to no good. I grabbed his machete and worked my way toward the entrance door.

"Don't let her get away!" someone called out.

I saw another *gordo feo* running toward me with arms outstretched. He'd been on a starvation diet. Ugly loose skin where fat used to be flopped all over the place on his face and torso. I must have looked like the best meal he'd have since last week. I moved aside just in time. Slash, slash! Turned and ran. Slammed the front door shut. I was panting, hyped up with adrenaline, but plotting. I smiled. Slipped my whip through the door handles and tied knots in the rubber hose that would only become tighter when they tried to open the doors. Navy had taught me the knot, but couldn't remember its name.

Didn't stop until I was on the motorcycle and heading back to the 405 along Santa Monica. Still had the machete. That could be useful in the future. Mind played tricks on me as I rode: Remembered another time I could have used it…

ↄ৽ঌↄ

Sailors could become rowdy on shore leave. This time Ned wasn't there when I had a row with a drunken ship's mechanic in a San Diego bar. Afterward, though, Ned would tell the story to anyone to impress the person with what a spitfire he had for a girlfriend. Fortunately I already had him as a boyfriend. I figured that rep he was giving me would have destroyed any chance of ever getting one.

Some drunks were nasty; some lost all inhibitions; and some needed to have parents who weren't bigots, because big bigots breed little ones. I learned later that this sailor shared all those characteristics, a spoiled brat who grew up in Buckhead, a rich suburb of Atlanta. He had no use for African-Americans or Hispanic-Americans, so I was a double target for his bigotry. That night it seemed to take the form of his thinking I was some whore that would give him a blow job for five bucks. He likely lumped all women with my heritage in that class, at least in his drunken condition.

Generally you ignored shitheads like that. I made the mistake of telling him to go join the Ku Klux Klan and that he didn't belong in Uncle Sam's Navy. Knew by the grapevine that his parents had sent their only child to a posh private college, and he had flunked out. Daddy, over Mommy's objections, had made him join the navy. *Maybe the most commonsense choice the old man ever made for his son?* He sure had failed at raising him.

A bear hug around the waist from a drunken lout with foul breath was a turn-off for any woman, I imagined. I received a lot of that foul breath too, because he called me everything under the sun, including "Spanish *puta.*" Bigots tended to lump all Hispanics under the label Spanish, which was an insult to all of us, including people from Spain. Of course, you didn't expect a drunk to appreciate nuances in language or a bigot to be politically correct.

There was a standard way to break an unwanted hug—slapping ears hard and then gouging eyes. That only made him more furious. I stole a bottle from the bar and smashed him on the head. *Tutti finito!* That ended the confrontation.

I spent two days in the brig until details about the incident came to light. My wannabe paramour spent a month of grace and then received a dishonorable discharge. Guess he went home to Mommy and Daddy after that. I was expecting to be served with a lawsuit—he'd required some stiches and might have a scar for life on his crown—but that never happened, probably because the Buckhead parents figured I didn't have any money, and they couldn't sue the navy because they were "patriots."

∽∾∽

I regretted ignoring the results of my finger-pointing exercise with the map leading to the visit to Beverly Hills and West Hollywood. Malibu had left me wary of being anywhere near the rich and famous people's abodes, so Beverly Hills hadn't been appealing, but the incident at the radio station showed West Hollywood was also too dangerous for staying a while and seeing the sights.

The pileup on the 405 on-ramp even blocked my motorcycle. There was no other solution: I struggled up the ramp walking on top of damaged cars, some burned out with crispy critters inside. It became less congested on the freeway, but now I had to repeat a portion of my trip on foot.

I'd made one big circle, more or less, and had lost a day without accomplishing a damn thing. My stomach was growling too. Guessed running for your life was good cardio-exercise though.

I stopped and had some water and a pack of chocolate chip cookies, looking around at the scenery, if cadavers covered by flies and broken-down vehicles could be called that. Later found a rear-ended car with a functioning radio and listened to my message. *Okay, los locos didn't figure out how to turn it off.* Not surprising. I'd seen their red eyes even in the dark station. And the one who had received the machete blow was well away from any dead lights. Heroin, meth, cocaine…who cared? They were so high they could be flesh-eating zombies—flesh-eating at least, especially *el gordo.*

Having done my good deed for the day, I decided now to heed my finger-pointing results. Started walking north, picking my way through the obstacle course of the 405. As I walked, I realized that SoCal without some kind of vehicle was a huge place to move around in. I commiserated with all those service people who had bused to Malibu to take care of the rich and famous.

Hiking along a body-and-vehicle-strewn freeway wasn't a fast way to go anywhere. Still made good time, though. My deputy's conditioning paid off—more from diving and swimming, of course. The nap in the station had helped too. Just before I arrived at the 101, I left the 405 and walked north on Sepulveda.

Slept the night in a Jack-in-the-Box. It was in better shape than that McDonald's.

❧❧❧

A cat fight awoke me from a fitful sleep just before dawn. I watched them duke it out in the neon lights just outside the entrance door, feral cats or cats becoming feral, posturing, clawing, howling, and spitting while dancing in rainbow hues. Poor babies were likely starving. They'd probably already scavenged trash bins and killed any feral rats in the vicinity—the great circle of life was broken. Already knew the only food inside for them was frozen.

A cold and clammy wave swept over me, and I shivered. After all the dead human bodies, some created by me, and here I was feeling sorry for cats? Okay, I liked cats. Why did anyone have to die? Pets were taken care of by humans. With them gone, the poor pets' worlds were turned upside down. Maybe it would have been better if animals had died too? A sobering thought. I went to the restroom, sat on the pot, and had a good cry. When I walked out, I noticed urinals and shrugged.

On the counters by the registers, there were brownies and cookies in little packs designed to tempt customers while they paid for other purchases. *Mommy, Mommy, can I have a brownie?* I remembered my own *Mamacita,* bless her soul; I'd badgered the poor woman like that. A little kid didn't understand that Mom is dirt poor and can't even put a healthy meal on the table. Tried a brownie. A bit stale, but it was a high-energy breakfast at least. *Sorry, Mamacita! Your kid still eats crap and likes it.*

I walked to the front and peered out to see if there were any dead cats and saw headlights approaching. *Too fast!* Backed up in a hurry. An SUV smashed into the front of the Jack-in-the-Box and came to a halt just in front of the register counter I was standing behind. Someone was slumped over the wheel. I opened the door, and he fell out.

I checked for a pulse. Weak. He had the symptoms. Whatever plague was unloaded on us was still working. For some reason, this guy, who looked like a construction worker, had taken a bit longer to succumb. Or hadn't been exposed immediately? *My future?*

Cursed and searched my backpacks where I found the box of rubber gloves. When he died, I checked his eyes and then closed them. Good-looking Hispanic guy. Seeing the unknown plague in action had been sobering. Definitely not the Second Coming. I tossed the gloves and hugged myself. *Penny, are you lucky? And is it good luck or bad?*

I ate some more brownies and then a pack of oatmeal cookies, downed a bottle of water, and decided it was time to go. The Jack-in-the-Box didn't seem like a safe place anymore.

I didn't feel dizzy or nauseous about seeing Death in action, though. *Am I becoming inured to all the death and violence? Is PTSD or some other state of depression in my future?* Knew it happened. Didn't know if anyone could do anything about preventing it. I'd almost butchered the fat kid. Didn't think much of it. Then it hit me. *What have I done?* My hands started shaking. *Delayed reaction!* I sat down. It took five minutes or so for the shaking to stop. I needed to leave that place pronto.

Epiphany! I put another pair of gloves on, pulled the guy's body from the SUV, hopped into it, and tried to back it out. It was imprisoned by all the little tables, each supported by a heavy metal pole. *Epiphany deflated!* The SUV was a maxi with three rows of seats. I knew I wasn't strong enough to push the behemoth out either.

Didn't occur to me to yank its battery and use it for a car in the parking lot. Was in a hurry to put some distance between me and the fresh body, recently succumbed to something lethal.

❧

The San Fernando Valley had always been a random mix of strip malls, grocery and convenience stores, gyms, hair salons, condos, and a lot of little one-level houses that all looked alike. Always thought the area looked worse than New Jersey where I grew up because the gentle SoCal climate lent itself to shoddy construction. You could find one-hundred-year-old houses in the Northeast that still looked nice and where people still lived in comfort. Nothing in SoCal was one hundred years old. Discounting a few missions here and there, everything looked beat up and rickety, and no one lived in comfort. Too many people, too many cars, and inflated house prices. *That's the name of the game in SoCal. Or was.*

Still, SoCal had been my home for a few years, I had found a job there, and the lifestyle had been easy for the most part. Already said I wasn't a surfer, but I could have been. Mountains weren't too far away either. *Where else can you be just hours away from surfing and skiing?*

I thought of all these things as I searched for a new place to live. I found it. All those people who owned those little ranch-style houses needed to landscape, and that often meant DIY work—landscapers were often too expensive. I found a nursery and decided to make it home for a while.

"A while" could be a long time.

PART 2

One Plus Two Equals Life Change

"The family is the nucleus of civilization."
~ Will Durant

CHAPTER 8

Penny, old girl, you've found a treasure trove!
I'd entered a sprawling ranch-style house in the hills through a gaping hole in its outside wall, not expecting to find much of anything, and there it was in plain sight: canned goods in a sagging cupboard not long for this world—reminded me of my boobs. The last quake probably did the cupboard no good because its door hung open on one hinge. Its excuse. I thought my boobs' excuse was malnutrition.

Lucky me! Scavengers going through that neighborhood before me must have missed the house and its treasure. I grabbed a can of SpaghettiOs, found a hand-operated can opener in a drawer—that was luck too—and went onto the deck to wolf it down. One side of the deck had collapsed, but the other seemed safe enough. There was even a weathered lounge chair. *Heaven!*

Five years and a few months had passed since that unlucky dive, civilization continued its descent into the maelstrom, and I kept swimming against the strong current. Those few days in Malibu and the battle at the radio station seemed like a memory of purgatory if I ignored the hellish encounters with wild boy bands. Now endless days seemed only like a climb through purgatory, not any kind of heaven or hell—but still only a few bus stops away from fire and brimstone. Those days and years had become a boring routine. Scavenge, eat, sleep, and then scavenge some more. Better than dead maybe. During some nights of insomnia, I wondered about that.

When you're famished—a sophisticated way of saying starving—anything looks like a banquet in a five-star restaurant. I'd eaten a lot of things during the last five years. My ribs showed more of the deprivation than my boobs, but I was still alive. Scraped my sandals in the deck's thick layer of dust and stared at arid landscape and mostly dead city. Sat in that chair and thanked my good karma, if that's what it was. Knew I didn't have much left, but the bad had beaten me up for so long that the meager feast cheered me up.

Restaurant with a view even. What a view the BBQ guests at the house must have had! I enjoyed it for about two minutes as I polished off my entrée. Found my jar of dirty water in my old backpack and washed it all down. Belched and smiled as the echo bounced back to me from the canyon's nude walls. *You learn to celebrate small victories.*

I then returned to the kitchen and fetched a can of cut green beans—"Gotta eat those veges," *Mamacita* had always said. I ate the beans more slowly than the entrée, though—not as tasty and they needed butter and salt. Looked at the can. "Del Monte Fresh Cut Blue Lake Cut String Beans." Sounded a bit redundant. Wondered if the world had any blue lakes left. Maybe where people had never lived? And probably not in California.

I went a bit slower with the beans, though, just to enjoy the view some more. Didn't worry about bright sunshine—my mulatto skin was more ravaged by blown grit and dry air than sunshine. I still could imagine myself as a little housewife out there on the deck, though, sunbathing in the nude and enjoying margaritas or strawberry daiquiris, puffin' weed, and dreamily looking off toward the hills bordering the ocean with the blue Pacific peeking through canyons in spots. Spotted Mulholland Drive. Remembered how it used to look like a string of pearls at night with traffic moving along it—white pearls anti-parallel with bright red rubies like some starlet's million-dollar necklace. Remembered the detour from hell to the radio station. Still had that machete, but hadn't had to use it since the chop-chop on *el gordo* at that station.

Yes, a great view. Okay, maybe residents of the house had more smog back in the day and couldn't enjoy that view. With no cars to speak of, Gaia had reduced that old atmospheric affliction to a gray bank miles away floating just above the horizon, its hue almost matching the indifferent and polluted Pacific. I didn't see one person in that wide expanse of land still blackened in spots by old wildfires. That wasn't surprising. People wanted to be invisible nowadays, or they could become food.

There were stories about cannibalism. I learned that from a dying and terrified woman I found who had run so hard from them she'd had a heart attack and collapsed. I tried CPR, but it didn't work. Not everyone was lucky enough to find my kind of treasure. Some thought even old human flesh was more nutritious as long as it was fresh. Maybe they were right, but not my thing. The day I considered it as an option would be the day I'd off myself. The only cannibalism I ever wanted to see was the ritual Catholic one where wine and crackers were turned into the blood and body of our Lord and Savior Jesus Christ. And maybe not even that if only ghost priests said mass. Wine? I hadn't done a good search for that. If other scavengers had left vittles, they might also have left wine.

I didn't find anything but empties in the garbage cans. People probably had thrown a party to celebrate the coming Armageddon and drunk all the reserves? *Why not?* A toast to the end of the human race!

I packed the rest of the cans into my old backpack—about twenty cans worth of assorted treats—and then decided to search other places in the house where other useful items might be found besides food and drink. *Maybe even some good drugs?* Thought about that and shook my head. Had to stay alert. I might forget my troubles that way, but more might find me too. That choice always was a conundrum.

Bedroom closets contained mostly useless junk, toys and sporting equipment included, but I did find a laundry basket in the garage where the washer and dryer were. That basket was filled with soiled clothes. I shook them out. Kid's clothes for the most part—not much need for those anymore—but there was a woman's bra, jeans, and T-shirt. Tossed the soiled bra to the floor. I have certain scruples, and I never wore bras now anyway. *Let 'em sag, I say. Who's gonna care?*

Both jeans and T-shirt were a little large for me. If the rich woman of the house were still alive, they'd likely be for her too by now. Even more so if her skeleton was nearby. Near-starvation diets or death didn't pack pounds on.

Normally, I cut pants legs off above the knee, but I left these intact. Liked that quality feel of almost new Levi denim…well, new when the pants went into the basket, say five years earlier? No chance to wash them either unless I walked miles to the beach. Not advisable with the gangs there, and inland the water was too scarce otherwise. I didn't have enough water to do more than a PTA bath occasionally—that's pits, tits, and ass for the acronym-challenged.

Visiting the shore was never advisable, not even right after the sky fell on us. From the beginning, there were gangs there that would have raped me and then served me for dinner—and I wasn't just talking about wild, savage males either. The dying woman's horde of cannibals had female members just as wild as the males—or so she said. I was not about to test her dying memory, although by now my meat was pretty tough. They wouldn't have much to chew on unless they ate the organs too. *Ugh. Pâté de foie de Penny sans gras.*

I visited the half-bath in the entry off the garage. Toilet was empty and dry—no odiferous problem, though. Put down the lid and used the toilet as a dressing room stool. Stood up and admired myself in the mirror. "Admire" was the wrong word, of course. I still looked like shit. Never was a Hollywood beauty, and five-plus years of neglecting my body had left me in worse shape. Cinderella had to look better when she was slaving away for the old stepmother and evil stepsisters. Hell, a twenty-five dollar whore on an ME's slab after she was beaten to pulp by her pimp would look better than me.

I laughed. Didn't imagine any were left. Pimps, whores, and johns were all gone, victims of the same plague that had killed almost everyone.

☙☙☙

I went onto the deck one last time in my new duds. Hooked my thumbs in the pants' waistband and strutted a little, pretending I was the rich homeowner. A bit of nostalgia slapped my mind hard as the dry, hot wind slapped my face. Five years ago this house represented the middle class dream—husband, wife, 2.5 children, dog, and cat, all living in an overpriced multi-million-dollar home, with Mom and Pop sitting on the deck smoking and drinking whatever while watching their kids and pets play.

As if it were a zombie rising from the dead, that deck shook a bit, moaned, and shifted, waking me from my daydream. Kept my balance and went inside just in time. With that small tremor, the remainder of the deck collapsed into the canyon. The house started to shake too. I grabbed my backpack and left in a hurry. So much for the multi-million-dollar view! The whole house would probably go now. *What a coincidence!*

But I didn't believe in coincidences. Figured my meager forty-five kilos plus the little tremor had been enough to destabilize that already weakened deck. I made a namaskar to Namagiri once I was outside the house, shifted the backpack over my shoulder, and left for home.

Went around rusting cars, some now with only skeletons at the wheel, and jumped over cracks in the asphalt. Wondered how much longer I'd last. Couldn't imagine jumping around like that when I was fifty.

Strange that mortality didn't worry me much anymore. What did I have to live for? Was I lucky to be alive in this world filled with death? What quirk of genetics had set me apart from the billions who died? That woman in the mirror hadn't looked special. Her background wasn't special either. But she had survived. For what?

CHAPTER 9

I was so deep in thought that I didn't see the feral dogs. Was often on the lookout for them. A single dog was a coward if he thought you were more threatening than he was. Packs ran by mob rule, though, each one encouraging the other, all so everyone could dine. A solitary canine could be frightening; a pack of them surrounding you and snarling froze your blood.

I didn't see them but heard their snarls. Unsheathed my machete, swung the backpack of can goods off my shoulder, and prepared for battle. Knew running wouldn't do much good. That would just tell them I was frightened prey—which I was!

Which one would come at me first? Spotted him just before he lunged.

Warning to anyone left who wants to make a movie about my life—yeah, I know—absurd—but consider what I was doing: I abused those animals! *Also warning to any SPCA or PETA members who are left alive.* Dispatched number one with a machete hack across the eyes deep enough to reach the front of the brain. Number two soon followed. Clubbed him with the bag of can goods, crushing his skull.

I backed up a bit but still facing them so the others

could sniff their dead companions. *Do dogs want revenge?* I didn't think the remainder of the pack had any real love for numbers one and two. Why would they? Alpha and Beta had likely bullied Gamma and his companions. By eying the hanging fruit, I could see the females were staying back now while the males circled. The bitches were probably also abused by numbers one and two.

When the others were through sniffing their dead companions, they turned to me. *Okay, maybe they do want revenge.*

"Come and get me, you scrawny devils!" I said.

That startled them, so I said it louder and advanced a few steps, but I knew a few were circling me from behind. Scrawny didn't mean stupid. Nowadays stupid dogs in the wild didn't survive.

But that meant the ranks ahead of me had thinned a bit. I rushed them and jumped onto some concrete blocks, probably remnants of a building that hadn't survived that last quake. That put me at an advantage. I could swing that backpack with a bigger arc and could wind up for a good machete hack too.

❧❧❧

Dogs were domesticated wolves. I knew their genetic lines were distinct but fuzzy, and feral dogs in the boonies often interbred with their kissing cousins—more coyotes than wolves in the LA area. None of these dogs were small, though. They were enough like wolves for me. Guessed the little yip-yap dogs had already been eaten by their bigger brothers and sisters, and huge dogs that some people needed a second mortgage to feed, just needed humans feeding them too much, or had died of thirst.

What I was facing was a pack of hardened survivors like me, except none of their kind had succumbed to the contagion that fell from the sky.

I tried to determine how this pack of dogs was different from packs of wild humans I'd seen. Surviving had made these dogs more cunning. Could I say that about feral humans? Nope. They'd sunk to dog level. Maybe God had just become Dog, a backward deity for a backwards time? I thought of that Egyptian god with the dog's head. Didn't have time to remember his name as number three jumped onto the concrete block and faced me. *Or is he the Alpha now by default?*

The area on top of the block was tight quarters. I couldn't maneuver, but neither could he. I swept him off the block with one machete chop. His friends couldn't circle the block because one side was barricaded with a pile of rubble. So they paced. *Stalemate?* They didn't seem to want to repeat number three's antics while he was still a twitching reminder of my lethality. Couldn't blame them.

❧❦❧

Pacing went on for about fifteen minutes, maybe twenty. I then had an epiphany. I started throwing rocks at them. I'd played some softball and always won some worthless stuffed animal at those carnival booths, so three more went down. *Are the dogs maybe thinking this scrawny human isn't worth the trouble?*

Either my aim went to hell or they became better dodgers, but subsequent stones didn't find their mark. They'd stopped pacing, though, congregating some distance in front of the cement block to talk it over. Reminded me of an NFL huddle to decide about whether to go for the first down.

The new quarterback came forward a little. Those angry yellow eyes stared at me. I swear he gave me a sly wink. *Respect?* He and his buddies then slinked away.

I was cautious. I waited on the cement block for about twenty minutes more to see if it was a ploy and whether they'd come back. They didn't.

I slinked away too, keeping a watchful eye and turning at every noise. There weren't many noises, though, which was a good thing. My nerves were frazzled enough. Figured I was lucky.

Time to go home.

CHAPTER 10

There wasn't much to come home to. I still lived in what was once a nursery selling plants to LA's middleclass homeowners so they could spruce up their little boxes on the hillsides and in the valleys and waste as much water as possible. There were all sorts of pots spread around three acres or so, all with shriveled, dead plants in them. Lots of hoses, dry and cracked by the sun and heat too, attached to faucets that no longer delivered water. My water supply was obtained by collecting what dew there was overnight and straining out the crap with a cloth.

That took place outside and inside my swanky abode, a large shed used once to store fertilizer, mulch, peat moss, and so forth. The original pungent odor still lingered a bit even though I'd cleaned the shed out long ago. Always figured no one would look for me there, and no one ever had. Nomad people tended to avoid bad odors. That no longer meant decaying flesh, but still…

I hadn't counted on a visit from a kid. Not a kid really, but a pubescent teen. He was sitting on the steps leading to the business entrance to my shed—I kept the sliding doors of the loading dock shut and padlocked. He sat regally on his throne, but like the descendant of the emper-

or who had no clothes. *Maybe a tween?* I made sure my machete was in hand as I approached him with a smile.

He said he was fourteen and looked six, worse than any waif in a Dickens orphanage. Looked hungry too— all skin and bones with visible ribs, more so than mine. He was dirty, and he needed a haircut right down to his balls. I wished I had a hose to use on him.

He had the shakes. I knew he wasn't cold. *Drugs? Drug withdrawal? Careful Penny!* I decided it was just nerves, a lost puppy happy to see a human being again. That was my gut feeling. He didn't look mean like the kids at Malibu or the radio station. Didn't look like a rapist or murderer either, although he was fully endowed.

I told him my name, and he said he was Samuel Hunter, so I called him Sammy, preferring to avoid that last name. Kept it friendly although I knew from experience his kind on the beaches were like packs of wolves feeding on just about anything, including other human beings. Or like the dogs I had just fought off.

He smiled. Cute. Freckles and dimples. Red hair. Noticed other details. Teeth missing. Missing finger. Partially missing ear. I was remembering Golding's *Lord of the Flies*, though, and not just because they were buzzing around his head. Long hair and needing a bath screamed gang member *de las playas*, but the smile seemed genuine enough. Golding's angelic choir boy.

I cleaned him up a bit and dressed him with some kid's old pajama bottoms I had planned to tear into rags. Smiled at the erection. He seemed a bit embarrassed by it, so I let him finish pulling the PJs on. *Maybe he's honest about the age?* I wasn't going to encourage anything. Found some old flip-flops for him. Had scavenged them earlier. They fit him okay. No idea how long they'd last—kids were always hard on shoes. *Mamacita* always said that.

I gave him some of my treasure—a whole can of Bush's Baked Beans, in fact. Used my finger to taste some sauce from the can 'cause I knew that was the last can of baked beans I'd see for a while. Figured I could leave the door open if he started to fart, but also had figured he needed some protein in a bad way. *Who doesn't these days?*

"Will you be my mom?" he said after the beans—no farts yet, but anytime now with the beans hitting an empty stomach and that good old fiber starting to work.

What to say to that? "No, but you can stay here with me. I'll take care of you. And I'll give you a few hugs if you give me some. Just don't get any ideas beyond that."

He hugged me. "Don't worry. I'll take care of you too, Penny."

My heart melted. "You'll need some training." Feral animals always did, and it was always iffy. You never knew when they'd turn on you. I finished putting my treasure in the crates I used for shelving. Ignored dents in the cans corresponding to blows to feral dogs' heads. *How will I feed both of us?*

Still slept with my machete.

᪣᪣᪣

Two days later, the situation worsened. Sammy found a dog. Considering my recent experience, I was wary, but the mutt seemed okay. A boy and his dog. Lassie and Timmy. Rin Tin Tin and Rusty. Astro and Elroy Jetson. Scooby-Doo and Shaggy Rogers. Mothers of poor kids used reruns as babysitters and told them never to open the door so Child Services didn't discover they were alone. *Mamacita* was no exception.

We were exploring a strip mall not far from our humble abode. The kid was pretending to be a cowboy with one of those mechanical horses that took quarters—*Do quarters exist anymore?*—and the mutt came running around the corner, wagging its tail, emaciated and dirty like the kid had been—still was—only the canine had a spiked hairdo from dried feces. The tail wag said "friend" instead of "I want to eat you" like that pack of feral beasts. I knew I needed water for both of the kid and dog, even dirty water. For me too. A Saturday night bath was in order. Would use beer instead if I could find some. *Why waste good water?*

The beer problem was solved when that observant kid found the liquor store's cellar. The store proper didn't have anything left on its shelves, of course. Maybe the first item to go when the shit hit the fan and survivors became thirsty? Two overripe and mostly skeletal cadavers in the alley showed signs of being in a fight over something, liquor being the safe bet. Only strings of desiccated meat, human jerky, were on the dry bones. I wondered if the dog had been chewing on them—there were bite marks. Would have to brush his teeth too. *Ugh!*

I guessed the store had received its liquor shipments and other merchandise at the back via an extra-wide door. Stood up and contemplated bodies awhile before pinching my nose—soon realized it was dog feces, not the skeletons—and went to see if there was anything on them they no longer needed wherever their sad souls were now. When I returned, Sammy pointed to the rectangular outline in the floor.

"Secret vault," he said.

Smart kid. Big vocabulary for a feral whelp. I decided to continue his education. "It's called a cellar or basement." The store was small. *Where else could they put their inventory?*

I expected the cellar to be as bare as the store proper, but it wasn't. Used two cases of beer I'd always considered a rotgut brand to give Sammy and the dog a bath. Decided I'd wait, but had to join in when the kid starting shaking beer bottles and squirting me. The kid thought it was great fun. Imagine, drinking some of your own bathwater! The dog hated the procedure, although he lapped it up from the floor. Both boy and dog became tipsy, but they were cleaner. I felt cleaner too.

Wondered if it would improve their doggy breaths. *Isn't mouthwash mostly alcohol?* Certainly improved the dog's odor. The beer was full of hops. I had managed to remove most of the dry dog turds from the dog's hair. I'd just hacked off the remainder with a switchblade I'd lifted off that biker dude's cadaver many years ago—protection in a pocket. I still had the machete, and those kitchen knives from earlier days were still useful for home defense.

Kid and dog made me begin to think of dental hygiene. Never gave it much thought for myself because figured I'd die of something else before my teeth rotted and fell out or the rot reached my brain. Had good teeth anyhow. *Look, Mamacita, no cavities!* But now I had to be a surrogate mom and caretaker of a boy's pet. *Responsibilities!*

Next to the liquor store was a drugstore. All good inventory was long gone, but dental floss and toothbrushes, likely not considered luxury items like opioids, were scattered all over. The beer had been a good choice, though, because there wasn't any shampoo or bars of soap. Go figure: Why would people steal shampoo if there wasn't any water to bathe in? Maybe they bathed in the ocean…or beer.

But I cut people some slack. It had been pretty hectic after the world went to hell. Still was. What few survivors there were had to make do with what they could find. I supposed all the brilliant politicos who caused the attacks were safely in bunkers in the nation's capital when it happened. Too bad I wasn't in DC. I'd smoke 'em out and ask "What the fuck were you thinking?" before I killed them. Or handed them over to cannibals.

Sammy stayed in his flip-flops, but I carried the pajama bottoms and a case of beer. He smelled like a sailor on a shore-leave binge, without the obligatory visit to cathouses, but he was clean. And I was now equipped with implements for our dental care. Figured we'd brush our teeth in beer and come back for more from our secret cache as needed.

જ્જજ

The kid had been an infant when the world went to hell. That made him an innocent, assuming he wasn't a member of a beach gang. Said he wasn't, and I believed him—for the time being. He and the dog became good friends. Kind of liked the stray myself. We named him Mutt.

"Do you remember your parents?" I said one morning as we shared a can of dog food evenly—a third for the kid, Mutt, and me.

The kid wrinkled his nose. "This stinks."

"Read the label. 'Real meat or meat byproducts with vegetables and cereal added.' It's the nearest thing I have to corned beef hash, which is the all-American breakfast meat besides bacon."

"What's that?"

"Which? Hash or bacon? Never mind. Eat up or starve. And answer my question."

He frowned and took a few tentative bites. I dug in, ignoring the voice inside my head telling me that I was eating canned crap. Mutt had no problems at all.

"I sort of remember them. Dad more than Mom. She

died of some disease—what everyone else had, I guess, but a bit later. Dad said it was from drinking unboiled water, though. He worked as a male nurse—you know, before—so he might be right about that."

"And what happened to him?"

"Gangs killed him." Sammy used an oily rag to wipe away tears and blow his nose. Scratch one rag from the household inventory. "He pushed me away and told me to run as fast as I could. I did, but I stopped to watch." More tears streamed down his cheeks.

Maybe Dad didn't want his kid to see his body turning on a spit? Or Dad didn't want his kid to be the appetizer for the main course? I'd have done the same thing. No wonder the kid awoke screaming and shaking at night sometimes. "You should have been here all along. On the shore, you never know what you'll run into."

"We knew our way around," Sammy said, glaring at me. "Dad was good at keeping us safe. The gangs had predictable movements. Dad said they're like herds of wild animals. He was in the Peace Corps in Africa."

Ha! Now there's an ironic name from the past. A lot of good that Corps did in keeping peace in the world. 'Course they depended on funding from Washington, and we all know how that dried up faster than California aquifers.

Those thoughts made me wonder about all those desalination plants offshore again. Hadn't thought about them for a long while. Looked toward the ocean. *Are they still functioning? If so, where's the water?*

"To change the topic," I said, "living where you did, did you guys ever see anything offshore?"

"The gangs have small boats, and they go fishing sometimes. Is that what you mean?"

"No, I'm talking about big things in the distance, maybe like islands on the horizon."

"I still don't understand."

I explained the concept of island and horizon.

"Sure. We could sometimes see those old oil rigs."

"Anything else? Anything bigger with lots of pipes and stuff?"

"Yeah. I have no idea what they are. I never talked to Dad about them."

One thing for sure, if they were desalination plants, that fresh water was no longer coming ashore. *But are there engineers on them still, tending to all the machines and computers?*

"I might have to go and see for myself," I said. Or find high-power binoculars or a telescope.

Sammy looked horrified. "Please don't do that! You'll end up like Dad."

I ruffled the mop of red hair, a bit shorter now, because of my expertise with some old rusty scissors likely once used to trim rose bushes. I'd even given my kinky curls a whack and a prayer too.

"Don't worry. We'll plan carefully."

He didn't look like he had any confidence in that. Mutt stole the remainder of his breakfast. Taught Sammy a lesson about eating and not talking so much.

CHAPTER 11

Sammy and I became farmers. I knew UC once ran an Agricultural Extension Service, but we were all DIY, using the old tried and true techniques of by-guess-and-by-gosh. Later I also remembered a few techniques from a previous visit to Israel.

I'd found some seeds one day scavenging in an already scavenged grocery store. Ignored flower seeds—couldn't spare the water and couldn't eat flowers. Took seeds for vegetables and tubers. I once read a sci-fi novel titled *The Martian* about growing potatoes on the red planet—thought I could grow potatoes too.

SoCal wasn't as bad as Mars yet. Soil around our humble abode was a bit red, though. Lots of bags of fertilizer from the nursery to use too. Big assumption about whether their contents had any poop left—pun intended—no expiration dates I could see, but we didn't eat well enough or have time to collect what that novel's hero used.

We had plenty of air, sun, and the necessary tools, though, just not much water. I'd developed two new ideas about getting water. We had enlarged my dew distillation setup. We also boiled the alcohol and carbonation from the beer. It was a lot of work and maybe a waste of good beer. Breaking down nearby construction for kindling was therapeutic.

Sammy and I bonded. We were curled together on our front porch looking at the sunset one night, Sammy's head on my belly that was growling from hunger, when the kid became practical.

"We'll run out of beer," he said.

"I'm down to one bottle," I said in agreement. I'd been watching our stock. "It's a race. But we still have the dew collector."

"I wish it would rain."

"Not happening, unless we have one of those Pineapple Expresses like we had years ago." I saw his puzzled expression. "Forget it. We need a desalination plant to send us some water."

"I don't think they work. We can check."

"I'm not going near the shore," I said, "at least not yet, and not with you."

He sat up. "Never do that, Penny! Promise!" The second time he'd gone crazy about that idea. I nodded. He gave me a hug and then scratched the top of his head. "I think I know where one pipe ends. We can open the valve and see if there's any water in it."

In the old days when cars were ubiquitous in the LA area, that pipe's end would be about as far as the daily trip for donuts and coffee—nothing to worry about. Walking, it took us many hours, mostly because of a littered landscape.

The kid was right, though. Only the pipe didn't end. It was connected to a pumping station. The station was no longer pumping, but I figured that was because there was no electricity and nothing to pump. Valve before the pumping station was more than just shut—the shutoff valve was rusted tight.

Kicked the damn thing and danced around a bit. Old

sneakers weren't much protection, and I wasn't wearing socks. Put my butt on the ground, took off my shoe, and rubbed the sore foot.

"That wasn't practical," Sammy said. "You could have hurt yourself."

"I did. Do you know what frustration means?"

"Sure. It always slaps you in the face when there's no obvious solution to a problem." He smiled. "But I have one."

"A little late in telling me, don't you think?"

He shrugged and pointed to a piece of rebar. "Give me a big enough lever, and I can move the Earth."

"Your dad teach you that?"

"My dad was a smart man."

"So the answer is yes, Master Luke. Your Yoda-dad read it somewhere, but teaching you the principle was good too. Let's go to work." Kid had no idea who Luke and Yoda were either. I'd seen the first movie, episode whatever, about twenty years after it came out. More fantasy than sci-fi. *The Martian* was better.

It took us another two rebars and an hour to break through oxidization and open the valve. No reward for all that effort. Jammed the third rebar into the seam between the pipe's top and valve. Still nothing. We had a good opening now, but I couldn't even put my arm inside.

"Let me." The kid reached in until his arm was in almost up to his shoulder. "No water."

"You at the bottom of the pipe?"

"No. Lift me up and closer."

I complied.

"It's wet at the bottom." He withdrew his hand covered with mud.

"Sludge," I said. Sniffed. Foul stuff. Probably a five-year-old pool of stagnant water saved from evaporation by being confined to the pipe. "But let's fill something with any mud you can dredge up and take it back to our plants."

"Are you kidding? That'll weigh a ton."

I sat on my butt and tried to keep from crying. "Guess that's not practical either. It's a shame to waste it, though. The plants wouldn't care if it's sludge."

Sammy sat beside me and patted my shoulder. Good kid. He knew my moods now. I didn't know if that was good or bad, but patting helped.

My eyes followed the pipeline toward the shore. Bet there were more pumping stations along the way. *Maybe we can follow the damn pipe all the way to the desalination plant?* I filed that possibility away for future reference. Thought of the new breed of beach bums. Sammy wouldn't be on that trek, and I would have to invent some way to arm myself. Thought of the NRA and almost broke out laughing. Unless they had fled to bunkers with other DC bigwigs, they were all dead. *What is that Second Amendment again?*

I was no stranger to SoCal. Knew it was likely there were guns around in ranches north of the city. The local supply was probably exhausted—the ammo, if not the guns. Filed that away for future reference too. That weekend excursion north to Six Flags seemed an impossible dream now—the amusement park was in the middle of gun country, meaning ranches of orange groves, cattle, and horses. The ranchers would all be gone, but their guns should remain. Ironic. Appropriate?

I patted Sammy on the back. "Come on, Kemo Sabe, we need to get somewhere safe. Tomorrow is another day."

ೲೲ

I hadn't seen a chipmunk or rabbit since I moved into

my old fertilizer shed. Wouldn't you know they were just waiting for my crop of vegies? Mutt chased the critters away. Thought he was chasing an intruder at first. A woman alone with a kid—who wouldn't be paranoid? But the appearance of fauna in the flora gave me an idea. *Traps!*

"You have to have bait," Sammy said.

Always a critic! The skinny kid stood up with hands on hips eyeing my first masterpiece, an optimistic trap—it was big enough for a rabbit.

"Okay, genius, what should I use for bait?"

"Leaves. They're likely after them. Rabbits probably won't eat tomatoes and they can't reach the carrots and potatoes yet. Try some fresh leaves."

"Seems hurtful to the plants. What about weeds?" They were shooting up everywhere. Knew they were sucking up moisture the good plants needed. They would have choked out those good plants if I didn't go down on my knees every day and pull the damn things out.

"They won't touch some weeds."

"Picky little critters, aren't they? Which ones will they like?"

"Don't know. Try a mixture. Ever cooked a rabbit before?"

I grimaced. "Heavens no. But it must be good protein."

"Maybe. Don't worry. I'll prepare it if we catch one. My dad taught me. I'd let the chippies go, though."

"Not much meat there, I'll agree. Critters are skinny, just like us. What's a rabbit taste like?"

"Chicken. Leaner. No dark meat."

But the critters seemed to know Mutt was guarding the vegetable garden now, so they never came back. I kept working on the weeds and watering. Damned vegetables took a lot of water. I'd rigged transparent tarps to act like

little greenhouses and dripped the precious dew conden-
sate right around the roots. Saw that in a kibbutz in Israel
on one leave, but hadn't paid enough attention to details.
My technique must have been a close approximation,
though.

Our foraging trips became less frequent as we became
vegetarians. Learned to grill carrots and potatoes—
couldn't boil them for lack of water. They took forever to
cook and were still bland. Thought of using sweat as a
salt source—how did our bodies find it now?—but that
idea grossed me out. Sammy discovered a weed that we
could press to make some kind of oily liquid. Brushed
that on our barbecued tubers. Also used remains of
canned goods…maybe the salt source?…and beer. We
replenished our supply of the latter as often as possible.

On one foraging trip, though, we had a new adventure.

ↄ℈ↄↄ

We were about ten klicks from home base when
Sammy spotted the downed chopper. "Think it will fly?"

"Can you pilot one?" I asked.

He shook his head.

"Neither can I, so it's a moot point."

"What's that mean?"

"Irrelevant. Not important. Whatever. If there's no one
around who can fly it, it won't fly. Period. Probably no
fuel nor batteries left either."

"Guess that's right. Can we look inside?"

I saw the red cross on the plane's side with the letters
U-S-A-F E-M-S below. "Good idea. It might have some
medical supplies we can use."

The pilot and patient's eye sockets were empty where
carrion birds had feasted. They couldn't reach the pilot's
or patient's bodies, though, but fly maggots could. An

EMT uniform protected the first from birds, and the patient was in a thermal bag to keep him warm. All that implied, in my expert opinion, that the whirlybird had crashed recently.

I figured at least one other EMT was among the missing but soon spotted two. A man and woman had crawled away from the helicopter, likely thinking the gas tank would catch fire. They'd been stabbed and left to die as near as I could tell. Meant the attackers hadn't been cannibalistic. Also meant they hadn't shot down the chopper, so it must have suffered mechanical failure.

The whole scene smelled like decay and death, mechanical and physical. Because the chopper probably crashed a few weeks earlier, somewhere something military was functioning after all this time. I remembered the call I'd intercepted long ago about picking up refugees in Oxnard. Swatted away flies and peaked inside.

"If you're coming in, hold your nose. It's ripe in here." I entered the chopper and began to rummage.

"Flares," said Sammy from the back. "Bet they're still good. Wonder why the knife-wielders didn't take them."

I shuddered, thinking about the violence. "Grab anything you find that might be useful. I'd like to take medical supplies back, but I don't think I can carry them."

"We can drag them on a medical stretcher," Sammy said, pointing to one side of the whirlybird where two of them were stored.

Damn, how did I ever get along without this kid?

"We can take a lot more if you can pull one," he said.

"You'll have to help me lift it over rubble, but sure. Why not?"

That was what scavenging was all about: finding useful items and taking them back to home base.

I found some small shovels that might be useful for the garden too, especially for Sammy who had a hard time handling adult-sized tools. Being a boy, he might grow some more—my brother had grown two inches in his twenties—but at that time Sammy needed some Hobbit tools.

I thought about burying the crash victims. Decided against it because I didn't want to be out after dark. Alone, I might have taken the chance, but now I had to think about Sammy's safety too.

"What about some electronics?" Sammy said.

"Useless. Runs on whirlybird power. There are good batteries somewhere like those in cars, but also too heavy to take back. We need more manpower. Who are we going to call?"

"Ghostbusters? Dad used to say that."

I smiled and then frowned. Probably a lot more ghosts now. We'd need the original guys and the new gals from the two movies and an entire army as well to chase the ghosts away from LA. For sure it wouldn't happen in my lifetime.

♋♋

I gained an admiration for farmers. We had worked like hell to produce a few vegies, using a lot of water and fertilizer, and now they were almost all gone. Kind of depressing, to say the least. Had seeds left for another round or two, but didn't know how to obtain more. *How do they make them to put in those little packages?*

Sammy popped a small red tomato into his mouth, made a happy face, and sucked some juice that had escaped his chapped lips. "Maybe they'd be bigger next time if you thin them?"

I remembered the name on the package. "They're cherry tomatoes, so we're lucky they're bigger than cherries. Remember, the others came in bigger. And the beefsteak ones were bigger than a hamburger. Those babies drank a lot of water."

I saw his raised eyebrows. Explained what a hamburger was. Realized I was neglecting the kid's education. I popped a slice of cucumber into my mouth. Knew it was like watermelon because it contained a lot of our precious water. That gave me an idea. "We can recycle our pee to produce more water."

"Ick. How do you do that?"

"Don't know. If I had a computer, I could Google it."

"I'm not sure what that means, but before computers there were books. My dad said so."

"Might be some still around if we can find a library. They were becoming scarce, just like bookstores. Books would make good fuel."

Silence reigned. Hopelessness created it for me. *What do I say to the kid? We're living on borrowed time, Sammy, so prepare to die?* Not of the plague but starvation. We both had some kind of immunity that allowed us to survive the contagion they'd bombed us with. But were we better off than all those who had died? We were becoming listless, silent zombies, the walking dead. Even Mutt, who had a steady diet of cockroaches to complement his vegetarian diet. *Those bugs will inherit the Earth!*

A crash interrupted my reverie. Mutt started barking and then yowled in pain. I grabbed a shovel as a makeshift weapon and headed out the door. A naked man was carrying our dead dog. He stopped and stared at me. I raised the shovel.

"Put down the dog or I'll bash your head in."

"I'm starving," said the man.

Long ago he might have been good looking, but now he might as well have been an emaciated Robinson Crusoe. He looked worse than we did. Looked worse than the actor in that old castaway movie—Tom something or other.

This fellow's stench reached out and grabbed me by the throat. Gnats swarmed around his head. A tangled beard was in worse shape than Mutt's fur had been when we found him. Splotches were all over his body. *Scurvy?*

I took all this in while wanting to kill him for taking our dog's life. Mutt had been good company for Sammy. *Shit, he had been good company for me!*

"Put him down!"

"What will you do with him?"

"Bury him, dipshit, right after I bury you!"

"No!" He came at me.

I slammed the shovel against the side of his head. He went down. I was ready to plunge the shovel's blade into his neck when I saw Sammy.

"Don't do it!" Sammy ran over and looked at the unconscious man. "His name is Ben Hur. He must have followed me here."

Lassie come home? I looked at the kid and broke out laughing like an insane person. "You know him? And he told you that was his name?"

Sammy shrugged. "My dad called him that. We didn't know his real name. We saved him from a gang. Ben tried to save my dad when that other gang attacked Dad, but Ben had to run for his life too. I haven't seen him since then. I think he's crazy. You know, like mentally disturbed. He can't remember his real name."

I bent down and took the man's neck pulse. Faint, but still there. Saw the scar. Followed it through the matted beard up the right side of his face and halfway across the top of his head. It was the remnants of an old and serious head wound.

"Brain damaged maybe? With that kind of injury, he's lucky to be alive."

Ben Hur regained consciousness with a start, put his hands up as if to protect himself, and tried to push away from me by doing a backstroke on the ground with his scrawny, hairy legs and arms.

"Easy, Benjamin. Sammy's here. You know Sammy, right?"

The kid bent over him. Recognition filled the old man's eyes. He teared up. "Sorry about the dog, Sammy. Didn't know he was yours. I've been looking for you for a long time."

"You'll be okay now," said Sammy, patting him on the shoulder.

That chopper's medical supplies now came in handy. Soon Ben was bandaged and slurping beer-flavored vegetarian soup—no meat except for some big ants' butts, but a fair number of vegies. I even opened a treasure-trove can of corn for him.

CHAPTER 12

After Ben finished eating, we had a funeral service for Mutt. I wanted Ben to officiate, but he looked pale as if he would upchuck all the good food I'd fed him, so Deacon Penny had to do it again. I felt a bit weird saying the same words for the dog as I had for Angela, George, and the others, but I didn't have a Bible around to look for different material—not sure the Good Book mentioned dogs much. St. Francis came later— didn't know anything he wrote either. I should have paid better attention when I was young.

You could argue the words were wasted. Any deities were far away and prayers to them seemed futile. I said these words out of respect. Mutt had no choice in being born a dog, and he'd been part of our little family. I'll have to confess I wanted to see Ben's reaction. He and Sammy seemed bonded, but I still didn't trust the old man. Being a mental case was no excuse if he became psychotic and killed Sammy and me. We'd still be dead.

So I made my spiel, Ben said "Amen," and I gave the boys the job of burying Mutt. I sat on a concrete block and made sure they did it right. I didn't want a pack of feral beasts to dig up our dog's body. He hadn't been with us too long, but he'd been a loyal friend.

"Should I make a cross?" said Sammy.

"No. I have one." I went in back of our humble abode to where there was a pile of those palm crosses they put on graves for Palm Sunday and Easter. Before the apocalypse, nurseries had done a good business selling them with flowers. I often used them as kindling, but there were still a lot left. Wished I'd had them for Angela and her kids. George hadn't needed one, of course.

I still thought about taking one to Leo Carrillo State Park, though, diving down, and sticking it by George's body. Realized that wasn't too bright. First, couldn't go there easily. Second, the body might be unrecognizable by now among other bodies there. Three, where would I obtain tanks and a wetsuit? Going for mine would make the journey even longer. And the big number four? I had no desire to do more diving again.

Decided that remembering George, Angela, and others in my thoughts was good enough. After all the bodies I'd seen without names, my prayers for my friends seemed like something special. I wiped away tears, thinking that maybe in the future Sammy would be remembering me, hopefully just as fondly. *What more can we ask for?*

❧❦❧

I figured Ben Hur to be about twenty to thirty years my senior, maybe making him the oldest man still alive? I hadn't seen anyone older. Maybe all older survivors had been eaten by younger ones? Or just withered away in the dry heat, joining the generalized boneyard that was SoCal?

I never could figure why some survived and others didn't. I dove into deep water when the world was still alive. I surfaced and found it dying. I was only under about twenty minutes. A whole substation of deputies was gone when I came up. I remembered the victim. Figured that bringing to the surface a murder victim some gang members from the valley had probably weighted down and dumped was no longer important with all the other dead people lying around.

The navy taught me to dive. It was the only real skill I had. America's armed services had always been strange institutions. The USN, for example, told people to join the navy and see the world and even promised those who enlisted a chance to learn skills that would give them a job when their tours were up. They took a high-school grad and turned him into a cook or mechanic. But the cook never learned the culinary arts needed for a restaurant career. He only learned to cook great quantities of crappy food—they called the eateries mess halls for good reason—and all that quantity was needed for thousands of hungry sailors. The mechanic never learned the skills necessary to fix a car either—the navy didn't do cars.

Tio Jose—a great uncle—was in Vietnam. He even had a degree in American history. They made him into a janitor in Saigon. I guess that gave him useful skills—he was a janitor for forty years in a posh girls' school. At least they didn't put that gentle soul on the frontlines to kill Viet Cong.

I survived two deployments in the navy and then found a job with the sheriff's department. Ironic because I was afraid of water as a kid. Bobby, my older brother Roberto, had knocked me into the pool—not on purpose, but he laughed his head off until he realized I was drowning. He dove in and kept my head above water long enough for the lifeguard to save me. He stormed off when the lifeguard chewed him out for even letting me near the adult pool. But that was on me. I'd been tired of the wading pool—I was already potty-trained and the other little brats weren't. Amazing what parents would let their babies do in public pools in that respect. Guess chlorine handles urine more or less, but kids' turds created visible havoc.

Big brother Bobby liked to be in bathing suits. And girls liked to see him in them. He should have been a lifeguard or surfer. Fewer of the latter on the East Coast, of course. Never knew him to have a permanent relationship, though. He either had commitment problems or was trying to mimic a sheik with his harem.

Bobby was swarthy but not as dark as me. Great teeth too when he smiled, which wasn't often. Broad shoulders and a lean, muscled body made him athletic, but, except for a bit of swimming to justify strutting along a pool's edge or at the beach, he was lazy and didn't even play intramural sports. Some siblings were role models for their younger siblings. Bobby wasn't mine, and later events associated with my mother's care confirmed that he was just an asshole. Too much of Dad in him, maybe.

I couldn't ask Ben how he survived—he wasn't all there. I couldn't ask Sammy either, for that matter—he'd been a baby. Lucky kid, to have a father who survived too. I thought about Angela's baby-to-be. Would that kid have been the next great physicist or great musician?

That plague they hit us with was designed for humans, but maybe they didn't find the perfect formula, because some of us survived. It didn't kill any animals either. Dogs running wild and carrion birds had a field day. Even feral cats. You've heard that part, but I was reminiscing—better said, reliving the nightmare.

Flora and fauna didn't last long without water, though. California had droughts before, but this one was a killer. It was already in full swing, but it became worse after that crap fell from the sky. So did the quakes. I wasn't a scientist, but I thought there was too much coincidence there. *Or maybe just Gaia getting even with us?* Probably no one around anymore smart enough to figure it all out.

Ben was like a little kid. He played with Sammy a lot. No wonder the kid liked him. Ben could talk okay, but sometimes the words didn't make much sense. His conversation was often at a kid's level too, perfect for Sammy. Problem now was I had two kids to care for and no Mutt to help protect us. Not that he had been much protection, but he offered undemanding love and barked like crazy at anything strange, even a horrible invading insect—cockroaches were an exception—he knew what to do with them.

Having a bit of a technical background—the navy had been patient about teaching yet another recruit who hadn't paid much attention in high school—I couldn't help wondering how generalized the attack had been. Suspected it wasn't just SoCal. *Otherwise, you'd expect the Huns to come claim the conquered lands, right?*

Was it the whole US? Europe? Asia? Did things just go crazy all over? Between the initial attack and retaliatory ones…were there any?…were we only a handful left on the planet? I didn't expect to answer those questions anytime soon. Maybe never. We were too busy surviving.

I figured we'd eventually have to move into new territory. Become nomads. Scavenging the area was producing less useful stuff. Staying in one place could also be dangerous.

Ben turned out okay, but next time we might not be so lucky. Moving around could be dangerous too, but if the choice was between starving or dying of thirst and fighting someone for food and water, I was ready to choose the latter. Might as well go down fighting instead of whining about things I couldn't control.

I began to plan for our move.

ာso

Stay in one place, you accumulate stuff, a lot of it useful in some way. Move on, you have to decide what's indispensable and what's disposable. Move a lot, and the time you have to accumulate and decide diminishes. Being a nomad isn't easy.

Sammy resisted, Ben was indifferent, and I lost myself in logistics. I knew the LA area. It was decaying even before the shit hit the fan. Back East, they complained about one-hundred-plus-year-old infrastructure needing an upgrade. Things in California didn't even last twenty years. They never built to last in the Golden State, good materials weren't used, and too many people used and abused what was built.

Urban sprawl had created a dependence on polluting cars and trucks, or were cause and effect reversed? Public transportation never amounted to anything, so when that contagion had rained down, bodies just stayed in their cars. Some survivors just abandoned their cars and stumbled away, dazed by the horror of it all until they died or coped. Cars couldn't go anywhere. Even if they could, there would be no gas when they arrived there. That was distributed by tanker trucks, and their drivers were dead too.

We walked west along 118. We'd taken a little sightseeing detour to the San Fernando Mission—I'd never been there. The crumbled structure had wasted away from fire and drought—no water for firefighters even if there were some. The baking sun hadn't helped either. I crossed myself in front of a cracked bell with some inscription in Latin on it and felt foolish. Ben became emotional and cried. Sammy wondered what the big deal was. Maybe Dad and Mom hadn't taught him about religion. Maybe he was a Buddhist. And he might be better off. No one gave a damn about religion anymore.

I thought Ben was crying more for the mission itself.

A statue of some dude…Fernando?…was lying face down in a dry fountain. I didn't even check inside buildings. Didn't want to take the chance of a wall falling on me. God had forsaken that place. I didn't want to find dead monks or nuns either. If they hadn't made it with God blessing them for their dedication, who would?

Made me think about heaven and hell too. Given our circumstances, heaven seemed a nebulous concept. Were all my friends and colleagues somewhere being pious and playing harps with angels? Maybe. I imagined them floating around with bloated red faces and swollen tongues—not exactly angelic. Hell seemed an irrelevant concept. Better said, I believed human beings made their own hells, and my little family was trying to survive those created by the devils who had unleashed pestilence upon us. Who was to blame? Figured I probably would never know, but you could summarize their activities by calling them agents of Satan. Collectively, they were Satan.

The Ronald Reagan Freeway, 118, goes to Simi Valley. That was one option. But I wanted to go into the hills first, so we did that via Tapo Canyon Road. Higher was cooler, enough to make it worthwhile for a time. There would be some rich houses along the way too. Wasn't Reagan rich? He must have been. He had a highway named after him. Then I remembered he also had a library farther out just off 118. Never been there either. Tourism for another day. Doubted it would have books on how to distill pee or grow vegies in Death Valley conditions. Maybe it would have a copy of *The Martian*, though, so I could improve my potato-farming skills.

Okay, I was being a nasty critic of the book. I remembered the movie. I liked Matt Damon, a guy my size and also a dedicated family man. But the book and movie were about exploring Mars. That was a laugh. California was starting to look a lot like Mars. And space exploration was some whim of past generations that seemed now to be as logical as a belief in fairy tales.

Brushfires started by dry lightning had scorched a lot of the area. A lot of million-dollar houses had gone up in flames. Didn't bother to check on those because I didn't think Sammy should see crispy critters, many humans among them, that hadn't escaped in time.

I expected a lot more skeletons left over from the attack. Couldn't avoid those because they might have fallen dead right in their houses back when Sammy was just a baby. 'Course they would all look like Halloween ornaments now.

We explored lots of houses not touched by flames. Picked one that had most of its windows still intact. Ben helped me shove the owners' skeletons into the street. What carrion birds and rats hadn't chewed away had become mummified jerky in the arid climate. *Might as well feed feral dogs and coyotes.* Many we saw looked like crossbreeds. Just what I needed: even more vicious dog packs like the one I'd fought!

ⱷↈⱷ

"It's pretty lonely here," Sammy said. Ben nodded.

The three of us were on the deck looking across no man's land—acres and acres of once bustling city and roads. I liked decks with a view. Why have a deck if the view sucked? We each had a warm beer. Figured there was no cop around willing to give me trouble about giving Sammy the straight stuff. *What else is he going to drink?* Even hard liquor had some calories if your body could still process the alcohol.

"Not any lonelier than where we were," I said. Ben nodded again. "Maybe no gangs, but lots of ghosts and evil spirits." I laughed. Ben smiled. Sammy looked worried. "Hey, I'm just kiddin'. Worst we'll see are a few stray dogs and cats, rats, and other critters that have adapted to a world without human beings."

"My dad told me about a lot of different kinds of animals that were wild. Aren't they already adapted?"

"Maybe he was thinking about zoos. I'm pretty sure those all died because there aren't any zookeepers anymore to take care of them. The animals either died of starvation or thirst in their cages."

"How 'bout coyotes?"

"Wild dogs. Local, so maybe. Maybe they ate pet dogs and cats and then died of thirst and starvation. Maybe they all interbred with pet dogs and made a super canine. Who knows? You can wonder all you want, but that doesn't change anything. In SoCal, all animals, even wild ones to some extent, depended on human beings, and human beings let them down."

"Sorry 'bout your dog," Ben said to Sammy.

I shook my head in wonder. He would listen to a conversation, and it would trigger a memory and maybe a comment. This time there was a strong relationship to what was being said. *Maybe some improvement?*

"We'll find another one," said Sammy.

"Yeah, Mutt the Second," I said.

My legs ached. Finished my beer while I wondered how much to unpack. Thought I'd leave the medical stretchers all packed until we decided whether we were staying awhile. We had three backpacks, though. Time to go to work.

Next time I was on the deck in back of the house, the boys were dozing. I'd found some blankets in a linen closet. Used two to cover them. Chilly, was low fifties there—the outside thermometer still worked—not freezing, but a bit cool for leaving them uncovered. I didn't want to move them. I went and curled up by the front door. Anyone coming in would hit me with it. Wasn't expecting the neighborhood welcoming party from the Elks' ladies' auxiliary, though. And I liked that we were even farther away from coastal gangs.

The following morning it rained. That only meant a heavier dew with less ash content. Worked for me. It was easier to obtain water. Not so much ash and other crap in the air higher up either.

Nomad Station Number Two started to take shape. I had decided to count my nursery digs as Number One.

⁐⁐⁐

Three days later, Sammy woke me from my exhausted stupor and pulled me to my feet.

"They're working! Come see."

Ben was at the other side of the house. The deck wrapped around the back to the two sides. From where he was standing, one could see ocean on a clear day. I made a bet to myself that, like that other house, the ocean was more visible now than when the house was built. He was shading his eyes and staring into the distance.

Offshore I saw what had caught the boys' attentions. There was gray smoke coming from a desalination plant. Maybe it was just the horizon effect, but it looked huge. I wondered if they were under attack, or that was normal operation. If so, would there now be water gushing from that pipeline?

"I don't think that's supposed to happen," I said. "The EPA would never allow that contradiction."

"What's the EPA?" said Sammy.

"Never mind. Dead and gone, I'm sure. Pretty well emasculated years ago too. California kept up the good fight, though."

"What's the contradiction?" said Ben.

That surprised me again. Normalcy was becoming more frequent. *Maybe hitting him on the head with a shovel did some good?*

"Polluting the atmosphere to make drinking water," I said.

"Water took precedence over pollution," Ben said. "Just like what happened for energy production. Power and clean water were essentials. Essentials take precedence."

Those were the most logical words he'd ever said to me. Never mind that I disagreed with them because smart people should have discovered how to desalinate water without polluting. I remembered that it was all with solar panels. Conclusion: my kneejerk reaction about being under attack might be the correct one. Decided not to argue—the whole discussion was irrelevant to our lives now.

"Think someone's out there?" said Sammy.

"Yeah, someone is," I said, "and they're probably up to no good. C'mon. Let's have some breakfast."

Mama Penny had heated dog food for her boys.

CHAPTER 13

Life was chaotic after that—interruption after interruption. We had a tremor that cracked a deck support. I was underneath trying to figure out how to mend a four-by-four—no handyman to call—when I heard the whump-whump-whump. Took me back years to when the chopper landed on the carrier and what was left of Ned was taken off in a body bag.

Ned wasn't only my lover, he was my best friend. He was my Adonis too. You couldn't see much of his blond hair because he always had a military-grade buzz-cut, but he could have been bald for all I cared. His piercing blue eyes were so damn expressive. They could stab someone like icicles and make that person turn away from his cold stare. They could also be warm, moist, and appear to be laughing at some private joke.

Of course, he was in great shape, but not after that last mission.

We'd talked about a lot of things, but he never said much about parents or other relatives. When I met him, he appeared to be a bit aloof and pissed at life, not to mention being wound tight.

I confess that I first thought he was a conceited prick, but I later learned that was his shield to keep from getting close to people. But he did his job well for Uncle Sam—a man dedicated to protecting all those threatened by the bad guys in the world.

My pet SEAL often went off in choppers on TOP SE-CRET missions. Not knowing where he was going because of the mission's classification was a blessing. I would have worried more. I was all for the general policy of secret ops and drone strikes replacing boots on the ground. Terrorists wanted the latter. More targets close at hand. Massive troop deployments maximized their number of victims. I always knew the majority of the 1.6 billion Muslims in the world wasn't comprised of murdering savages, but we weren't fighting the peaceful ones. It didn't feel like we were fighting the Crusades either—the messes we became embroiled in didn't have anything to do with religion. And that maelstrom had swallowed my Ned because the general policy I described hit me in its specifics.

Christian, Muslim, Buddhist, Jew—what did it matter now? I knew many of the 1.6 billion Muslims were long dead, along with most everyone else. We had forsaken God, Allah—whatever you call Her—in our rush to destroy the world.

I shook my head to clear the funk from my brain and grit from my curls and listened some more. Not a pissy little news 'copter, but a big military one. *Bad news or good?*

Ned's had been bad. Body bags were always depressing. Knowing someone you love was in one took you as about as low as you could be without dying. I had just wanted to be dead and join him in that bag. Morbid, I know, but when you feel like your life might as well be over, you think like that. Or worse.

Probably my fault. I'd loved someone who made his living staring Death in the face. Maybe loving someone was a mistake. Was I making it again with Sammy and Ben? I looked skyward as if Ned would zap me an answer to that question, but saw only the deck's bottom. He had been good at giving answers, about why we must do certain things even though they were painful things to do. I still missed him. Maybe I no longer needed my happy pills, but the ache was still there. Decided I'd have to keep Ben and Sammy around. They dulled that ache, more so with time.

❧❧❧

I'd had a talk with old Sheriff Hancock about loving someone and then having them die. I was sitting on a swing set he had in his backyard. The annual Christmas party was in full swing inside his sprawling ranch home, but I wasn't in the mood.

He chose a swing next to me. Seemed to support him in spite of his bulk. "We're lucky we're in SoCal," he said. "Imagine barbecuing for a Christmas party Back East."

"Not usual practice, I guess." My words were mumbled. I wanted him to go away. "They tailgate at football games even in the snow, though. And most of the time the weather is bad for the tree lighting in Rockefeller Center too. Californians are too soft."

"That's what I say to my wife. She's from Sacramento. I'm from Colorado."

"Denver Police Force," I said, remembering his creds. "What made you end up here in SoCal?"

"You go where jobs are. I don't see much of you, Penny, because I waste a lot of time hobnobbing with politicos." I smiled at that. He was elected too. "You okay? Don't seem to have much of the holiday spirit. How about some eggnog?"

I hugged myself. "Just missing someone. Best Christmas I ever had was on an aircraft carrier."

"I know the feeling. We lost our daughter just before Christmas years ago. IED killed her in Iraq. She was a translator."

"I'm sorry."

"They say time heals all wounds, but it doesn't, right?"

I nodded.

"Time just files off the rough edges from your hurt. Who did you lose?"

I told him about Ned. "I had a safe job in the navy. He had one of the most dangerous. I should have known better."

"Maybe you did, but you couldn't help loving the guy. That's the way life is. My wife and I tried to convince our daughter that Iraq was a dangerous place, but she insisted on enlisting after Nine/Eleven and going there to help. Didn't make us feel any better when we learned that Hussein had no relationship with al Qaeda, but it's likely she still would have gone."

"She studied languages?"

He smiled. "A real knack for them—Arabic, Farsi, and Pashtun. Me, I can only stumble through kid-level Spanish, and I need to do better with that because of my job. She knew a lot of songs in those languages too."

"Strange. Those cultures don't treat women well."

"Hispanics don't treat women well either. But we men can't keep you down, can we?" He smiled. "I'm writing yearly evaluations of personnel now, with inputs from substation heads. Your captain, for example. I like what I'm seeing about your performance. I'm not liking seeing you maudlin, though."

"I'll get over it. Like you say, time files away rough edges. Seems like a slow process, though."

"You have to move on. Your Ned would want that. We knew our daughter wanted that too. Think of it as a New Year's resolution."

I did. But I was never good at keeping those resolutions.

⋙⋘

I came from under the deck, shaded my eyes, and looked up. Sure 'nough. A whirlybird was flying over. Its black color had faded to dark gray and markings were illegible, but it was a sign of civilization. *Or danger?* Someone had a big-ass helicopter and they were flying it. That meant there was fuel somewhere. I thought of the message I'd overheard to Wolfpack years ago.

Considering our situation, slow starvation to the point we didn't have enough energy to distill water for drinking, that refugee camp I'd imagined still sounded good. Making a quick decision, I waved. Maybe not a good idea, considering our exposed situation, but it was a reflex, like when the fleet doctor used to hit me on the knee with his little rubber tomahawk. Testing my sea legs, I guess. He'd be aghast at my physical condition now. Sinewy muscles from hard work and vegetarian diet—knew the dog food was vegetarian too, maybe with a few meat byproducts—but without an ounce of fat. All our ribs were showing now. Like I said, slow starvation.

My farmer boys were tending the garden on the house's opposite side at that moment, like good little serfs. After tearing out the lady-of-the-house's dead flower garden, we found good soil there. We had found some more seeds in a nearby strip mall. It was an addiction. For some reason, I thought of that song in the off-Broadway play *The Fantastiks*—not the one everyone knows, "Try to Remember," but the one about planting a garden, called "Plant a Radish." Always tried to have some radishes to add a bit of spice to vegetable dishes. The little turnips were also easy to grow and didn't need water all that potable.

I wondered if my boys saw the chopper. Sammy had seen the one on the ground. This one was different—not for medevac. I wondered if Ben remembered them. The poor guy had interesting gaps in his memory. It was a coin toss—if I had a coin to toss.

My waving or sagging boobs didn't change the chopper's flight pattern. It was heading northeast over the mountains. Thought about where they were heading. *Maybe Edwards? After all these years?* That was the most likely scenario. Wouldn't you know it? The people who were better off now were in the military. Edwards was a good place to hide a refugee camp too. *One can dream.* I should have joined the air force!

ʚঌৎɞ

Three days later I awoke with a start. Read once that the left brain sleeps while the right stays vigilant. *Or is it the opposite?* At any rate, it wasn't any great skill. The marauding gang was making enough noise, partying from house to house, ascending the canyon road. Woke Sammy and Ben Hur.

Fight or flight? That ancient question of survival had always haunted me, these last five years especially. With my newly acquired family, the answer had changed to always erring on the side of caution. We gathered what we could and slipped around and past the festivities. Couldn't help liking the aromas, though. Smelled like something between roasted chicken and duck. I knew it wasn't. Who had they caught? I had thought we were alone. Or was it one of their own who had incurred the mob's wrath or had more meat on his bones?

Better question: why were they here? Couldn't the savages fish anymore? Or stay on the beach and eat their own people there? Why leave the shore? I thought of the chopper. Maybe a cleanup had been attempted? If they had gone after savages on the beaches—the big bird had been too high to see if it was a gunship—would gangs of feral humans ascend into the mountains in fear? Lots of questions without answers, but I wasn't waiting around to ask gang members for them.

The three of us made good time, even with the one medical stretcher we brought with us. We made it back to 118 and headed west. I thought it might be a good time to visit that library. A bit of tourism to forget about yet another gang. *Maybe more than one by now!* Seemed like every time I was getting comfortable in a place, peace was disturbed big time, only now disturbances seemed more frequent.

When we arrived at the library early next afternoon, it was obvious that the beautiful building designed to house a famous man's memorabilia was in sad shape. Fire had scarred some of it, and quakes had done some damage too. Two graves had been looted and desecrated. I'd seen that before and couldn't understand the motivation, but drug-crazed cannibalistic hordes didn't reason like normal people. I doubted they were political activists. From what I knew about the man, I was ambivalent, but I respected him. A politician with some moral fiber. Go figure.

We'd lacked that since his presidency, no matter the political party, each one now irrelevant to our lives.

Inside it was cool. "I don't suppose they have any books on gardening," Sammy said, admiring the modern architecture. "Who was this guy?"

"He was a controversial figure," I said, "but some considered him responsible for the demise of the Soviet Union that ended the Cold War." *Give credit even if it's maybe not due. Who wants to speak ill of the dead?*

"What's that?" Sammy said.

"Commies," said Ben Hur.

"Never mind," I said. "It's ancient history and no longer important. We'll camp here for tonight. We're all tired."

In the remaining daylight, I studied one old map I'd kept from some time ago. I'd known my original area around the nursery, but I was extending our nomadic range now.

From where we were, I planned to find Highway 23 and then follow 126 into the mountains back toward I-5. Felt the need to move farther from the coast and gangs, especially if they were moving into the hills now to murder and pillage.

I also wanted to obtain some firepower. Maybe a *ranchito* along 126 would at least have some squirrel guns. Or, maybe we'd find a survivalist's compound. I smiled at that. Wondered how they'd made out. Always thinking that their government would disarm them and take away all their rights when it was some genetically engineered virus or bacterium without any brains at all that did everybody in, present company excluded.

Sammy came and hugged me. "We'll be okay, right?"

I showed him the map, following the route with my finger. "If we go into the mountains, we should be okay." I hugged him back. His nightmares and nighttime sweats weren't as common now. "Did that business last night bring back bad memories?" He nodded. "Want to talk about them?" I asked. He shook his head in the negative. I shrugged. "Okay, why don't you and Ben gather up some books to burn so we can have a hot meal?"

"Which books?"

I shrugged again. *Does it matter?* Books were irrelevant now. They were most likely on history and politics. *Who cares about that anymore?*

We left a lot of scorched tile and ashes on the library's marble floor. I looked back once from the road, thinking it was all symbolic. Once-beautiful grounds were now filled with shriveled dead plants and a few hearty weeds. The library had been built in memory of the dead and now was death itself. I had no regrets as I left the place.

❧❧❧

We saw a few camps during our trek. Not gangs, just desperate people like us. Although I was happy to know we weren't alone, I didn't feel like talking to them. You couldn't trust anyone anymore. People desperate for food and water did desperate things. They might not do it as savagely as gangs, carrying some shreds of morality with them from the old days, but, if they killed us, it wouldn't matter if they did it in unthinking rage or deliberately and methodically.

It took us over two weeks to make the outskirts of Fillmore. We hadn't been in a hurry. Didn't know what would await us—only knew what was behind us. Seemed prudent to take our time and live off the land a bit.

That trek included examining cars and trucks abandoned on highways. The dead had become skeletons in the hot, dry air, of course, some still grasping steering wheels. We found a shotgun and pistol during our scavenging. Also found a truck that had been carrying cows. The cows inside were skeletons too. They'd been trapped in the truck so they didn't survive—otherwise, you'd have feral cows if they avoided predators. A catch-22, I supposed.

Most vehicles still had gas in them, but they wouldn't

start. I couldn't figure that out. Didn't think the plague from the sky went after motors. Maybe it liked ignition wires?

"Electronics," Ben said, as if he were reading my mind. He waved a board covered with chips he yanked from under the hood of a car. He crumbled them in his hands. "Some kind of rot."

I thought a moment. "Come and wash your hands." He joined me by the stretcher and reached for the water jug. "No. Use gasoline."

A pickup truck owned by Mr. and Mrs. Sampson had provided us with two five-gallon cans of regular gas. It was the only thing we had for sterilization.

"You think the sickness did that?" Sammy said.

I nodded. "Maybe just gook left over, but I don't want to take chances." I handed Ben our thin bar of soap. "Now soap and water."

"Wouldn't everything be covered with gook?" Sammy said.

Ben nodded and smiled. "Sammy has a valid point."

"Okay. You're right. But maybe the weather broke it down in the open while what's under hoods stayed around to fester longer."

Ben shook his head.

"Okay, I'm being paranoid, but it's only paranoia—"

"—if it's not true," said Ben.

I smiled at him and nodded. "Okay. Let's pack up and move on. There's no chance for a ride here."

CHAPTER 14

P retty once," Ben said.

We were sitting on someone's screened-in back porch, looking across sloping hills once covered with a grove of live orange trees. Scraggly remnants of those fruit-bearing producers of that golden elixir now looked like skeleton armies marching in perfect columns, all the soldiers' bony hands beckoning to us in the slight breeze to join them in their dance of death. A bit spooky in the waning twilight.

But Ben was right. Once it must have been pretty. We had stayed at the ranch house between Fillmore and Castaic for three days. It was beginning to feel like Nomad Camp Number Three.

Upstairs had been scavenged clean, but all furniture and windows were intact. We had also found a gun collection in the basement. The collector had been a responsible owner of guns, but I couldn't understand why looters hadn't busted the padlocks like we did. Okay, they were good quality, but not that good. Didn't have much use for the old colonial and Civil War pieces, but there were three shotguns, two hunting rifles, and several handguns, all with boxes of ammo.

I had two burning questions to settle: Should I trust

Ben with weapons? And should I teach Sammy to shoot? While I was happy the orange grower had been a gun collector, I hated guns. Worst part of basic training for me. Guns in the military were for killing, of course. Guess they all were designed for killing something—this rancher's newer shotguns and rifles were intended for game hunting. I had no idea what they would do to people. Had a good idea what the handguns would do, though. I'd been a diver for the sheriff's department, after all.

Guns killed people. I remembered seeing that firsthand underwater on an early dive…

☙❦❧

We had an eyewitness who said a body had been dumped off a pier. We had our doubts because the witness had been drunk and had crashed his pickup into a shipping container, but we did have the case of a missing person to consider. George, my friend the sheriff's deputy, called on me to take a look. No boat needed. I was still a newbie. In three previous dives, I was looking for guns. This was my first search for a body.

The waters were so murky that the beam from the light on my head disappeared within two or three meters. I'd had the feeling before—like you're in a haunted house about to open a door to a room where spooks are ready to grab you, or vampires, zombies, whatever. Childhood paranoias exacerbated by my earlier fear of water that I had overcome, no thanks to big brother Bobby.

Many piers had underwater junkyards under them. This one was no exception. Soda and beer cans; old tires; what looked like the rear axle of a car; one single car seat, likely from a van; a kitchen or bathroom sink; a toilet without a lid; and rotting timbers and pieces of concrete left over from the pier's construction. There were also masses of gray seaweed that managed to eke out an existence in that toxic environment among rocks and sand not covered by debris. It wouldn't be easy to dive there even in good light. With the dim light from my beam and what little sunlight filtered through thirty feet of murky water, I swam a pattern, a square spiral expanding out from the pier.

When that spiral had a radius of about twenty yards, I puked into my mask. I'd spotted body parts. The upper torso was intact but without arms. A head rolled along the bottom pushed by the weak current produced by my fins. Some other body parts were scattered about too.

I treaded water a moment, removed the mask, and washed it out. Used the air hose to blow out the filthy water the best I could before I put it back on. Dangerous, but choking on puke and drowning was too. The mask still was about one-third full of seawater. I steadied my breathing and looked up. Decided to surface and use my body as a marker, letting the dinghy come to me. I'd need a bag for body parts anyway.

On the next dive, I played the role of a ghoul, scooting around the bottom and collecting the victim's remains. Almost lost it again. The head had belonged to a young female. When I latched onto it, crabs escaped from the eye sockets and the bullet hole in her forehead. Collected a military-style knife and a gun too.

That initiation into forensics diving had steeled me for almost anything.

∽∾∽∾

Finally, I decided to teach both boys how to shoot a gun. Sammy couldn't handle the shotguns—the recoil always knocked him back on his butt. Might not have if he'd been normal weight. Didn't want to waste much ammo, but they got the hang of it. I figured if they missed their opponent, it would still rattle him until I could take care of the bastard. Could be a female bastard too. You never know. There might be kick-ass females like me running around among the cannibals.

I smiled at that. Shouldn't call myself a kick-ass female. I was a gentle soul who didn't like guns or violence. In the flee-or-fight choice, my general reaction was to flee and fight another day, especially if odds weren't in my favor. Wouldn't have worked for that dog pack, though. My—no, our—situation had toughened me, of course, but my basic nature was still the same: there's a fine line between foolishness and courage or practicality and boldness. I knew my time on the planet would be a lot shorter now, but I still would try to make it last as long as possible now that I had my new family.

I had also caught the nomad spirit. Now I became antsy staying in one place. Decided we should work our way to I-5 and then back to the San Fernando Valley. It would be quite a trek but I figured we could take our time again, scavenging along the way. I hoped the gangs had returned to the beaches, or that chopper had strafed them out of existence.

We visited Six Flags on the way. Not a happy scene. Roller coaster was down and twisted from the quake, and many facilities had been torched. Later brush fires? Roving gangs? Who knew? Some evidence for what might have happened could be found by observing that the only human remains were charred skeletons. The Grim Reaper ran that park for his own amusement now. I wanted to leave soon because he might become pissed. We weren't paying customers.

Both Ben and Sammy were disappointed, but I didn't let them mope. Rides ran on electricity, a non-existent power source now, except for gasoline-fueled generators.

We moved on. We were doing a lot of camping now like those other people we met. Somehow I felt more secure in the open.

We had hiked along I-5 for two days when Ben grabbed my arm, cupping his hand to his ear. I stopped and listened. Maybe a far-away truck, the sound of its straining motor echoing off denuded foothills like we were in some huge theater with surround-sound. *Good guys or bad?*

We left the broken pavement, crouched behind a berm covered with a thick stand of surviving dry manzanita, and waited. Soon we saw an old army flatbed moving at about forty miles per hour. I pushed everyone down more. *They aren't good guys!*

"We'll let them pass," I said in a whisper, hoping they wouldn't spot us. We were only about a 100 yards off the road. I could see Sammy getting nervous. "Guns ready!" I said.

The truck passed. I could see everyone aboard was bare-chested, even women and kids. They had fancy old cowboy hats and blue jeans on. *Going to a rodeo? County fair?* I smiled at my own black humor.

There weren't many guns, but I saw lots of machetes, some bigger than mine. Hard to hide them, but I suspected there were also knives and pistols hidden among those devils. Everyone was greasy and dirty and in need of haircuts and a bath. We weren't spic and span ourselves, but I now tried to keep a hygiene program going in our little band. These feral humans would likely think we were just healthy, non-GMO, free-range chickens.

But the truck stopped alongside the highway and the cannibal troop jumped down. Potty stop! Females squatted and males stood up—probably the most liquid that site had seen in months. Maybe years?

I heard Sammy squirm and reached to calm him. Kid

maybe was imagining his father on a spit. Always wondered if he'd seen it and was blocking it out, causing nightmares. In a sense, Ben was blessed. Who knew what he'd seen and forgotten?

Disaster! Somehow Sammy's gun went off! Cannibals looked around and quickly buttoned up.

"Stay down!" Ben said, his voice a hiss. "Humans can't determine the direction of a distant source of sound so easily, especially with those echoes."

I looked at him and nodded. Again he'd surprised me. *Humans? What are we? ETs?* I fell to the ground and readied my rifle. "If they move toward us, let'em have it, boys!"

"Maybe they're friendly," Sammy said in a hoarse whisper. Ben and he had followed suit. Kid was in tears. "I'm sorry, Penny."

"Shit happens. Let's see how they react."

❦❦

The group's leader, an older fellow with a long, black beard streaked with gray hanging halfway to his belly button, reached into the truck's cab and found binoculars. Scanned around, confirming Ben's theory by looking over and beyond us. Said something guttural. He and another five men fanned out in search mode. Now I saw revolvers and automatics. Forget machetes. If the enemy has guns, you use guns.

"Russian," Ben said.

"They're speaking Russian?" I said to confirm.

He nodded. Way back when, the LA area had many Russian immigrants. Like many ethnicities, they sort of banded together. Maybe even more so after the sky fell? Maybe these were ex-Russian mob members. SoCal had those too. I used to watch an NCIS spinoff where navy boys would fight them. Thought that had been over the top. I remembered NCIS agents as pretty boring gals and guys doing pretty boring things, mostly picking on us, the enlisted sailors.

Only Russians I'd known owned restaurants. The usual Russian fare was boring too. Czars and Bolsheviks had liked to starve their people, after all, and Putin later had followed that time-honored tradition, but, after the Soviet Union's breakup, "Russian" immigrants brought a wide range of good ethnic food from all over the old USSR with them to the US.

I could even count one store owner from Georgia—the country, not the state—as a friend. Wondered what had happened to him.

These Russian men looked like old Putin on steroids— big, ugly guys with bulging muscles that made their tatts dance, but still with ribs showing. If they were hungry, we'd end up on a spit. They'd sacrifice a few of their number to receive a square meal.

"Do you know Russian?" I said to Ben in a whisper. He nodded. I smiled. "Stand up, but without making too much of a target, and tell them our band has them covered and outnumbered."

"Handguns don't have the range," he said, rising.

He let loose with a speech that reminded me of that old news clip of old bald-headed Nikita in a rage, pounding on the table with his shoe. The cannibals stopped in their tracks. The leader yelled something.

"He asked how many are there in our band," said Ben.

I made a quick count of our enemy and doubled it. Ben passed that number on to the leader. He added something else.

"Told him we all have Uzis."

"I wish."

But the leader shrugged and gestured to his five companions. They backed their way to the truck, still looking around with guns ready.

"Guess we have détente," I said as the truck continued on its way. "Next stop for us: the UN Security Council."

Sammy helped me up.

"When the safety's not on, the gun can go off," I said with a hand on his shoulder and a smile. He nodded. I ruffled his mop of red hair. "We'd best be heading in the opposite direction. Thanks, Ben. And how do you know Russian?"

He shrugged. "Can't remember. Just recognized it. Maybe I was an international spy?"

"Yeah, and I was the first female Prez of the US of A. C'mon. Time's wastin'."

CHAPTER 15

When we arrived at the junction with 405, I had to make a decision. Did I want to return to the same area we had left many weeks ago, or go elsewhere? In some sense, it didn't matter. As the Russians had proven, nowhere was safe. We had a good arsenal now, but wouldn't have won the battle with the Russians. They would have taken casualties, but they had the numbers to overwhelm us.

I decided on elsewhere, leaving that cracked old freeway and heading toward the Van Nuys Airport. The San Fernando Valley didn't have tall buildings because of the earthquake risk—an old neighbor had lost his wife in that Northridge quake—but the valley still had lots of places to hide.

Right then I wanted to have that option, and I liked having those foothills between me and the coast. So, back home in a sense, arriving not far from Nomad Station Number One.

That first night we holed up in an old laundromat. Next day we scavenged around for a change of diet. Found it in an unusual place—a dry cleaner two shops down. Found a lot of imported can goods, even Polish hams.

"Makes up for those eastern Europeans on the Four-Oh-Five," I told my boys.

We had a sit-down feast at a small table with three rickety dollhouse chairs the owners had in the rear. I could imagine they had been hard-working immigrants, maybe working fourteen hours a day, living and slaving away in their little shop. A double bed and cot completed the meager furnishings there. It made me sad. They had come to America to have a better life only to perish in an attack not of their doing.

Sammy liked canned ham but didn't much care for cold sauerkraut. I wondered if he would like it heated up, but decided it wasn't worth the effort. Didn't want to chance a fire either. Fires made smoke, and smoke could be seen, even from far away. Managed to convince him to eat some pickled beets, though. Ben ate everything with great gusto.

"Where to next?" said Ben after a burp and pushing away a little from the midget table and patting his stomach.

"Nomad Station number whatever. Someplace more secure than here."

"What about Cal State Northridge?" Ben said.

Speaking of Northridge! "Why would that be more secure than anywhere else?" I said.

"Like staying right where we are," said Sammy. *Is he tired of being a nomad?*

"Don't know. I just think of universities as being secure."

I wondered about that. Was Ben some kind of academic? "Maybe you're right, unless wild bands of students are hanging around there," I said.

"Wild bands of students were always present at universities," Ben said with a smile.

"I mean like the Russians or those guys in the mountains we ran from." I saw they were waiting for my opinion. "Okay. We move tomorrow to obtain our college education."

∽∾∽

CSUN—that was the acronym—wasn't far. It also was a ghost town. I didn't know if all ghosts were students and professors, but the place was deserted. Most buildings were intact with a bit of quake damage here and there. Californians had learned to build buildings that withstood quakes—maybe not "the big one," but good enough that I just saw books and lab equipment tumbled from shelves and tables and cracks in walls among the skeletal remains.

We wandered. I found a practice room with a piano. Tested it with a few runs over the keys and some chords. The dry and constant climate had kept it almost in tune. I played a bit while Ben and Sammy listened.

"That was nice," Sammy said when I finished. Ben nodded. "Did you write it?"

I smiled at Sammy. "I wish. No, a Polish composer named Chopin wrote it in Paris. He has a bunch like it. They're called mazurkas."

"Not as easy as it sounds," Ben said to Sammy. "You must have had a good teacher," he said to me. "And a good memory."

"My grandmother," I said. "Stayed with her a lot when things went bad at home. She taught piano."

"What's 'Polish,' other than a name on those hams? 'Composer' I understand." Sammy looked from Ben to me.

"A person from a country called Poland," I said. "Or products from that same country. I suppose you want to know what 'Paris' is too?"

"No, I understood that. Dad told me about the Eiffel Tower. I want to climb it someday."

"Montmartre is more interesting," said Ben. "That means 'martyr's mountain.' It overlooks Paris too."

"Lesson Two in my CSUN class about world civilization will be about martyrs," I said, "but we'd better move on." I hooked arms with Ben as we walked along the corridor. "Have you been to Paris, Ben?"

He thought a moment. "Maybe, and maybe more than once. I associate it with something called NATO." He frowned; his brow wrinkled.

"Don't worry about it. I doubt if NATO has any meaning anymore." We were now in a corridor joining two buildings. I stopped and looked outside into a courtyard that would have been shady at one time. Now all the trees were dead, so there were no leaves. Dead branches produced fractal shadows on parched ground. "We're exposed here. I don't like it."

"It's a great adventure for Sammy. We'll be okay."

We explored different buildings, an eerie experience. I imagined the place once vibrant with student life. Ben gathered up some books from the Delmar T. Oviatt Library and Matador Bookstore—guessed the school mascot had been a matador—but we settled into two apartments in the University Park complex.

I passed a spooky night dreaming of Russians dressed as *toreros* who wanted to skewer me like a bull—I mean rape, like a Minotaur, not in a ring in Madrid. Would have been kinky if it wasn't so frightening. I decided our new digs were a bit too peaceful, leading my mind to compensate, but thought the boys needed some peace and quiet for a change—or less excitement at least.

Next morning Ben had breakfast waiting.

"Found a little store at the Student Union," he said. "It was vandalized, of course. All valuable items were gone, but I found some canned fruit. We don't even need an opener—the cans are pop-tops like soda cans."

I nodded. Student snacks.

"Soda cans too. Guess vandals thought that was all too heavy."

"Hard to run with cases of soda or canned fruit," I said. "What are you reading?" Ben used a finger to mark his place and showed me the cover. I blinked. "*The Elegant Universe*? Sounds deep."

He shrugged. "A bit elementary actually. I picked it up for Sammy."

"Sammy can read?"

"His father taught him." He scratched his head. "I don't know how I remembered that."

I nodded at the book. "I don't know how you can say that's elementary."

He shrugged again. "It's old, but well written. A popular science tome."

Again I wondered about Ben's past. Remembered the NATO in Paris comment. Was his past gone, or was it locked in his head ready to come out?

Later that day, we visited a place called Nordhoff Hall, home of the Campus Theatre—I thought "theatre" wasn't spelled right. Ben surprised me again when he jumped on the stage and started spouting something that sounded Shakespearean. I was no expert, but Sammy, sitting in the first row, applauded the soliloquy.

Chopin and Shakespeare. We were starting to relax.

୧৩୧৩

I was explaining to Sammy what racquetball was in Redwood Hall when I again heard the whump-whump-whump of a chopper and then silence. *Must have landed, but where?*

"North Field," said Ben, as if he were reading my mind again. "Shall we go see?"

I felt like running the other way, but was remembering the chopper we'd seen near Nomad Camp Number Two in the foothills. If Sammy was tired of being a nomad, would he feel better as a refugee? I was curious too. Unlike cats, I only had one life, so I was also cautious.

It looked like the same chopper, but the first had been high up, so it was hard to be sure. Five guys in air force fatigues were having lunch on the field that was once a lawn but now was filled with weeds and hardpan.

"Stay here," I told my boys, "but be ready to run like hell."

We were hiding just off the field in something called the Center for Adaptive Aquatic Therapy, which made sense because Redwood had pools in addition to racquetball courts—pools were all dry, of course.

I handed my rifle and other weapons to Ben and went to greet the flyboys. I approached them with hands open at shoulder level, palms facing them. As I approached, I noticed they were all clean shaven and healthy looking. They were also concentrated on their MREs. I'd hated them in basic training, but there were many times in the last five years I would have liked to have some. They were a bit better than dog food.

"Where were you guys when the shit hit the fan?" I said. That brought them to their feet with handguns ready. "I'm unarmed, you fools."

"Who are you?" said one who came toward me. *Maybe the leader?*

"Give me name, rank, and serial number, airman."

He smiled and lowered his gun. "Master Sergeant Rodriguez. Just name and rank for now. And who are you?"

He was average height, trim, and square-shouldered. Looked well fed and in good shape. Not too muscle-bound, but muscular enough, like George had been, projecting authority without flaunting it too much. I liked the ready smile set above a strong jaw. A nose bent to his left a bit told me he'd either been in a few bar fights or had seen combat. That and a scar on his right cheek meant that he wasn't the perfect Adonis. Still the best looking guy I'd seen in years. Even compared well to my brother, who wasn't as dark as I was and was a hunk who looked a lot like Eric Estrada, that actor in that old SoCal series *Chips*.

Mr. Master Sergeant either had a good sun tan or it was genetically provided. And his skin wasn't dry, blotched, blistered, and cracked like mine.

"Penelope Castro, but you can call me Ensign Penny. Was in the navy years ago. Why do you guys look so prim and sassy while I'm looking like a twenty-buck whore from North Hollywood?"

"Too scrawny," he said with a laugh. "Are you alone?"

"No, we have you covered, so don't try to take advantage of me, you brute." I said it with a smile, though.

Another flyboy approached Rodriguez and whispered in his ear.

"Jones here found your service record," Rodriguez said. "Says you look a bit different now compared to your pic. Guess you are who you say you are, though. You people aren't members of a beach gang, are you?"

I ignored the question. "How'd Jones manage that?"

He waved at the chopper. *Dumb question!* They had radio contact with someone, and that someone likely had access to some military databases. Each airman also had a com unit dangling from his belt too, unusual nowadays. *Nowadays?* I hadn't seen one that worked since the apocalypse.

"I take it you guys crawled into bunkers somewhere

and sat out the worst of whatever hit us. Is there any country left to protect?"

"Not much. And we do the best we can. We're running short on just about everything, though. It's hard to keep going when companies that supplied the Pentagon no longer exist."

"That makes sense. Anything I can do for you? I'd like to help you so you have a bit of pity on us and help us too."

He shook his head. "There's a refugee camp near the base, but we don't have room for a big group in this Pave Hawk. It's been retrofitted for weapons. We're on patrol."

I smiled. "How many people can you take?"

He raised his eyebrows in the other airman's direction. "Four max, maybe a few more if you don't have a lot of shit," Jones said.

I smiled again. "How about a teenage boy, an old man, and me, along with a few backpacks? Unless you want your medical stretcher back."

CHAPTER 16

Our lives took a turn for the worse at Edwards. Not what I expected. My little family was just getting to know other refugees when Rodriguez appeared accompanied by other AF security. They grabbed Ben.

"What's going on?" I said to the handsome airman, watching my father-surrogate squirm in fear. I felt my face getting hot with rage. I'd growled the words like a she-wolf protecting her cubs.

"Settle down, old man, or we'll have to tranquilize you," Rodriguez told Ben. He offered a lame explanation. "Your Ben Hur is Benjamin Thomas, a physicist. He was at a meeting in Vandenberg when the sky fell in."

That might explain some things. I wondered if Ben had met my brother. "So what?" I said. "He's not a spy, is he?"

Rodriguez smiled. "Hardly. He's a national security asset. They want him back at Andrews."

I approached Rodriguez. "You can't have him!" I stole the airman's gun in a flash and started waving it. "Ben's a member of my family now."

Four other guns were now leveled at me.

"Let me have the gun, Penny. You've lived through a lot. Don't throw all that away now."

I handed him the gun and sank to my knees, bawling like a baby, my rage dissolving into frustration and help-lessness.

Sammy, who had stood back watching, now moved forward, threw his arm around me, and glared at Rodriguez. "You're no friend at all! I know how to shoot. If I had that gun, I would have shot you between the eyes. Next time I see you, I'll kill you!"

"Don't make idle threats, son. We're not going to hurt your friend Ben. We just need him to do his job."

"And what happens if he can't?" Sammy said. "He doesn't even remember his real name." Ben had been muttering "Benjamin Thomas" for a while, as if he were a Buddhist monk seeking enlightenment with that mantra. His fear had turned into puzzlement about his Universe. "What will you do to him if he can't help you?"

Rodriguez shrugged. "Not my call. I just follow orders."

I struggled to my feet with Sammy's help and approached Rodriguez again, staring him down. "You're a bastard's marionette then." I spat in his face, turned, and headed back to the tent. Sammy followed me inside after calling the airman an asshole and a few other choice words in English, French, Spanish, and something else—maybe an African language like Swahili? I wondered where he'd learned all that. *Not from me!*

"What will we do?" Sammy said as we peered past the tent flap to see them give Ben a tranq with a needle, even though he was subdued and still muttering, and haul him away.

I put my arm around Sammy. He was taller than me now—a good-looking redhead who often reminded me of that actor on *CSI Miami*. Yeah, more old TV shows—what else do you watch on a navy aircraft carrier? "When the moment comes, the USAF will feel my wrath," I said.

"Right now we still should integrate with other refugees while I work on a plan."

That plan would take a lot of work. I had no ideas yet about how to save Ben from the clutches of what remained of the US government.

People often felt disconnected from their governments. Sometimes it was their fault, of course. In the "great democracies," voters became excited about their elections, supporting their favorite bloviating politico, and then forgot about government as they struggled to achieve some semblance of a normal life—2.5 kids, putting food on the table, finding somewhere to live, and encountering means of transportation to arrive at a boring job, only to be caught in traffic jams and subway and commuter rail snafus. Or they returned to living off government welfare programs or working menial jobs because they neither had the energy nor skills for anything better.

In the great fascist states like China and Russia, people lived regimented and resigned, also completely indifferent about their governments. They knew they couldn't do anything about them, and they also tried to achieve some semblance of a normal life, "normal" being defined by their mendicant existence.

The various kinds of government had this in common: they had incompetent bureaucracies, and they were beholding to special interests and formed some kind of oligarchy, all of them not giving a damn about people except for making sure they paid their taxes and provided soldiers to fill their armies.

All this seemed to have been the human condition from ancient tribal societies forward. I didn't think Roman citizens even gave a damn when Goths invaded the empire.

The crap that fell upon us from the sky almost ended

this glorious human history. Maybe we would be better off if it had.

☙❧

Many refugees had seen the altercation. Many still looked angry about it. We'd already learned that refugees in the camp didn't have a lot of love for people on base. Many held the government responsible for our predicament. Refugee camps were much the same everywhere, filled with people whose hopes had been shredded by events beyond their control. They were angry, depressed, and frustrated. Couldn't blame them.

They'd already helped me develop a paranoid theory about the major reason we were there. Some of them had heard rumors, told me, and we commiserated long enough to believe them: We were going to be guinea pigs. Our government wanted to know why we had survived and others hadn't. *Will they retaliate with a new and improved version of the same plague that was launched against us? Retaliate against whom? Or do they just want to develop a vaccine against it?* After what just happened, I suspected the former. And somehow Ben was supposed to help them. I doubted he would, but that might spell trouble for him.

"And Rodriguez?" asked Sammy.

"He's air force, isn't he?" My growl was now the feral one corresponding to the bitch dog who had been abused too long. There had been some in that pack that had attacked me, so the metaphor was even more appropriate— human alpha males were now abusing me!

Thought there might be some satisfaction in turning Rodriguez over to a beach gang. Couldn't wait for him to roast in hell, so why not in this lifetime on a spit? I'd even provide the barbecue sauce! Had decided that giving him to that dog pack would be a quick death—wouldn't want that!

☙❧

The other refugees were good people from all walks of life, survivors like me. Among them were two doctors and three nurses. They had all survived several years of wandering and had first welcomed refugee status off-base at Edwards. One doc, Pat Nagi, had been in the camp for four years. She gave me a physical.

"You're not in bad shape," she said as I dressed. "Your weight's too low, but all parts seem to be functioning." She had already given Sammy the Good Housekeeping seal of approval. Must have been all my TLC.

"Great. I'll find me a man here and have a dozen kids."

She frowned. "I'm not sure that will be possible. Fertility is low among us. You've probably noticed Sammy doesn't have many friends, younger or otherwise. If human beings are going to make a comeback on this planet, it will take some time."

"So, I don't have to worry about the little pills?"

"Only to the extent that they're no longer available. No one makes them now, so no one takes them. Women have become pregnant, but there are a lot of miscarriages. I hope it's more caused by malnourishment and not some insidious side effect of whatever hit us, like that Zika epidemic a few years ago. But anything's possible. Pregnancy is rare, and babies carried to term that aren't stillbirths even rarer."

"Yeah. I heard that. What's your theory on why we survived?"

"That needs research. I'm guessing it's a combination of genetics and reduced exposure. Scientists in good labs will have to examine a lot of survivors before any conclusions can be drawn. On the West Coast, we received a direct hit. Many people died in their tracks. I'm not sure about the remainder of the country or world."

"Rodriguez mentioned that the remainder is fucked too. Maybe it's better not knowing the extent of it. What's your story?"

"Same as yours, basically. I was an intern at Northridge Hospital. Among all the personnel and patients, the accountant, a leukemia patient in for chemo, and I were the only survivors. That leukemia patient later died from cancer, not the plague."

"An accountant? Ralph Ballesteros?"

"Yep. Old Ralph, our fearless mayor. Elected fair and square."

"Nice guy." I looked past the flap of her tent. "I miss Ben Hur."

"He was nice. Did you discover what happened to him?"

"Janet Miller, who works on base and seems to show some compassion toward us, told me they took him to Washington. I'm afraid Sammy and I will never get him back."

"At least you know he's alive for now."

❦

Pat Nagi became my BFF and Ralph Ballesteros my BMF. The other refugees were nice enough and would talk to me when talked to, but usually they walked around in a daze. We were taken care of—the USAF supplied food and water and some medicines—but the refugees' zombie-like attitudes were understandable. That occurred in just about any refugee camp anywhere in the world as people uprooted from what they considered their normal lives tried to adjust after months or years of stressful existence. I could sense their despondency growing with each passing week.

The mayor was paranoid. He worried more than me about becoming the government's guinea pigs, for whatever reason. He was sure we'd be used to improve similar biological WMDs. Of course, the Russians on the Grapevine and beach cannibals had somehow survived the attack too. But we were the ones the USAF had on hand for their testing, so I could understand his concern.

The mayor was a strange fellow. He had started life as a Catholic but by the time I met him he had no religion to speak of. Yet he was a philosopher of sorts. I had a discussion about the meaning of life with him one night as we polished off two-thirds of a bottle of bourbon some constituent had given him.

"My problem, Ralph, is that we're born to die."

"Meaning," he said, his speech a bit slurred like mine, "that once we're born and self-aware, we know our fate. That's the curse of all human beings, my dear Penny."

I pointed to his ugly dog, some kind of terrier and Chihuahua mix that needed a good vet. "Think Rascal knows he has to die?"

"Probably not thinking about it now, but animals know about mortality. I used to have a cat too. Rascal lay beside old Pete and comforted him when he was dying. Are you afraid of death, Penny?"

"Maybe. I don't know. Maybe I'm more afraid of life. Death seems pretty final. Life seems like a game of poker—all random and unpredictable, especially now. Sometimes I think life is just a big joke on us. Why bother? Why go on? What difference will it make if I off myself right now?"

"Hmm. Maybe none for you. For me, a messy tent. People around you will feel the emptiness, though. If we ever think about it, most of us do what we do for other people around us, assuming you don't have a sociopathic personality. I don't think you do."

"In a thousand years, who will care?"

"Given current conditions, it's likely no one will care in twenty years. I think people around us care, though, right now, and in our immediate future."

"Are you a pessimist or an optimist?"

"Neither. I'm a practical man. The only thing we know for sure is that we only have one chance here on this planet. We'd better make the best of our time here. To do otherwise is insanity."

I couldn't pin him down on how I could determine if I was doing my best. He'd sunk into a drunken stupor. Never had occasion to pick up that conversation again, although we often talked about other things.

∽∾∽

But the USAF's little refugee camp provided us with a safe and secure place to live compared to the numbing scavenging and violence of existence in the outside world. Both Sammy and I started putting on some weight. I started an aerobics class—Penny's easy version of boot-camp calisthenics—and Pat reminded us about good nutrition and sleeping habits. There were still a lot of people sitting around looking despondent. I'd pick on them a bit, emphasizing there was nowhere else to go that was any better. Moods seemed to improve a bit.

USAF security refereed the inevitable skirmishes. A couple of guys tried distilling their own vodka—yeah, we had potatoes and they used even the peelings. Wasn't bad, but some people were bad drunks. Rowdies slept it off in an air force brig.

I saw Rodriguez again at that time. He was studying

me, looking a bit forlorn. I turned my back on him and returned to my tent.

The mayor knew about all the depression, of course. I thought one reason for his organizing a protest was to alleviate that a bit by giving people a cause. One source of depression was the living conditions. Almost all of us were in tents, but the base's buildings had those government-style cinder blocks and corrugated steel roofing and some more modern ones, so Ballesteros developed the idea of having buildings for community use and maybe some better abodes for bigger families. Base VIPs said no. Protest was the result.

It was a bit pathetic. Someone made some crude signs and we invaded the base, chanting "Fascist Pricks!" and the like. Two refugees, an old man and woman, collapsed in the heat. Leaders of the protest, mayor included, spent a night crowded into a few cells in the brig. The event helped some people forget their depression just like Ballesteros planned, and we received some cinder blocks and roofing for more latrines.

I wondered what it took to make cinder blocks? Knew even cement was scarce. Easy to understand—there weren't any functioning cement factories far as I knew. And you had to give an arm and a leg for a window frame with real glass. One family had two sitting in their tent for the day when things would get better. They must have found it elsewhere and brought them along with their meager belongings. Safe bet that Uncle Sam's Air Force wouldn't be giving away windows anytime soon. Family donated it to a community center when we had one.

The flyboys were susceptible to the general depression too. Heard from Janet Miller that an AFB security guard and colleague of Rodriguez went bonkers. *What do you do with an insane airman?* No shrinks around, so the only thing they could do was throw him into the brig where he was left to wallow naked in his waste products. Janet said that what put him over the edge was the boring routine. Maybe. I could imagine hundreds of other things.

In camp or on base, too many people thought there was no future. Thought it was a little bit like being in those Russian *gulags* Solzhenitsyn wrote about—days and days of laboring in mind-numbing despair. Our only advantage was that it was dry and hot, not snowy and bitterly cold. Janet suggested that males' depression might be traced to the plague's gender bias. I heard about the theory from her—didn't know if it was true, but a version was included in my list of hundreds of other things that drove that airman crazy. Janet even had some scientific hearsay to back it up: some geeks...back in DC?...thought there were more female victims than males. That correlated well with low birthrates, but I figured they didn't have reliable stats. Couldn't imagine little geeks touring the country and counting skeletons of males vs. females, not with feral humans all over the place.

Adding to my own depression, I yearned for news about Ben Hur. Could I weasel it from Rodriguez? I didn't know the other air force security guards that well. Thought I knew him too well.

In spite of the overall depression, I began to recover from five years of malnutrition. Muscle tone improved and I couldn't be called scrawny anymore. My skin improved, wrinkles smoothed out, and I felt much healthier. Some of that was due to saving what calories I obtained from the food I ate instead of spending all of them and more looking for more food. The exercise routines I followed, which contained a bit of Yoga and Tai-Chi, seemed to help too.

Part 3

Saving Ben Hur

"Go up in an airplane. Go high enough,
and it's like we don't exist."
~ Muhammad Ali

CHAPTER 17

Things kept improving. The base provided our community center with an old upright piano. Made me think of playing for Ben and Sammy on that college campus, but I managed to tune it and play a bit, just to ease my depression.

Sometimes I attracted a crowd, so I'd play some pop songs from memory. Always ended with "This Land is Your Land" and "We Shall Overcome." Some people would cry with those, but I thought they were still optimistic songs. The last one had brought a lot of black people some comfort in facing a lot of stressful situations produced by bigots and racists. Figured it might do the same in our case, although the enemy in our case seemed to be the USAF.

People weren't too much into classical music. Good thing too, because I was out of practice and the pieces were often so complicated that I'd have needed sheet music for ones I never played much. They loved Joplin, though, but I could only remember a few more pieces besides "The Entertainer" from *The Sting*.

I had to simplify a lot without sheet music too. Funny. I could still play a bit of Chopin from memory but had to do pop standards like a klutz—right-hand melody and left-hand chords. Old memory was a bit rusty when it came to fancy chords too. I let the flyboys know that if they found any sheet music lying around to make me copies—or just give them to me. That was mostly for my own benefit. The refugees wanted to hear the same old songs over and over again for the most part. They sang along better with time; I played better too. A bit of medicine to relieve the boredom.

ⱷⱷ

Sammy and I would often spend time together watching planes and choppers takeoff and land, more the latter than the former. I wondered when fuel would run out. Maybe not too many assets around that needed it, though. Saw a C-5M Super Galaxy once—Sammy was impressed more by that monster than by two fighters we spotted.

Seeing those fighters started me thinking. *Are they flying back and forth to DC?* I saw Rodriguez helping an old woman flip an old mattress one day. Olga was about Ben's age I guessed, spoke some Slavic language, not Russian, and hardly any English, but still had pink skin and rosy cheeks, a rarity in the Mojave-like environment. Liked to hug a lot. Sammy and the small number of other kids were often beneficiaries of her hugs, which was okay by me. My kid was lovable and needed to forget a lot of things—the more hugs, the better.

I waited to talk to Rodriguez. He was surprised.

"You must want something," he said. I turned and began to walk away. He grabbed my shoulder. "Wait! Talk to me, damn you!"

I turned back toward him. "For me, you're the enemy, and I don't trust you anymore. But sometimes the enemy can be useful. I need some information."

He probably decided that was better than having me

turn away. "I'm not the enemy, Penny. I just have a job to do. You know how it is. If you're in the military, you take orders if you're not giving them. It's nice to talk to you again, so ask away, but don't ask about classified stuff."

I smiled at that. Always wondered how a civilian was supposed to know when something's classified. Half that shit was so arbitrary—I knew from my navy days that many classifications were just in place to cover someone's ass if plans went south—maybe multiple high-ranking someones like admirals and generals who had and were big asses.

"What my brother was doing at Vandenberg was classified. What you people are doing with refugees is more akin to guarding internment camps, to put it nicely."

"You mean, like flipping Olga's mattress for her?"

"Okay. You guys can apply some useful muscle sometimes." I decided to avoid the chatty argument about military versus refugee life where we always seemed to be at the bottom of the pecking order. "Did they take Ben Hur to DC in a jet?"

He nodded. "There are a couple of flights per week. Why do you ask?"

"I want to see my mother. She's in southern Jersey. Just wondering if I could hitch a ride sometime soon."

He thought a moment. "That's a reasonable request. We can't ferry every refugee who wants to look for a long-lost relative, but I can mention it to the brass. There's often a space available in the taxi. And southern Jersey's not far from DC."

"Even nearer Andrews. Just up the Pike, and I'm sure Delaware's not collecting tolls anymore. And, by the way, my mother isn't lost. I know right where she is." That wasn't a lie.

He leaned against an old pickup that no longer functioned. *Where does rust come from if the air's so dry? Maybe that dew I used to collect?* "What about your brother at Vandenberg? What did he do there?"

"My brother and I are estranged. Haven't seen him in years. We had a falling out about my mother's care, so I don't want him seeing *Mamacita*. Bobby's like you—a complete jerk who follows orders no matter what they are. Guess the military doesn't always make people better."

Rodriguez frowned. "His name is Roberto Castro, I suppose. I can check with records. Needless to say, they aren't complete now. I'm not even sure what happened at Vandenberg. Right now it's offline. Been that way for some time. We need to send a team there to reconnoiter."

"Whatever happened will likely be classified," I said with a grin. "But Jones found my name okay, and I wasn't even active. Go ahead and trace Bobby, but don't ever think I give a shit about him." My grin had turned to a frown, remembering his domineering and abusive manner. "Let me know what you find out about a ride for me. I'd appreciate it."

I walked away then with a bit of swing in my hips. I could tell he liked me. That meant I could use him to further my own agenda. If flirting with the enemy returned Ben, so be it. I hadn't lied about my brother. I didn't give a shit about Bobby—that SOB had shown his stripes long ago—but I now was scheming at full steam, focused on that possible jet ride to Andrews.

❧❦❧

I'd cast a fishing line for Rodriguez, decided I had him hooked, and began to reel him in. More in a flirtatious way at first. A gal had needs same as a guy, and I hadn't been intimate with a guy since Ned. That was a long time ago, long enough that I began to wonder if all the old plumbing still functioned well enough to have some fun. Like I said, not serious. I was still mad at the big ox. But he did take my proposal to the base VIPs, so I decided to reward him a bit—and myself.

Invited him to dinner. Scooted Sammy off on an overnight with a friend and likely prepared the worst meal a woman could prepare a man. If the way to a man's heart was through his stomach, I was in trouble.

How did some *arepas* made from old corn meal, a can of *chili con carne*, and three Coronas I swapped my pillow for sound for a menu to you? Oh, I forgot appetizers: a five-plus-year-old can of stale peanuts. Cooking involved waving the *arepas* over a candle—they were already baked over a "wood fire" where most of the wood was broken up sagebrush and dried cacti. Heated the *chili* over same.

"Sorry, Alex, the supermarket was closed. Must be a holiday."

He laughed. "Better than MREs. Better than some food base cooks serve us too. Always of questionable provenance." The smile turned to a frown. "We're equal opportunity here. Base personnel and refugees alike are equally hungry."

He was sitting beside me. We were in front of my tent, watching for an occasional shooting star among the many in the heavens. Didn't believe they brought luck, but I could sure use some.

"Am I on your good side again?" he said, putting a tentative arm around my shoulders.

I leaned on the arm. As thin as we had all become, his biceps were still hard and as big around as my thigh. Private joke: he was built a little like Popeye. Guess I was scrawny Olive. "I'm not sure I have a good side anymore in the general sense." I winked at him. "With respect to *entreteniendo al guapo*, as my *Mamacita* used to call it, all my sides used to be good. It's been a while, though."

He started fooling around with my refugee-camp perm AKA dry, withered hair that bore a resemblance to those sagebrush specimens. "Me too. I have a confession to make. I wanted to get in your pants the minute I met you. I'm sure the other guys did too. We were talking about you afterward."

"I'm not into inverse-harems," I said. I brushed his cheek. "But maybe I could manage all of you over a few days."

"I told them you probably weren't that kind of girl."

"Woman. I stopped being a girl a long time ago. Are you thinking what I'm thinking?"

"Maybe a little bit of fun?"

I nodded.

We retired to the tent. Two hours later I was on top making up for his quick explosions the first two times. It was good to be back in the saddle again.

And then he ruined it. I was resting my sweaty brow on his curly-haired chest, sated and mostly forgetting what our life had become.

"I still haven't heard a response to your request, you know."

I sat on his pelvic region and pounded his chest. "Do you think I was fucking your brains out so you'd promote my petition? I'd almost forgiven you for kidnapping Ben. Now I'm not so sure." I swung off him. "I needed some comfort. Thought you did too. Infatuation can go both ways, and it's hard for me to give into it when you're such a prick. Pardon the double meaning."

"I rub you the wrong way sometimes, I guess."

"You were doing it the right way before you opened your big mouth. When we first met, you said I was too scrawny to be a twenty-dollar whore from North Hollywood. I'm a bit plumper and the tits a bit fuller now, so where's my hundred dollars?"

"Don't be like that! I wasn't accusing you of anything. I just wanted to inform you that base VIPs haven't decided anything yet. It was completely innocent."

"Okay, maybe it was, but it didn't sound like it. Let's call it an evening. I'm no longer in the mood."

We dressed. Before he left, he gave me a kiss. I reciprocated a bit, remembering the great feeling of him inside me, but I had already decided to cool off our relationship again. I felt guilty. Having such a good time, I'd forgotten all about Ben. Promised myself that hormones in the future wouldn't take away my focus.

☙☯❧

You have less patience as you age. I was never too patient with the slow-turning wheels of military bureaucracy. Now they'd lose a race with a snail swimming uphill on a waterslide covered in molasses, if any snails still existed. *Poor French!* I wondered if any were left to cook gourmet dishes…or to eat them. Some surely had tasty recipes for human flesh. *Gens au vin!* That thought almost made me barf.

But about two weeks later, Rodriguez and two of his colleagues came to our lovely abode.

"Pack your bag, Penny," he said. "Just one, a small one. You lucked out. Because you have an exemplary service record and quality years with law enforcement, base honchos approved your petition. Keep that to yourself, though."

"I have to tell Sammy."

"Of course. Pat and Ralph too."

"So, do we have a new visitor? Or did they send an empty jet just for little ol' me?"

"New base commander. Major Roger Landon."

"What? Not a general?"

"We have a personnel shortage. Major's a temp as I understand it. He has some experience with disasters and insurgents."

"Disasters I understand. We're suffering from one. Who are the insurgents?"

"The roving gangs that plague the area are considered terrorists and insurgents."

"Don't forget their cannibalistic inclinations."

"I'm not, but I don't think anyone in the modern air force has much experience with that. You'd need old navy in the days of tall ships."

After packing and goodbyes—big hugs for Sammy, Pat, and Ralph produced some tears—I left the refugee camp with Rodriguez and his colleagues. Hadn't visited the base since the day we were brought in from the San Fernando Valley. Didn't see much difference except that the road was bumpier and filled with more potholes now. Wondered if they were losing jeeps to broken axles. Probably didn't have equipment or supplies to repair potholes. Or vehicles. Except for air force planes on runways, Edwards could have been a local air field in the Sahara. Likely dustier too, because Africa had more rain.

I didn't have the chance to meet the new base commander. Didn't much care. I was driven right onto the tarmac to a sleek fighter jet. The pilot, a nice guy named Harold Hooper with nickname Hannibal, took charge of me. Rodriguez and company left.

Hannibal looked me over. "Ever flown in a jet?"

With his handlebar mustache and a pilot's uniform from the World War One era, Hannibal in a *Flugzeugwerke* Albatross could be Snoopy's Red Baron. He was sloppy and lean but small and compact like me, and he spoke Texan, not English. USAF *esprit de corps* and spit and polish had taken nose dives in the last five years, but they probably had fewer fighter pilots than generals, so I supposed Hooper was given a pass.

"Commercial. Not the same thing, I'm sure."

"And no longer flying," he said, "which is why you're allowed to hitch a ride, I guess. Good enough for me. I like the idea. I often don't have a passenger on the return trip. Either way. Come on. Taxi meter's running." He put me in a picture frame with his large hands. "I'll need to find you a flight suit. You'll be my copilot as we travel east. I want to pick up two extra oxy masks too—hose on mine is a bit brittle; I don't trust it."

Maybe we shouldn't trust any of them? I tried to banish that thought from my mind. "Oh goody, your copilot, just like in *Top Gun.*"

He made a sour face. "That was navy."

"I was navy. But we're on the same side, airman."

☙☙☙

The flight wasn't leisurely sightseeing, by any means. Hannibal pointed out the Grand Canyon; I caught a glimpse of it. There was no sonic boom. Felt stupid when I realized we wouldn't hear it, just people on the ground—the plane was outrunning its sound, except for the onboard engine noise. Received a lecture from Hannibal about the old F-15's motors and weapons systems. Cared about the first, not so much about the second. He wasn't carrying weapons. He was just a glorified taxi driver. Didn't tell him that, of course. He worried about oxygen masks; I worried about old masks and parachutes and whether he would eject me!

We stopped only once at Whiteman Air Force Base in Missouri to refuel and find restrooms. I needed one in a bad way. The tin cans Hannibal and other pilots used—

were all previous passengers males?—weren't unisex. That base had fewer personnel than Edwards. A few pilots slummin' around, maintenance personnel, and lots of security.

"Kind of biased toward security types," I said, stopping on the way back from the head to study four armed guards with serious firepower.

I hadn't been impressed by the head, maybe because the ladies' room hadn't been used in a while. Squatted, didn't sit, but I was used to that from my nomadic life. Likely exposed myself to a whole new breed of germs, though.

I'd had a lot of injections in the USN and boosters later while at the sheriff's department, but you never know. Figured I was immune to the lethal contagion that killed most everyone else. Otherwise, I'd be dead.

"Middle of the country is pretty wild," said Hannibal. "Lots of survivors fleeing the chaos in KC, St. Louis, and Chicago have become nomadic marauders. No one farms anymore. It's too dangerous, unless you're protected by a military base nearby."

"I'm not going to ask what nomads eat. How long do you think 'til order is restored?"

"'Nother ten years at least, ma'am, but maybe it'll take the remainder of this century. Who knows? We just have a few refineries left. Pumps at oil wells have to run with generators. It's a vicious circle now, and it's shrinking away to nothing."

"And no corn to make fuel either," I said. "Guess airplanes couldn't burn that."

"That's why we have so few flights. Only the essential. Maybe we can start making fuel from bio-waste and retrofit the old props, break the vicious circle, and have more oil wells and refineries running. My career is endangered if things don't get better." He made a gallant gesture toward the plane. "Your steed awaits, my lady. I have a schedule to keep."

"How 'bout some snacks? I figure we have the same distance still to go."

"Coffee? Donuts?" Hannibal said. "Probably old and stale, respectively."

He headed toward some out-buildings and gestured for me to follow.

Someone had kept the little canteen supplied. I passed on coffee—caffeine made me pee more and it looked as advertised, at least a day old, and maybe not coffee but boiled bark?—and ate a stale donut.

Most important lesson I learned in survival training way back when was not to pass up on a chance to eat. That mantra had come in handy during the five-plus years I had to survive as a scavenger and nomad.

"The Midwest was always underpopulated compared to the two coasts," he said, continuing his explanation of the local situation, "but you know what took the worst hit?"

"This a history lesson?" I said, washing down the dry donut stuck in my throat with some lukewarm water.

"A bit. The worst place was Chicago. The jet stream sent all the plague winging their way for several days and then plunged south. You folks out West were caught by surprise. All the people in Chicago and here just had to sit and wait on Death Row because the dispersal lowered the density and made it act slower. Same for the East, I guess."

"How did you survive?"

"I was on a NATO training mission in Europe. It was more of a 'we're still here' message to Russians. Funny that they all suffered the same fate."

I thought of Ben Hur's NATO memory. Wondered if he'd recovered enough to give me more details.

What did a physicist do for the USAF besides design, build, and test bombs?

"Yeah. Hilarious. So Europe is in bad shape too?"

"The contagion dispersed throughout the world. I spent three years in fallout bunkers outside Paris."

"I'd love to hear you speak French with a Texas drawl."

He frowned. "A lot of people died. Many people who survived feel guilty about that. I do."

"Me too, until Sammy and Ben Hur found me." I explained a bit who they were. Didn't mention that Ben was in a cell somewhere on Andrews AFB. "The apocalypse is in the past. We need to forge a new future where these things won't happen."

"Won't receive any arguments from me." He studied me a moment. "Any man in your life more your age?"

"Maybe a fellow named Rodriguez back at Edwards. Nice guy, but I have to decide whether I'll forgive him for being an asshole."

Hannibal snapped his fingers. "That's the story of my life. Someone else gets the gal."

"You'll find her. Maybe even me if I can't forgive Rodriguez."

"Not by flying old politicos back and forth across country," he said, not following up on the last remark. "They were quick to save their own asses when the shit hit the fan. I don't have much sympathy for their kind."

"Why do you keep doing what you're doing?"

"Something in me hopes they can make things better. I'm afraid it will be up to people like you and me, though."

CHAPTER 18

I hated to lie to Hannibal. Okay, not a straight lie, only a lie of omission. Didn't even consider he might receive some flak from the brass, but when I did, I decided I didn't have a choice.

He was the kind of character I could relate to—a free, independent spirit, though dedicated to his job. I'd seen similar personalities in navy pilots. Ned was also that way, although he had no love for terrorists who made it a habit of maiming and murdering men, women, and children alike. He'd preach about how the *Koran* didn't condone any of that and how radical clerics were just using religion to brainwash ignorant jihadists. Hannibal didn't preach at all, maybe because now most jihadists were dead like all the others who succumbed from the plague's dispersal. Wouldn't put it past them to become cannibals before anyone else, though. Couldn't remember if human meat was like pork for Semites, but I was sure religious fervor flew out the window with the arrival of the plague.

"Dedicated to his job" might be an understatement. He called his jet Molly and would touch controls like they were the nipples and genitalia of his special love. Gave me goose bumps to watch. I missed Rodriguez, the SOB. 'Course I didn't know how he'd touch me on a repeat frolic in the sack—for the first go at it, we were out of practice—but I hoped it would be like Hannibal and Molly. I then became maudlin over Ned. Round and round, crazy thoughts would run in my mind. By the time we reached our destination, I was exhausted mentally and physically.

He had taxied after landing his jet at Andrews to where ground crew waited to take care of his plane and helped me down. *Where is everybody?* Andrews was once the busiest military airport in the world and contained many non-military civilian employees as well, including those of the NSA and CIA—their main HQ was in Langley, of course. Not far away were NASA installations and the University of Maryland. It had been a busy little corner of the DC burbs. Now it looked like a ghost town.

I wondered if VIP ghosts still convened there. Did SCOTUS ghosts hear cases appealed from ghost courts around the land? Did ghosts of majority leaders from the House and Senate still mount their soapboxes and bloviate to other congressional ghosts? And then there was the military. Did ghosts of admirals and generals still walk the halls of the Pentagon? I figured they would still be around. They wouldn't be in heaven or hell because they deserved to still be here in the hell of their own creation. I'd been a member of the government. Funny how I didn't give a shit about it anymore. We'd been reduced to little tribes of survivors. Anarchy ruled the land of the living. The ghosts of government could continue with their bureaucratic nonsense.

Hannibal had flown over the Mall for my benefit. The White House was a charred and burned-out husk; the famous rose garden was dead and filled with hearty weeds, not delicate flowers; and there was no sign of life, at least from the air. Lincoln's statue had its face smashed in and the Washington monument was cracked in too many places to be called safe. Between there was stagnant water. The Capitol Building looked okay outside, but I could imagine it was a shambles inside. Abandoned cars filled the streets. I thought that was strange because they sure had more warning than SoCal—the jet stream moves fast, but not that fast.

So where is everyone? Do we have a seat of government or not?

As if reading my mind, Hannibal explained. "Some representative from the old Maryland legislature's now interim president. The last interim was the president's press secretary. Figureheads with six-year terms now, if they last that long. What's left of the military is running things, mostly from Edwards on the West Coast and Andrews on the East. Figureheads are there too. Even a small Congress at Andrews blathering along as usual."

"Mimicking the old system?"

"Guess so."

I would have taken the opportunity to make some radical changes in that old system. Bloviating politicos never accomplished anything, so I would limit speech time and axe all bills where debate went beyond one hour. *Can't agree in that time, why waste more?* I'd put some cabinet secretaries on continuous probation too—reassess every six months or so their job performances and fire their asses if they didn't accomplish anything. Couple all that with a bit more power for those same secretaries and make them more independent of a crazy POTUS and you might get something done. I didn't like the idea of the military in charge, though.

Noticed two World War Two fighters taking off from the base. Hannibal caught me eyeing them.

"They were mothballed, but mechanics did some creative repairs reminiscent to what Cubans used to do with those old cars in Havana. They have those old fighters flying again. They're headed for New Jersey on recon, but there's no room for you. And you wouldn't want to land where they're flying recon."

"What are they looking for in New Jersey?"

"They do recon sorties up and down the coast. Heard a crowd was tailgating at the Meadowlands as we speak, so recon was ordered."

"A football game? You're kidding. And why are they going there? For a flyover? Don't tell me fans are singing the national anthem as they pass over the stadium."

He frowned. "Nothing like that, I'm afraid. The tail-gating is done inside the stadium now. Some religious zealots are making sacrifices to God so that He's more merciful in the future. Makes the old Super Bowl halftime shows look pretty tame. I just see it as an excuse to barbecue people from another sect who became care-less and were caught."

I turned pale. *Now cannibalism in the name of religion?* I'd always thought that the Eucharist was symbolic cannibalism, but what Hannibal had just told me was over the top. "How'd the air force learn about it?"

"Cheyenne Mountain still has some sat-imaging go-ing."

I figured the satellites must be many-years-old. *How much longer would they stay up?* Decided that was a good question.

"Even the space station is still up. The three astronauts and two cosmonauts who were stranded there are dead by now. They all have some automatic orbit-correcting ca-pabilities, and most are responding to signals from the Mountain still."

"So they have power at the Mountain?"

"Generators running on fumes, for the most part. The Mountain is the last refuge in Colorado. That and other

Southwestern states are dust bowls. The Rockies don't have much snow in the winter now, less than the Sierras." He smiled. "No skiing at Aspen."

I wet a paper towel and rubbed grit off my face. You know it's bad when you see dirt on dark skin. Couldn't say I accomplished much. I needed a bath.

"Does anyone know how the water shortage and what fell on us are related? Or California quakes?"

He shook his head. "I've heard that empty aquifers cause quakes, like fracking in Oklahoma did earlier. If the plague and lack of rain are related, no one has a theory—not one I heard of anyway. The ecosystem is complex, so who knows?" He winked. "Maybe it's like plagues in the *Bible*?"

"So those crazies in the Meadowlands might have something then? I hope not. They might as well start worshipping the Devil. God has washed his hands of us, I'm afraid, and with good reason."

℮ↄ℮ↄ

I saw the blurred poster of the new interim president—probably a blowup of a security badge's pic—after Hannibal and I washed up inside the hangar. She was an older woman with lots of white, unruly hair who reminded me of a stern teacher I'd had in high school. Not very photogenic, this new ruler of the free world, not that "free world" had much meaning anymore.

A daughter of the *Sons of Anarchy*? Sounded like a good title for a sequel to the TV show, if someday there was any TV.

"Weren't POTUS and members of the cabinet in bunkers?"

"Stupid fools thought the whole blight was confined to the West Coast because that was where the missiles headed. Maybe not so stupid. They had just chosen to listen to scientists who told them they were safe. That lethal contagion just settled down and made itself at home. Now we think it was still reproducing and propagated from victim to victim too. Deadly bioengineering. The only good thing about it is that it backfired and killed the bastards that hit us with it."

"What happened to the first interim president?"

"She died from rabies. A feral dog bit her daughter. The daughter bit her. Teenagers, you know."

"And no vaccine," I said, shuddering. Could imagine how the woman and daughter died. Didn't know what more to say to all that. Maybe what Shakespeare's Puck had said: "What fools these mortals be"?

"After we check in, I'll see if I can find you a car," he said. "There are plenty around, but they aren't all functional. Like everyone else, mechanics are working their butts off in this new hub of the nation. We're shorthanded."

I nodded. "Thanks. I'll make it a point to stay away from the Meadowlands. That's Northern Jersey. Guess I'll have to bring the car back if I want a ride west again."

He smiled. "Something like that. I hate to say it, but you probably won't find your mother alive. But you'll have some closure. Come back and fly again with Hannibal Airlines." He pointed to an old building about 200 yards distant. "We need to report in there. They'll assign us some temporary sleeping quarters."

"I left a duffel bag stowed aboard the plane somewhere. You go ahead. I'll catch up."

He nodded. Hannibal was a trusting soul. I walked to the plane and waited behind it until he disappeared inside the building. I then beat it for the brig.

༄ঙ৩

Back in the day, Andrews AFB's security was a lot better. Things like the CIA and NSA and the president's marine choppers made it necessary. I wondered if the choppers were still around, or if there were any marines left to pilot them. Could imagine them ferrying around the interim president—what was her name? Or did those interims even fly around the country?

I hid in an abandoned hanger. Enough cracks between aluminum seams to see who was looking for me. Security patrols, most likely doing just that, didn't think of checking an old, empty trash barrel. It was no longer empty. I went a couple of times to use the head. Did a few jumping jacks then, but by the time early morning rolled around, I was stiff and hungry. *Penny, querida, you're getting too old for this!*

Hannibal's story about Paris reminded me of two hectic but wonderful nights Ned and I spent there. Nice to relive it even when I was crammed into a trash barrel.

We had a five-day leave, so we rented a car in Cadiz and drove to Paris via Barcelona—Cadiz was near Naval Station Rota. I couldn't say we slept much on that trip, for multiple reasons.

The best memory I had about Paris was dinner on top the Eiffel Tower. Parisians were snotty, though. Seemed to know we were American sailors, not tourists. Helped a bit with some snots; hurt with others. Still felt sorry for them all. Even snots dying was sad. The plague hadn't been selective about eliminating snots.

I had my first *escargots* there. Wasn't too exciting. Rather have lobster for that price—the garlic butter's the same. Had to give it to the French, though. They could make a meal from anything. Those culinary skills probably had come in handy when the crap from the sky reached them. Not as bad as the Greeks maybe. I read in *Zorba, the Greek* that they liked bull testicles. Eew!

Thought of a few men I'd like to volunteer for that. Men II Boyz instead of vice versa—permanent job in the pope's choir! *Say, what happened to our pope?*

I had discovered an old base map hanging on the wall that showed where the brig was along with other air force installations—figured unlabeled parts were things like the NSA and so forth. Knew the brig had always been a temporary one—just holding cells for the air force's bad girls and boys, mostly men who were AWOLs and drunks. Terrorists, murderers, drug traffickers, and other assorted felons had always been held elsewhere, and not by the air force.

That brig was a long walk because I had to do it in stealth-mode, but it limbered me up, especially crouching and stretching my neck to peer around corners. By the time I arrived, I was running on adrenaline and ready for a fight. The USAF didn't oblige. Not much anyway. Ben Hur was the only prisoner, and three security officers who were guarding him were trying to keep each other awake.

"I need some more java," I heard one say.

"Your turn to make a new pot," said another.

I had no idea where coffee was made, or if it was even real coffee—Hannibal had said the coffee in Missouri was bad—no *campesinos* in Colombia to exploit anymore?—but I liked two against one better than three against one. One on one was even better. I found a janitor's closet and used its mops and pails to make a ruckus. Ducked in and waited. Knew with one making coffee and one guarding that infamous felon Ben Hur, only one would come to investigate.

Timed it perfectly. I imagined the guard was Rodriguez as motivation. Shoved the closet door into his face, jumped out, and put the old chokehold on him. When he succumbed, I stuffed an old rag in his mouth and tied his hands behind him with his belt. Borrowed his weapons, a pistol and a Taser. Took his walkie-talkie too.

Didn't have to become too violent with the lazy guy who wouldn't make coffee. I had an epiphany about how to avoid some future problems. Had him strip and I put on his uniform. Cap was a bit tight with my current hairdo—refugee-frizz I called the style, still short while longer than a buzz cut—and the shirt was snug in the chest, but figured no one would notice that early in the morning.

The next victim had set the coffeemaker brewing and was in a bathroom stall reading something while waiting to dump a load. I saw his uniform pants around his ankles. Surprised him. Gagged and tied, I sat him back on the john. Rolled up and stuck the old dog-eared copy of *Penthouse* between his bare legs, not caring what I hit.

I now had three guns. Almost tossed them. Had no desire to use them. If Ben and I could steal away before dawn, I wouldn't need to.

The cells were back where the three had been chewing the fat. No keys, just a keypad. Just my luck. Ran back to the bathroom stall, removed my third victim's gag, and put the gun to his temple. "What's the code for the cellblock? And, is there more than one?"

He gave me two. Second one was for their only prisoner's cell.

Put the gag back in and patted him on the shoulder. "You can do your business now, flyboy. Be careful with the centerfold."

☙❧

Ben was asleep. I stared at the old man with envy. *Penny girl is tired and sore.* I stood there watching him snore. The other third of my family. *What is his real story? Does he still not know?*

"Always lying down on the job," I said in a loud voice.

He stirred and then sat upright, an astonished look on his face. "Penny? How did you get in here?"

"A story almost as long as the *Iliad* and not as interesting. Grab your things. We have a continent to cross. Sammy needs you. Hell, I need you."

"I—I don't understand."

"I'm breaking you out of prison, old man. Or, do you like it so much here you want to stay?"

His puzzled face now acquired a grin. "Can't say I do. Thanks for thinking of me."

Thinking of him? Sammy and I loved the old fart. I'd never stopped thinking of him. "Let's move it, Ben. We have to steal a car somewhere."

He followed me, throwing a quick glance at bound guards. Didn't look surprised. Maybe he knew me better than I thought. Or maybe that was just the strange that had become habitual in his stranger than strange life?

I stopped when I spotted an open laptop at the guard station. *Does the USAF still have an internet?* Rather intranet, because a lot of their shit still should be classified. Sat down for a moment.

"You don't seem too much in a hurry now," said Ben.

"Just curious. Give me a minute."

There wasn't much on the laptop. That seemed to say computers weren't used much in the post-apocalyptic air force. Maybe most of them were at Cheyenne Mountain? I checked the connectivity. Just some Andrews LAN with no connection to anywhere else. Obviously the guards hadn't been among the connected privileged.

I found a few things interesting, though. A nice website for the base, showing the command structure, and a video of a speech given by the current POTUS. Looked haggard and on drugs. I wondered why. There wasn't much country to look after now. The presidency was no longer the most important and demanding job in the world. Maybe just being the fall guy in case the shit hit the fan again? I smiled. For some reason this all made me feel better. Maybe what was left of the Pentagon felt the same way!

⌘

I was worried about running into more guards as we headed off base, but getting away from Andrews was easy. *So much for security at the nation's seat of government!* Guess they had the same problem at Edwards—not enough people left even to clean latrines, let alone police the place. I knew Rodriguez always worked overtime.

For once in my life, DC traffic wasn't a mess. Would have avoided it by walking, of course. After a few hours of doing that for something less than a marathon's distance, we came to the College Park Metro just across Rhode Island Avenue. Thought it might be cooler in the tunnels.

Fumes wafting up the dead escalator provided enough reason for nixing that idea. The stench was unbearable, even after all the years that had passed. It couldn't be all from dead bodies, probably down to bones by now. I cupped my ear and listened. Heard water lapping against concrete. Soggy bones then. Maybe skeletons still playing like they're civil servants in storm-flooded subways heading toward Penn Avenue and vicinity? I decided skeletons weren't likely to float. Didn't want to confirm that theory or test fetid waters. Who knew what else was down there?

Ben made the same observation. "I don't think going down there is advisable," he said.

"No kidding. Stagnant and foul water at the very least.

It's still humid as hell in this swamp. Maybe even ga-tors?" I could imagine people's weird and/or illegal pets getting loose and heading for any water they could find. "Makes me yearn for arid SoCal. Let's look around, though. People parked their cars and rode into the city from here. Maybe we can find a car that still works. Han-nibal said there are lots around."

I had to explain who Hannibal was. All the time we'd been walking like silent zombies, I'd been thinking about him. Wondered if he'd ever forgive me.

CHAPTER 19

We didn't find any cars that started. Their innards were like those back in California—all corroded by whatever had fallen from the sky, the rot exacerbated by the DC area's swampy air. I remembered one prez had run a campaign slogan about draining the swamp. Bio warfare had done it for him…and to him and his successors? Pestilence had done away with most human pests! The real swamp had returned.

After checking a few cars, I decided maybe the aerosol bugs or whatever sent our way had just died and became some corrosive acid when mixed with the soupy atmosphere. I didn't much care, except for not finding any transportation. Becoming a refugee had taken away my nomadic stamina. And Ben was an old fellow.

But College Park had always been a thriving college town with University of Maryland students chillin' in downtown places and more senior professors with tenure still being able to afford to live in the area—*who knows where others lived?* DC was expensive. I knew the area a bit because I'd visited nearby Annapolis on one occasion and seen some DC sights. My traveling companion, a navy girl from Montana, had gone to Maryland—don't look for logic in college choices, or in the home state of a lover of the high seas. Some people just had a love for the ocean in their DNA, no matter where they were born.

On a quiet side street, Ben and I found a typical brick house with a car in the garage. Jostled it a bit and heard gas in the tank. Looked under the hood at its innards. Seemed okay. Must have been protected by the garage.

"Throw your things inside, old man. I'll see if I can find keys."

Saw it done a dozen times on cop shows, even by lady cops, but the door from the garage to the inside didn't succumb to my best kick. Almost sprained my ankle in my two attempts. Doors in those TV shows were probably similar to chairs in old Westerns' bar fights where the good guy just shook off a chair to the head, looked at the pieces, and then punched the bad guy out. I spotted a row of tools on pegboards, chose a hefty sledgehammer, and knocked out the entire door handle and lock assembly. It had been a good installation with a serious deadbolt, but nothing could withstand Thor's hammer, even when wielded by a small woman.

I looked in obvious places inside the house. Found a laundry basket with some clean, folded female duds. Shed the AF uniform and changed. Searched some more. No keys. I then found a skeleton dressed in jeans and plaid flannel shirt. His sneakers worked for me. I gritted my teeth and rummaged through pockets. Wallet from the hip pocket had a UM faculty ID. Side pocket had keys. *Eureka!*

I went outside and tried to open the car door. Nothing.

"Dead battery in the key fob," said Ben. "Can't open the trunk either." He pointed at his bag of belongings still on the garage floor. "I'll gather that up. We can try the next house."

"Stand back." My sledgehammer made short work of

the back window on the driver's side. Found a broom and cleaned off all safety glass shards, reached forward, and hit the start button. Nada. Zilch. Cursed in Spanish and English.

"Car battery's dead too," said Ben, "unless it can't start because of the fob."

"You mean I can't even start this vehicle by pushing it? You're the damn physicist. Think of something!"

He pointed to a charger tucked away on the workbench.

"You're assuming there's electricity?" I asked.

"Base has it. Why not here? We're in the seat of the national government, after all."

"But nothing's ever worked in this town," I said. "And the escalator at the Metro wasn't functioning."

"Probably shorted out or ruined from the flooding. Or just lack of maintenance."

"Okay, let's try charging the battery. What's it been? About six or seven years? How long does a car battery last?"

"You're lucky if you get five, especially in the Northeast where winters can be cruel. Let me check fluids first." It was low on those. "I'll assume the acid is still okay and all we have to do is add some water."

"Great! Something everyone is rationing. Although I don't understand why rationing's needed here with all this humidity. And the grand Potomac isn't dry, is it?" I couldn't remember seeing it when Hannibal flew me over the Mall, though.

Ben shrugged. "Usual water sources are likely contaminated. But we're okay." He went to the workbench and examined a bottle, showing it to me with pride after his inspection. "We need to use distilled water. This bottle has never been opened."

By the time we had the car running, the sun was showing in the east. We hit the Beltway. It was hard going because it was like an obstacle course, reminiscent of my experiences in the LA area. Cars, buses, and trucks with skeletons inside, hanging from windows, or reposing on the concrete roadway made for a huge DC traffic jam, the worst example of traffic tie-ups in the nation's capital I'd ever seen. A dead standstill.

When we hit the Virginia burbs and I-66, things became a bit easier. I was tempted to leave the interstate, but smoke from fires in the distance didn't give me a good feeling.

"Looters, gangs—maybe we can help someone?" Ben said.

"Forget it, old man. It's just you and me against the world until we arrive home."

"Are we going cross-country in this car?" he said.

"Do you have a better idea?"

"We could fly. There's a small regional airport nearby. It might be better to hop across country from one to the next. Overland's riskier by car. You never know who you'll come across on the roads. Remember the Russians?"

I shuddered. "Yeah, I do. How could I forget those SOBs? Precisely my point about those fires in the distance. Who will fly the plane?"

"Me. I know how to fly."

"Fine time to tell me. We could have stolen an F-15 at Andrews."

He smiled. "I can fly a small plane. I can't fly a jet. I'd be like an Amish driving an Indianapolis racer instead of a horse-drawn carriage."

Ben made me wonder about them. Amish, Mennonites, Mormons, Pentecostals—all enjoying their Second Coming, I hoped. The meek hadn't inherited the earth.

I wondered what my rock in Hell was inscribed with.

❦

Regional airports were a dime a dozen. Many of them were always questionable with respect to safety because they had no control towers, although we wouldn't be seeing a lot of air traffic.

The 9/11 terrorists had trained in such airports with their gullible trainers unquestioning their purpose. I'd grown up next to one in Lincoln Park, NJ, where two motherfucking jihadists had trained.

There were always little puddle jumpers parked in them. At the one in Virginia, we even found business jets with dead corporate VIPs inside, likely just down from Wall Street and ready to wine and dine with their congressional lackeys or hump their secretaries or mistresses.

Ben chose a nice looking Beechcraft S35 Bonanza. We pushed two desiccated bodies onto the tarmac, mostly skeletal with a bit of stinky jerky still on the bones, and tidied up the plane's insides a bit. We then stole fuel from another six planes. Old fuel had its risks, although aircraft fuel was a lot cleaner than car fuel—the trick was not to siphon all the way to the bottom of the tanks.

The craft was a lot easier to start than the car had been. We were soon winging our way west at a speed that would make old Hannibal have a good chuckle.

"Don't go to sleep on me, old man," I told him, studying a map I had found in the console. Felt a bit like Daniel Boone or Davy Crockett. *Westward ho, o pioneers!* Could see the land was reverting back to Nature. No crops or people in sight. Maybe looked like early nineteenth-century America? Gaia might be happy about that. She likely had never been too fond of human beings and their polluting, forest-killing ways.

He smiled at me. He seemed to be having fun. "Wouldn't think of sleeping in the air, Penny. On the next refueling stop or the following, we should take a good nap, though."

Sun was setting when we made that second stop. Parked the Beechcraft by the hangar after refueling—again, plenty of parked planes, but no live human beings. Wolfed down a couple of cans of cold chili—didn't want to chance any kind of fire—and passed out in the hangar.

A noise awoke me. I soon located the direction and the kind—scratching at the hangar's side door. The sound also awoke a memory.

"What is it?" said Ben.

"Not a gang obviously. Maybe Mutt coming back to haunt you?"

He cocked his head. "It does sound like an animal." He jerked a ghostly thumb toward the empty chili cans. "Maybe it smells the food. If it's a bear, that door won't stop him."

I thought a moment. "Bears tend to avoid humans and would normally stay away from places like this."

He considered that comment. "Probably not enough human activity here now to keep them away," he said.

"I'll take a look through the door's little window." He followed me. I looked. Turned to him and smiled. "It's Mutt reincarnated."

"As a bear?"

"No, another dog. A bit smaller. Just as ugly. Should I let him in?"

"Does he look dangerous?"

"No, but 'nice dog' might just be an act. Be prepared for anything."

"He might have a master around here." Ben, who had been holding a gun at his side, brought it up. "Open the door. I'll back you up."

"Just make sure you don't shoot me."

I opened the door. The dog jumped on me and

knocked me down, but Ben held his fire. She was licking my face—no dangling fruit on this stray. She was at least five years and without her master. Maybe I looked like her owner? 'Course, the owner could have been male.

"I wonder what the fem version of Mutt is," I said.

CHAPTER 20

We named our new canine friend Muttsie and fed her another can of chili. She earned her stripes right away. We were two hours from dawn when I heard her growl. I thought it might be painful dog farts brewed from chili in a starving tummy, but I woke Ben and went to the door to check the outside. Saw shadows.

"Zombies looking for blood," I said to Ben.

"Zombies aren't vampires. They're the walking dead, biting others to create more zombies. Or to eat them. All fantasy."

"You win. I stand corrected. But if they're still carrying that plague, they could infect us if we aren't still immune. I'm more worried about them making us into an early breakfast, though. Keep Muttsie quiet and cover me from the center. They'll likely come right through this door, so I'll be the first line of defense."

"Why not me and the dog?"

"Because you can't shoot worth shit, and the dog can't shoot at all."

I readied two of the air force pistols. Ben had the other. He retreated back to where we'd been sleeping, holding the dog's collar, confirming she'd once had another owner. She was still growling, showing her nice set of chili-stained teeth. Probably had never seen a vet. *Do we have one back at Edwards?* Another feature of civilization that had maybe disappeared.

There were four of them. I shot two between the eyes but the other two wrestled me to the floor and began to rip off my clothes. I knew women were often raped before they went on the spit. Men not so much. Unless the zombies were female. Heard that happened sometimes. Crazy thoughts about gay zombies as I struggled—maybe some future graduate thesis?

I'd never spoken to a rape victim one-on-one. Wondered if their experiences were similar to mine. I sort of became detached, a bystander encouraging the victim to resist the savage attack with all her strength and energy, to make him pay while knowing the victim would succumb. Women might be smarter than men, but men were often stronger, and when they became savage beasts intent on rape, that overwhelming strength seemed to sap the victims. I could understand why some might acquiesce and just let it happen, hoping to live through it. I could also understand the loathing that remained, the memories of the attacker's wild eyes and fetid breath. There was also the self-loathing, the filthy feeling that your body had become a cesspool. Your instant reaction was a hatred for all men.

I managed to kick one attacker in the balls as he fought to pull down my pants. Easy target when a male has an erection—it was like the flag pole on a golf course. He howled and relinquished his spot to the other assailant.

There were two shots. The zombie I had kicked was now writhing, the other dead. I struggled to my feet and gave the live one a kick to the side of his head.

"Still doubt I can shoot?" said Ben.

I grabbed my gun and finished the job. No remorse. It was like putting down a rabid dog. *Animals!* "Good enough," I said.

"Are-are you okay?"

"No," I said, buttoning up the best I could. "One asshole bit me. What can we put on the bite?"

"Aviation fuel?"

"Works for me. Go find some while I drag these bodies into the weeds outside." Of course, I made sure no more cannibals were lurking by taking Muttsie with me.

Dealing with dead bodies reminded me of Ned…

ᘓᘔᘓᘔ

SEALs did just about anything. In particular, they were divers too. That gave Ned and me something in common to talk about at first until we became hot and heavy in the sack and words weren't needed as much and time was often short.

Everyone except the brass knew about our relationship. Maybe they did too and just looked the other way. Maybe they figured that it was a way for Ned to relieve some stress while waiting to be assigned to a dangerous op as we cruised through the Strait of Hormuz and around the Persian Gulf making like intrepid foreign tourists. The brass likely weren't worried about my stress—just empathy with Ned, they'd say.

Just before his last mission, we were talking about marriage and family. He'd had three tours; I'd had two. I was search and rescue—no combat duties per se if you discounted where we were. He was all combat. Should have known better to nurture such a relationship, but Ned AKA Rambo, for all his tough-guy persona, had his kinder, gentler side that I loved.

Six SEALs went on a mission. Two live ones and four

body bags returned. Not a good day for Uncle Sam's Special Ops. I felt lust for revenge but couldn't even know how he'd died because of security. Worse, no drinking while in a high-alert situation—DefCon whatever.

"What will you do?" said Kathy, my best friend from ordinance, not a big job on a carrier either except in a combat-ready situation, but more important than mine—many bad guys would just love to sink a carrier with a suicide mission in a small motorboat.

"I'm leaving the navy as fast as I can. I don't want to see any more bodies."

She hugged me, I cried, and the chaplain looked helpless. Most people knew Ned and I were tight, maybe even the captain, like I said. No one ever had complained because it didn't affect either of our jobs. It was like a workplace romance, except both of us were in harm's way—Ned much more so than me, of course.

I was still in the navy long enough to see more bodies, though. In the sheriff's department, even more. You start developing an emotional callous. Tried to avoid that. After the plague fell from the sky, the callousness hit its max—the dead far outnumbered the living and I'd lost my meals a few times.

Sammy and Ben had changed all that. Ned wasn't around, but I was still in love, a mellower love for my newly adopted family. Ned was the past; they were my future. Okay, it might also include Rodriguez if I could ever get beyond his betrayal. That would take some effort. I doubted springing Ben would help with the pilot's tight-ass attitude, though.

⸎

Ben, Muttsie, and I had more chili for breakfast and

took off farting into the wild blue yonder. Muttsie paced in the plane's small rear area to begin with but soon settled down just behind our seats. I would have preferred her more toward the rear. She needed a bath. Of course, we all did. Stink from within and without all wrapped up in a flying tin can.

"Too bad this plane can't land on a lake," I said.

"We have plenty of water," said Ben.

"Not enough for a reasonable bath," I said.

"I'm cleaner than you," he said.

"Courtesy of what's left of the US government. We need to talk about why you were in jail."

"You've had chances to do so."

"I've been busy." The plane started jumping a bit. "Air turbulence?"

"Dirty fuel. A cylinder's misfiring."

"Are we going to crash?"

"It could work itself out. But I'll make a soft landing if it doesn't."

"Let's pick a spot without zombies," I said.

But the engine smoothed out instead, and we flew on.

"Want to be pilot?" Ben said about an hour later.

"I don't know how to fly this damn thing."

"Doesn't take much right now. Takeoffs and landings are the hard part. Change seats."

So I sat in the pilot's seat for the next hour or so. Ben was watchful, but he'd been right—there wasn't much to do. Straight and level was straight and level. They might as well have had a cruise control. Then I remembered they did sometimes, called an autopilot. Our plane didn't.

"Now, bank to the right," he said.

"You're kidding. You take the helm and bank to the right."

"Just jerkin' your chains." He pointed ahead. "Fires. We might want to avoid them. We don't need another encounter with locals. Change seats with me. I'm changing course to miss them."

"You're curious, aren't you?"

"Yes, but I want us home in one piece."

I smiled at that. *Home. What a concept! A tent in a refugee camp! Would Rodriguez still be hanging around like a lovesick puppy? Would he move into our tent?* That tent could become crowded with Ben and Muttsie.

I was still working on forgiving Alejandro Rodriguez but thought he would make a nice addition too. Would help me forget about being almost raped. Hoped I could move past that. Rape victims often had a problem in future relationships, especially if authorities blamed them for the rape, which was so often the case. *You shouldn't have been walking alone. You shouldn't have been dressed like a slut. What does it matter that he was a rabid animal?* Yeah, I knew, men were raped too, especially in prison. But women were the traditional victims of rape.

I'd shot the zombies without hesitation. *No problema* because no authorities to blame me, and Ben sure wouldn't—but I'd always remember the rage and lust of my attackers.

I remembered the girl in that drugstore too. That could have been my future…or lack thereof.

CHAPTER 21

The bite became infected but I didn't die. Wasn't about to let that zombie-rapist win. At the next rest and refuel stop, Ben found a medical kit and plastered the bite with ten-year-old antibiotic cream after cleaning it well. Problem was finding clean cloth to serve as a bandage. A skeleton's clothes in the tiny control tower provided a reasonable approximation.

Come morning, Muttsie woke me with a facewash. We had bonded. Human beings and dogs, buds through the ages. I knew a lot of them had gone feral, dogs too, but canines seemed to handle it better. Our furry friends seemed to keep it together when that thin veneer of civilization wore off. *Or maybe they're more tolerant after putting up with humans?* I was counting any previous encounters with feral dog packs as anomalies, of course.

"So, what's your story?" I said to Ben over our meager breakfast.

Ben looked at me, nodded, and swallowed some canned peas. He tapped his shock of wild hair. "Nothing in here, but they tell me I'm a physicist who retrained and became a national security asset in the missile program. They wanted me to work on their antiquated guidance systems."

"Antiquated? Aren't they only five-years-old or so?" I said.

"I guess most of them are older. They need someone to check that they're still functioning well and reprogram them for new targets."

"What for? Isn't that how this messy situation came about?"

"Retaliation. They could fire off a few for that purpose—or so I heard. They have some scientists working on a payload even now. They wanted me to make sure it arrives at their designated targets."

"And you refused? I'm proud of you!"

He smiled. "Don't nominate me for the Nobel Peace Prize just yet. I had to refuse because I can't remember any technical stuff. I was once a leading expert on guidance systems, though, especially newer ones that use both GPS and onboard inertials."

"Do we still have GPS satellites?"

"Guess so. Doesn't matter. I couldn't help them."

"Did they torture you?"

"No. Yes? I can't remember. I was a bit embarrassed that I couldn't remember anything, so I started doing some reading there in that cell. I was up to elementary mechanics when you arrived—you know, Newton's laws and their consequences."

I thought a moment. "Guidance systems must be based on all that, but they're a lot more complicated. You can't remember that stuff?"

"Nope." He touched his head. "I'm as innocent as Sammy now. I'm thankful for that. No way I'd have helped them. They didn't believe me, of course. That's why I was still at Andrews."

"They don't have anyone else?"

He laughed and rubbed Muttsie on the head. "Not anyone they can find. It's a real hoot they can't. We can thank the plague for that."

I smiled. A real hoot and poetic justice. I began to worry about those scientists working to reverse engineer what fell on us from the sky, though. *How sick is that? And are Edwards' refugees a clandestine part of that program?*

ᘛᘚ

Next night we feasted on junk food. I found and broke into a vending machine still loaded with all kinds of good snacks. The candy bars were like bricks—I almost broke a tooth—but Ben and I found trail mix, peanuts, and crackers edible and filling. Nothing like a healthy Mediterranean diet. There were enough crackers for Muttsie too. Everything was a bit stale, but you'd think they'd be worse after five or more years. Goes to show those expiration dates are pretty meaningless.

I was filling pretty chipper. Antibiotic cream seemed to be working on my bite too. I dreamed about camping in the backyard with my older brother, before he became an asshole. Shouldn't have been so hard on him, I guess. Our sot of a father had abandoned us—Mom couldn't even find him to put the squeeze on for child support—so Bobby thought he had to be the man of the house.

He became overly protective. I had to start hiding boyfriends from him. He smothered me, and, like any younger sibling, I needed my freedom. But college was out of the question, so I joined the navy. That was the last straw for him. Go figure. He joined the air force and then lost his temper when I joined the navy. His tirade on the phone reminded me of Dad when he got drunk.

I suppose he had some justification, though. In joining the navy, I'd turned down a partial athletic scholarship offered because of my swimming prowess. My senior year I had been captain of our high school girls swim team that came in second at the state championships, not too shabby for a girl who'd started life fearing the water. Figured competition at the college level was a lot tougher, though, and I'd still have to work a lot to supplement that athletic scholarship in a Div II school. Blew it off, hence Bobby's ire. First stop along the road to complete estrangement.

In the end, it was all over Mom's care, with Bobby saying it was a waste of money. Early Alzheimer's was making her into a vegetable. I found a lawyer and became her legal guardian, sold her house, and put her in a nice place in Southern Jersey not far from the shore she had loved. I then went off to war. Bobby had never lifted a hand to help her. He always thought she drove Dad to drink. Maybe. I didn't know. But you couldn't just abandon your mother like she was chicken shit.

Last I heard about Bobby, he was in Vandenberg, and I was in SoCal working with the LA Sheriff's Department. Had no desire to go see him, no matter how near he was. He made no moves to see me either, even if he knew I was nearby. My dream had been filled with his sneering face, though. So much like Dad, even if Bobby didn't drink.

I staggered around a bit when I awoke until Ben and Muttsie came in. He and the dog were wet. Muttsie shook herself making me feel the need for a shower too.

"I arranged for some bathing facilities," said Ben. "Keep the bandage on. I'll change it after you shower."

There was running water. Sort of. His setup consisted of a gravity tank made from a barrel you filled with buckets of water. I could take a quick shower. *Heaven!* Even gave the dog a better bath after I did my clothes. Good thing I knew Ben well enough to feel comfortable in my birthday suit. Nomad life with Ben and Sammy had ended any modesty issues they or I might have had.

The S35 wasn't fast. Adding in fuel stops, which involved siphoning fuel from several planes, we had managed about a 500-to-600-mile chunk every day, more or less, putting along at 200 knots. Hannibal's jet was much faster, but we were lucky we hadn't stolen a business jet—jet fuel was scarce.

CHAPTER 22

We had one more adventure before landing at Edwards—real turbulence. Ben couldn't skirt a thunderstorm over the desert fast enough. Reminded me of why I disliked small planes almost as much as I did helicopters. Ben fought the rapid ups and downs; I watched the spinning altimeter.

"What's happening?"

He was pale, so I didn't believe him when he said, "Don't worry!" His biceps bulged and his veins showed more than usual as the plane disobeyed him in its *Rite of Spring* dance with Mother Nature. I could hear Stravinsky's pounding music. The theater had a light show as lightning flashes lit up the cockpit, but no direct hits. Never heard thunder because driving rain mixed with hail pounded on the plane's old aluminum fuselage turning Stravinsky's music into a Phil Collins's drum solo on steroids. I feared the hail would crack a window.

"I'm trying to go lower and fly beneath the clouds."

The turbulence ended but thunderheads still dumped their innards on us. Ben pointed off to the right. "I'm going to take it down if I can. Something's not right in the back."

I was a bit green like that witch in *Wicked* by the time

he landed and we skidded to a stop. I'd seen the play's ads on local TV as a kid and never liked skin the color of a bromating pile of garter snakes.

"That experience will make a good story to tell Sammy. Let's take a look."

There was a black-rimmed hole about the size of a tin can's top under the stern fuselage. We both saw a frayed cable that reminded me of that cable on the diving cage so long ago, except this one wasn't broken.

"That doesn't look good. How'd that happen?"

"Most likely an indirect lightning hit when we moved through an upstroke," he said. "Maybe even the step leader, which can start from the ground too."

Huh? Ben was techno-babbling again.

"Are we walking the rest of the way?"

"As you saw, I could still fly the plane, but that frayed cable is binding in the pulley. Everything will be fine when I replace the cable."

"What about dents from the hail?" I said, rubbing my hands over the pocketed fuselage.

"Isn't a jet. Streamlining is more aesthetic and convenient than it is necessary. We don't have much farther to go as the crow flies."

"Let's just hope the plane flies as well as the crow."

I watched Ben work, but began to worry when he stepped back with hands on hip and shook his head. "The cable won't last too much longer. We need a new one."

"Where are we? Doesn't look too busy around here." I scanned the horizon. "Is that a ghost town?"

Ben shaded his eyes. "Let me check the maps." He climbed aboard and studied them, leaving me outside in the blazing sun, wondering how old the maps were and how long it would take him to find his bearings.

I trusted him but hated to be so dependent on him.

"I'm pretty sure that's Peach Springs, Arizona, and

we're between I-Forty and old Route Sixty-Six."

"Good. We can just hitch a ride with a semi heading for LA."

He smiled. "Not likely, but the town might have some tools and cable I can use. Let's take a walk."

✂✂✂

I was dusty, thirsty, and well done from the sun by the time we entered the town. Put my T-shirt back on because I sensed eyes were watching us. "There are people here. Friends or foes?"

"They might be scared of us too. Maybe you should take the shirt off again so they can see how malnourished we both are." He stopped and looked back to the side. An old man wearing a broad-rim hat with a large feather in its band was staring at us. Ben waved a hand. "Can you help us?"

Blank expression. "*Puede ayudarnos?*" I said, meaning the same thing.

The man turned and went back inside what looked like a general store from an old spaghetti western. I could almost hear the music from *The Good, the Bad and the Ugly* with old Clint smoking a cheroot and riding in on his piebald. Did I have the right movie? There were so many. Knew I had the right music bouncing around in my head. 'Course Ben and I were both good and ugly. Would we have to confront the bad?

"We might want to high tail it out of town, partner," I said to Ben.

But the man returned with a short woman with pigtails who was carrying something. They approached us.

"*Agua*," said the man. "Water," said the woman. She was offering a pail of water containing a ladle.

They were Native Americans from the Hualapai Tribe.

Their administrative center was Peach Springs. After Ben
thanked them in English and I thanked them in Spanish,
they took us inside the general store. Correction: what
had been a general store. Mostly bare shelves bore mute
testament to the general breakdown of supply chains in
the country.

Inya'a and Hala were nice enough but not too talka-
tive. We managed to explain our problem. Inya'a held up
a hand and said, "*Espere un momento*," meaning "Wait a
minute." He walked to the store's rear and went outside. I
tensed. Ben looked at me and shrugged.

Inya'a returned with a man he introduced as his son,
also named Ben, although that probably wasn't his
Hualapai name. Father, mother, and son chatted in Pai—
my Ben later told me that was what their language was
called.

Their Ben turned to us. "I have an old pickup. I'll find
some tools and cable and take you back to your plane.
We'll fix it."

There was a pause. Both my Ben and I were considering the possible danger. The other Ben was in a lot better
shape than us. My Ben wasn't in great shape at all and
my arm was hurting. Even if my physical health had improved a lot at the refugee camp, the last few days had
taken a lot out of me. I'd be no match for this muscle-
bound young man who was in great shape.

I studied him some more. Almost giggled like a teenager. Could imagine him as a prom date. I'd be the envy
of all the girls that night because Hualapai Ben looked
like he belonged in Hollywood—not now, of course, but
back when cute, leading guys were the rage of action film
enthusiasts. He was a combo of Tom Cruise and Matt
Damon in their prime. He was slightly taller than me and
looked like a coiled spring. I could imagine all the high
school girls licking their chops when looking at him and

cursing me when looking my way. What a night I would have had!

"Thanks," my Ben said. "I wish there were something we could do for you folks in return."

"You can." He jerked a thumb at me. "She's okay. She's part Native American."

Huh? How's he know that if I don't?

"But you can do me the favor of telling your fellow white devils to take their plague and shove it up their ass."

"I'm not responsible for that," my Ben said.

The other Ben held up a hand. "I'm not blaming you personally—you're probably just an innocent dupe—but the white man has been making us sick for centuries. This time it backfired. We're alive and most of you are dead. Mother Earth has finally brought us some justice."

I wasn't about to argue the point that the perps were more than likely yellow, not white. Didn't make a difference—his underlying thesis was still valid.

"I guess I can understand your reasoning," said my Ben, "at least historically. Why are you helping us then?"

"Like I said, your squaw is part Native American."

Squaw? Do I look so terrible that Hualapai Ben puts me at the same age as my Ben? Again, I bit my tongue. Come to think of it, Hualapai Ben's mother looked a lot younger than the father.

❧❧

"Did all your people survive the plague?" I said in the pickup on the way back to the plane.

"Those who didn't die of starvation or thirst. We're doing okay now, but we had to return to a lot of our old ways. That's good, I think. We'd forgotten how to live off the land."

"But you keep this old truck running," said my Ben.

"Barely. And only for emergencies. It's had more use as an ambulance and funeral hearse. We've returned to the hills for the most part, but my parents are old and stubborn. I won't leave them alone in Peach Springs."

"You need a squaw to help you out," I said.

"I'm gay."

"Oh, great, another one." Knee-jerk reaction.

"What do you mean?"

I saw his frown in the rearview mirror—knee-jerk reaction to my knee-jerk reaction.

I eased the tension. "Just when I find a handsome guy, I discover he's gay." I thought of my good friend, Joey. We'd kept in contact via emails for a while. Wondered what had happened to him. "It will sound trite, but one best friend in the navy was gay."

Now he smiled. "I've heard that comment among our young girls too. My parents don't know, by the way, so please don't tell them."

"Mum's the word," I said.

"Pardon?"

"*Tu secreto es seguro conmigo*," I said, meaning "Your secret is secure with me."

"Thank you."

"Teach us some words in your native language," I said. We had a bit of fun with that, but I soon changed the topic. "Why do you think I'm part Native American? I had no idea, by the way."

"I sense it. You are a strange mix, I'll give you that, but there are features. It's just a guess. And it made my parents feel better about helping you two."

That was a sobering thought. *What if they hadn't?*

When we arrived at the plane, our new friend examined the damage. He gave us his diagnosis, which confirmed my Ben's suspicion: the entire cable would have to be replaced or our rudder would be more than stiff—it would be useless. He and Ben worked on the plane's underbelly for about two hours and then declared victory.

We all shook hands. I added an embrace. "*Dejame saber si cambias,*" I said, whispering in his ear and meaning, "Let me know if you change." He smiled and gave me a peck on my cheek. He knew what I meant by "change." I could imagine that his tribe didn't much like gays. Poor guy.

We took off, made a U, and passed back over the old pickup, waving at our new friend, and then headed for SoCal. Ben began to hassle me again about not knowing how to fly and boring me by telling me how planes worked. Lift, drag, airflow—who cares?

"What would you have done if I'd had a heart attack during that turbulence?"

"Scream? Why do you ask? You weren't having angina, were you?"

"No, but you never know what an old adrenaline-laced body will do in an emergency situation."

"I'd prefer to have brought a defibrillator with us than be a copilot. I'm nervous enough as a passenger." Didn't want to admit that was an acquired phobia after Ned's death—any type of flying unsettled me, but especially the choppers that often ferried Ned into danger, and small planes. I'd needed to swallow my fears on search and rescue missions and dives from choppers with the sheriff's department, but there was a big difference between swallowing your fear and being totally comfortable.

I was happy when we landed at Edwards.

ୡୡୡ

Ben had me radio in for clearance like I was flying the plane. Told the control tower we were a possible biohazard too. He taxied to a spot as far away from the base's buildings as he could be. I then switched places with him, and he hid in the rear under a tarp.

When I saw two jeeps approaching, I deplaned with Muttsie and waited for the security personnel. All four had biohazard suits on.

"We'll have to leave the dog here," said one guard in a muffled voice.

"Got a rope? I'll tie her to the landing gear. What about me?" I was handed a suit. "I'm immune, remember?"

"Sorry. Complete chem bath for you. You could be a carrier."

I shrugged. It was awful to crawl into that suit in that heat. Seemed to waste that wonderful shower the day before, not that I hadn't sweated on that little walk to Peach Springs. Guessed air force medical staff were used to it.

PART 4

Expeditions

"Heroism on command, senseless violence, and all the loathsome nonsense that goes by the name of patriotism—how passionately I hate them!"
~ Albert Einstein

CHAPTER 23

I was given the whole nine yards upon returning to Andrews—scrub-a-dub chemical shower, both in and out of the suit, and complete physical, including blood tests. After a few hours, I was led to my debriefing where I finally met Major Landon, only now he was Colonel Landon. Fast promotion. Wondered what he'd done to deserve it.

I've always been suspicious of officers, even female ones. Thought too many of them considered troops or even NCOs slaves or cannon fodder. Put it this way: I considered them guilty until proven innocent. Always thought civilians should have the same attitude, even more so. Too many times in recent history people became rich off war. Even Eisenhower warned about the military-industrial complex. When the shit fell from the sky, the US had the deadliest weapons and sold more arms to the rest of the world than any other country.

That said, I'd known some officers I respected. Hell, Ned had outranked me too. Most of the time I didn't give a rat's ass—the navy was just another job, one where I'd learn a trade that produced employment afterward. Unlike many others, I couldn't say I ever put my life on the line either. Just focused on my boring job, trying to do it well enough to avoid being chewed out. Not a bad agenda for anyone's working life.

Landon wasn't a big man, but he was intense. Definitely type-A. Thin hair, large eyes, and sunken cheeks made him look a bit ghoulish. You know the type—someone without enough meat in his face, making you think of the skeleton's head underneath. My first reaction wasn't positive, but I'd learned to be objective about a person's looks. I wasn't Cindy Crawford, by any means.

"Hi there, airman," I said to the base's nominal head. "How are you today?" Didn't shake hands. He was frowning too much. I was still getting bad vibes.

"Where's Ben?"

"No greeting? How 'bout, Ensign Penny, how are you doing today? How'd you manage to make it back without us? How'd you manage to make fools of Andrew's security personnel?"

He smiled. "You did the milk run in a Beechcraft. I didn't know you could fly."

"I didn't either. Desperate people do desperate things."

"Your landing was a bit ragged, but not bad. Where's Ben Thomas?"

"Do you think I'd bring him back here? You were the guys who arrested him. And for no reason—he doesn't remember a damn thing."

"I didn't give the orders to arrest him, but yes, the air force needs his skills."

"To retaliate against a country or countries likely in as bad a shape as this one? Maybe worse. You'd think the air force would understand the jet stream and other air currents better than anyone else. They wafted the pestilence right around the world. Gee, let's do it again!"

"Personally, I might agree with you, but that's irrelevant. My superiors have different opinions."

I shrugged. "Yeah, I saw the poster with the new president's smiling face. Saw a video too. You can all go to hell as far as I'm concerned. Oops, maybe you're already there, and I'm here with you!"

"You have a bad attitude."

I ignored his comment. It was true. The air force had only given me and my adopted family grief so far, discounting the refugee camp, which was at least safe enough, even with all its negatives.

"What are you going to do with my plane?"

"Torch it eventually. Who knows what plague you brought with you?"

"Oh, we can pretty much guess which plague, colonel. How 'bout I collect my family and fly it into the Big Valley? You haul in the water from there, right? We'd be out of your life. The cannibals there might need some fresh meat too."

"Yes, we're filling tankers around Bakersfield. But without our security personnel, you wouldn't survive, as you insinuated. And who wants you to contaminate the human population there, the ones who aren't cannibals?"

"For your first objection, I'm willing to gamble. For the second, you'd have two fewer mouths to feed in camp, three counting my dog." I didn't count Ben, of course, but always knew we'd be sharing rations with the old man. No way was I turning him in after making that dangerous cross-country trek. "Let me have the plane, and I won't bother you anymore."

"Tell us where Ben is."

"I can tell you where I left him. New Mexico. He spent some time with a tribe there once upon a time. Wants to try and find them. Seems like he finds peyote soothing. Lord knows he needs some comfort. Nothing here for him except another jail cell. Or the one back at Andrews." I gave him the evil eye. "What's my punishment for helping him escape, by the way?"

"You mean breaking him out of jail, right? I'll try to obtain a pardon for you because of mitigating circumstances. Go say hi to your kid. You might not see him for a while."

Rodriguez-style goons ushered me back to camp. I saw the Beechcraft in the distance. No dog. Ben would be in hiding at the camp.

∞

With all that crowded humanity in the refugee camp, it was easy to keep Ben hidden. Two families had left. Heard they couldn't stand cramped quarters, so they decided to take their chances being nomads again. I claimed their tents for us and shoved them together making a canvas mansion with three rooms. One was general living quarters, the second was my bedroom, and the third was Sammy's. Ben slept on an old loveseat in the main tent when he wasn't hiding in Sammy's tent or somewhere else; and Muttsie became Sammy's permanent roomie and our security alarm.

Our lives didn't change much except for the constant stress of keeping Ben hidden. The air force goons were pretty lax, figuring refugees didn't have it so bad, considering how things were going elsewhere. I had to agree with those two families, though. The camp was overflowing with humanity subjected to all the accompanying inconveniences found in refugee camps everywhere.

Ben maintained a sense of humor about the whole thing. He even put on a disguise and went on a date. He admired a widow. When I learned about it, I encouraged him. She was Olga, of the flipped mattress. A pleasant, heavyset woman, she reminded me a bit of Robin Williams as Mrs. Doubtfire. She didn't like to do it, but she spoke Russian, so they could communicate better in that language instead of broken English—Ben's broken by bad wiring in the brain and Olga's by being a recent immigrant.

I heard from refugees with tents near hers about that odd couple finishing off a few assorted bottles of hard liquor together. Heard from Ben that they slept together but didn't sleep together, if you know what I mean. The terrible hangover—yeah, what he needed was more head trauma—cured Ben of seeking female companionship for a while. Can't say Olga felt the same way—she was always flirting with him. She was a nice woman, so I might have encouraged that.

Hiding Ben was a game Olga and other refugees helped me play. His disguises were stashed in many places around camp, and they allowed him to move around more freely when you added cooperating refugees to the little conspiracy. Provided some fun for a droll existence. Allowed people to smack the air force around too. And it gave Ben something to do as he became camp philosopher. Many times he would be eating a meager dinner elsewhere, discussing everything that came to his hosts' minds. That also helped Ben move along a road to recovery, if by inches.

Sammy gave us a scare. He was fascinated with planes, but not in the way I thought. When he disappeared, I put USAF Security on the case. Might not like them, but they could cover more ground than me. I figured he wouldn't go far. Outside the base and refugee camp, there was a lot of desert area to wander around in, but, because of his past, he would be afraid of gangs of feral humans. Hell, I was afraid of just about feral anything…well, maybe not cats and rats, although I'd seen some mean-looking rodents since the apocalypse.

A mechanic heard security's walkie-talkie chatter and admitted Sammy was with him. Don't know if I was more upset with his disappearance or that he was covered head to toe with oil and grease. He and Hank the mechanic had been reconstructing a chopper motor. Planes and choppers were a bit like those old cars in Cuba—they were fast becoming relics, so they needed a lot of TLC to keep them going. After my anger passed, I thought that might be a good career for Sammy if the base stayed functional. No guarantee of that, of course.

Hank had been a chopper pilot until he crashed one. Fuel for the chopper hadn't been clean and had fouled up the motor. Reminded me of why I hated the damn things. He'd made his buddies go into the desert and perform salvage because he knew any parts would be useful in the future. He was that kind of guy.

One leg broken in the crash hadn't mended well, so he limped around hangars a bit like Chester—more TV reruns from my carrier days, this time *Gunsmoke*. Didn't dress like Matt Dillon's deputy, though—always muscle shirts, cutoff jeans, and sneakers without socks, everything loaded with grime. I didn't know if he had a tan or it was all just grease. Still a good role model for Sammy. Couldn't hurt for him to know something about motors. I knew squat.

Hank wasn't unusual. Put a lot of humans together and they started to stink. There wasn't much water to wash either clothes or bodies. We were always digging new holes in the ground for new outhouses. There were materials for them—just those government-issue cinder blocks and sheet-metal roofing—but not for habitations to replace tents. The air force had first dibs on all materials anyway.

The canvas in the tents was beginning to look a bit frayed and weathered under the hot sun, something like Ahab's sails after encountering the white whale, I suppose. Having lived in worse conditions at boot camp and elsewhere, I could cope, but I felt sorry for others. Still, thought it was better than being nomads.

Rodriguez increased the frequency and length of his visits. Sometimes I felt he was looking for intel about Ben's whereabouts, but most of the time he just seemed to be a good hunk who enjoyed Sammy's and my company.

I struggled to keep it platonic. A girl had needs, but I still hadn't completely forgiven him for being an asshole. By the time I had a few "your man's here" comments from other refugees, I decided to cool it considerably. Encouraged him to spend more time with Sammy. I spent time with Ben, my other child.

Ben and I were teaching each other science and technology. I'd never been much good at it, but he showed me that a lot of what I knew about water, air tanks, and so forth had general applications. We avoided talking about missile guidance. His position as surrogate-father/son solidified. And he became almost as well-known as Mayor Ballesteros, but always in hiding.

એજ્ય

Some refugees helped the air force personnel—just volunteering in order to keep busy. Because I was bored and boasted that my nuclear family could make it just fine without the USAF, I volunteered for water detail once. It meant a trip to the Big Valley and the artesian wells that had begun to recover as the water table rose from lack of use, even with reduced snow packs. Three tankers with three people crowded in each cab made the trek.

The flyboys had the duty of patrolling the CA-58/138/I-5/US-99 triangle. Highway 58 led from Edwards to Bakersfield, which was mostly a ghost town except for gangs of feral humans. We took 58 over to 99, cruised through that desert city, and somewhere between McFarland and Delano veered off into what had been farm country. I was nervous the entire trip, thinking of danger, but I'd also wanted to see for myself what farm country looked like now. In particular, could my family and I make a go of it there?

What had been rich farmland was now desert, of course. Bodies we saw were mummies without bandages for the most part, not skeletons. Human jerky on their bones. I was surprised they were still intact, but the lack of water might have driven carrion feeders into the cooler hills on the coast or the Sierra Nevadas. Made me think we were seeing King Tut and all his followers. Wondered why they'd bothered with all the mummification techniques in ancient Egypt. Wouldn't putting old Tut and Nefertiti onto the Sahara's hot sands have done the same thing? Could have saved all that money and slaves needed to build those pyramids!

The truck drivers didn't try to be stealthy. We rolled up to an old irrigation station without incident. In the weather-beaten pump house was a new gasoline generator—the old pumps had used home-service electricity. The production cost of that electricity was now a lot more, considering gasoline was so scarce, but the generators weren't on all the time either.

Ignoring all that, I still had some questions. "Why don't you make all these operational and get some farming started?" I said to my driver who was hooking up hoses.

"Lack of personnel," he said. "Someone needs to protect farmers and equipment. We can't afford the manpower."

"Find farmers who can protect themselves," I said, thinking of my family's future. "Worked in the American Revolution. Worked in the Old West."

"They had guns and ammo in the Old West. No one makes them anymore. We don't even have enough for the armed forces."

I nodded. That was a problem. Hard to defend yourself against marauding tribes of cannibals with only a pitchfork, although I'd had that kind of limited arsenal once. Thought I might want to try it, though, just to put distance between us and the US Government.

"Maybe you don't give the good people in refugee camps enough—"

My driver's exploding head caused me to hit the ground.

"We're under attack!" someone yelled.

You think?

I grabbed my driver's pistol and hid behind the old pumps. Figured they could take a few bullets better than I could. The survivors—we'd lost three people in a few seconds—soon joined me.

"Where are they?" I had a general idea, but no specific information. The land was so flat, I couldn't figure why I didn't spot them.

"In the irrigation ditch," said one flyboy.

I saw a small berm in the distance. The pumping station was a major one, so of course there was a ditch to carry the water off to nearby fields. The standard technique was to open and close gates along the way on a weekly schedule when this desert had once been the nation's bread basket—maybe more fruit and vegetable basket, along with cotton and sugar beets.

"They have us pinned down," I said, stating the obvious. "We have to take the fight to them."

"And just how do you propose doing that?"

"Using a truck. We drive right up to them, jump out, and use the truck as a shield."

Another companion nodded. "Might lose a truck, but

what the hell. But we can only put three in a cab."

"I and…" I checked the little fellow's badge lying next to me. "…Taylor here can scrunch up on the back shelf. We're small." Most air force personnel were small fellows, especially the flyers, but Taylor was pint-size like me. Taylor reminded me of my pal Joey, although Taylor likely wasn't gay—I knew he had nudies in his wallet, and they weren't guys.

"Let's go for it."

It was a tight squeeze. Taylor put his arms around me, giving me a sly wink. I decided to ignore it until our firefight was over. It was comforting in a platonic way.

The truck's driver first headed parallel to the ditch away from our attackers and then made a U. Safety glass was flying all around by the time he stopped and we jumped out, using the old chassis as our shield.

My references to the Old West were on the money. Thought I'd time-traveled back to the OK Corral. My aim was a bit off at first, but I soon became used to the handgun. Went through my driver's clips and picked up Taylor's AR-15 when he caught a bullet in the chest.

He became the only additional casualty. Four tattooed savages were dead. One I recognized—the white-haired, wild Russian leader who was still shirtless. His tattoos would provide his burial bouquet.

I didn't feel any justice about that. Didn't think it was fair to exchange a few cannibals for Taylor. Didn't feel much at all. Puked instead. My hardened life as a nomad had softened in the refugee camp. But who'd have expected a firefight going for water?

I decided on the way back to put my family's move for independence on hold for a while.

CHAPTER 24

One week later, I learned the truth in the adage that you can be a victim of your own success. Even though I'd insisted that I didn't want any more violence in my life—the trip to the Big Valley was more about curiosity almost killing this cat—the USAF now considered Ensign Penny an asset, although a reluctant one.

"I've never been to Vandenberg," I told Rodriguez.

He stood before me looking a bit forlorn. I couldn't see him well from my camp chair with the blazing sun at his back. "If it's any consolation, I tried to dissuade the colonel because I knew you wouldn't want to participate."

"Why do they think I'd want to participate?"

"A convoluted reason: we airlifted someone from the Santa Maria area who had managed to cobble together a coded message we could recognize and broadcasted it at a radio station."

I thought of my own broadcast. Wondered if it was still hitting the airwaves. Thought a moment more. "I'm guessing he's from Vandenberg."

"She is. There's a Top Secret satellite there Cheyenne Mountain wants us to launch, and she knows where it is."

"So *La Femme Nikita* will be our guide to recover something completely useless?"

"Why useless? Cheyenne Mountain doesn't think it's useless. She doesn't either."

"How will you put it into orbit? Have the Hulk bounce it that high?"

He upended a pail and sat near but still facing me. He looked around. "We—she thinks there's still a rocket ready to launch there." His voice was a whisper.

"Gee, why don't you just use it to pay back the jerks who did this to us? Or bring back the astronauts and cosmonauts for burial?"

"The rocket can't handle that kind of payload. Besides, the satellite is more important."

"Describe it."

"I can't, but it will help this country get back on its feet again."

"You mean that no comsats are online?"

He hadn't changed expressions when I made that deduction. "They're still up there, but the Mountain can't wake all of them. There's some evidence that enemy anti-sat missiles blasted the ones now silent with EMP bursts just before other missiles carrying the plague hit the West Coast. And they weren't just comsats that were affected. I can't talk about details. Many are missing. Key people who had a lot of technical expertise died at the Mountain from the plague."

"I'll need details."

"You won't receive them. You're considered a civilian."

"But why should I help you then?"

"Patriotic duty? And because our survivor says your brother is in the group that took over the base? She barely escaped."

My brother is alive! "Wait! You want me to convince

him to surrender? No way. I can't do that. Do you think that's a valid reason?"

He nodded.

"My brother and I have been estranged for years. I don't want to see the SOB again—ever!"

"Would you at least talk to Rebecca?"

"Is that the woman from Santa Maria?"

He nodded.

"Why would that accomplish anything?"

"You'll see. Just talk to her. That's not her name, by the way. We created an alias just for you."

"Gee, thanks for all your trust."

ⱷⱱⱷ

I postponed my decision until I met the mysterious Rebecca. That gave me time to talk things over with Ben.

I'd decided I wouldn't mind encountering my scurrilous sibling. Slapping Bobby or spitting in his face would be worth it. Telephone calls were so impersonal. It would be great to call him an SOB to his handsome face.

"Looks like you could use some of this," said Ben, setting a half-filled jar of Dewar's on our little camp table that evening. Made our little tent in the refugee camp seem homier, not that we had enough to hang one on.

"Only if you share some," I said.

He pulled up the other camping chair. "You need it more than me, although I'll take a few sips. Want to talk it over?"

I didn't care about national security. Rodriguez had said it: *I'm a civilian!* I told Ben everything I knew. "What should I do, Ben?"

He took a sip—I'd already downed multiple gulps and was feeling the burn—and thought a moment. "It's your decision, but I'd consider it an opportunity." He waved a hand in a circle. "Everything has changed. The reasons for your estrangement with your brother are irrelevant now in these terrible times. It might be worthwhile to mend fences with the gentleman."

Gentleman? I smiled. My Ben was such a kind soul. How could he know how Bobby had treated Mom, how he took sides with Dad, and what a controlling jerk he had been in my life?

"You're focusing on my brother," I said. "What about that satellite?"

"If they'll use it to beef up com links, it might be justified as a way to stitch the country back together again. Right now Hannibal and his jet pilot friends are little better than the Pony Express was before telegraph and railroads. All the com here is pretty local, unless somebody is willing to chance bringing TV and radio stations back online. Don't see that happening anytime soon."

"Maybe having the whole country connected wasn't a good thing," I said. "People would just mount their soapboxes and proselytize and other people would become angry about it and do the same thing. You just wound up with everyone yelling at everyone else. No one listened to anyone else anymore. Smaller groups might get along better."

"From a sociological and anthropological point of view, you might have something there. In prehistory, small homogeneous tribes got along because members who didn't were thrown out. That's easier to do within a small group. But even Native Americans, Egyptians, Macedonians, Greeks, and so forth formed cities, states, and empires, ones often evolving into despotic regimes."

"Ben, I don't need a history lesson about why human beings suck," I said. "Small groups are like big families."

"And big families can be ripped apart by contrary actions and opinions, often stimulated by outside influences," he said. "Yours is a case in point."

"Which is why I'm happy to have had the opportunity of choosing my present family," I said with a smile. "Most people can't choose their family and often end with jerks ruining family get-togethers. I had a rare privilege."

Ben smiled and stole a sip. I'd long ago decided that Ben and Sammy were my family. Talk of my brother disturbed me.

☙❧

I spent a night of insomnia thinking about my choices, even with the pleasant buzz produced by that hit of whiskey. Didn't want to make a decision. And didn't want to think about the USAF, the navy, my government, or my brother. And I didn't give a rat's ass about Cheyenne Mountain.

Next day, Rodriguez took me to see Rebecca. I think he would have done it even if I'd committed right away, but not committing made it also a meeting for her to try to convince me. I was ready for a speech about my patriotic duty to God and country. There wasn't much left of the latter, and I was sure the former had abandoned us, so it was a given that such a speech would be useless.

I was left in a small conference room somewhere in the main base building in Edwards. Figured it belonged to security because it looked like the interrogation room in my old sheriff's substation. Waited about five minutes until there was a knock at the door.

A woman entered, moved around the table with measured steps, and took a seat opposite me. "You can call me Rebecca," she said, placing her palms on the table's edge. She seemed to be focused on the wall behind me, her gaze about six inches over my head.

Huh? I then noticed her hands. They were prosthetics, maybe the best I'd ever seen, but prosthetics nonetheless.

"You have heard the general outline of our problem. I'm here to answer your questions."

OK, no speech. That upset my preconceived notions about how the meeting would go. "I'll call you Becky," I said. "You were picked up in Santa Maria? Were you stationed at Vandenberg?"

"Yes. I'm a scientist. I was working there and living in Lompoc."

No expression. I stood up and went to the window to peer through blinds and bars at an expanse of tarmac, much of it now sprouting weeds in the cracked asphalt and concrete, about the only thing that managed to grow without water, although even the weeds looked dry. Her eyes didn't follow me.

"It's no different from other bases," she continued. "Andrews and Edwards are in better shape, though."

"You follow my sound. Are you blind?"

"I'd probably be called just 'legally blind' years ago, but that definition was used by authorities. Now it doesn't matter."

"Did that happen at Vandenberg?"

"Yes. A small group wreaked havoc, especially among the scientists. We were blamed, you see. A few others and I escaped."

Blame? I'd second that. I had nothing against science, but when it was used to kill people, it should be called prostitution with governments or corporations as the pimps.

"Did you build military satellites?"

"Some of them. The one we want to launch in particular. Do you want me to elaborate on what we'll use it for?"

"Military communications?"

"For now, the government is the military, and it's handling most of the nation's communications piggybacking on the military's available resources. This satellite will aid in that process and help stitch the country back together."

"And you think that's a good thing?"

I watched her body language. I had some interrogation training when I became a deputy. She didn't realize I was interrogating her and probably thought she was there to convince me. I appreciated the simple discussion and not having to suffer through some patriotic speech, though.

"It will help. It's not the complete answer."

Her sideways response to my question annoyed me.

"There will be no quick solutions."

Roger that!

"We're doing the best we can."

"We? After all that happened to you, you're still ready to aid the government? Don't you think they share some of the responsibility?"

"Perhaps. After careful analysis, though, I think they don't share much of it. The worst sin might have been guilelessness."

"You're blind and with prosthetic hands, and you still say that?"

"Our government didn't do that, Penny. I lost my eyesight and hands in an explosion caused by the group I mentioned. I survived. Many of us didn't."

"Okay, why me? I have no favorites in this fight. I just want to live whatever life I have left in peace with my family."

"Your brother was a leader in that group."

I returned to my chair and buried my head in my folded arms on the table. *Oh, Bobby, what have you done?*

I felt like crying because I could understand Bobby's sentiments. I often figured that somehow our government had failed us. Supposed the Vandenberg scientists and technicians were the obvious scapegoats. *Maybe all over the world? Maybe in whatever country or countries that launched the missiles carrying man-made plague?* Politicians would pay scientists tons of money to do their dirty work, but that didn't mean they were responsible.

"Okay, tell me what you want me to do," I said to her.

CHAPTER 25

Our caravan made slow progress on US 101, traveling farther inland from Malibu and Leo Carrillo State Park where my life had changed for the worst. Rusting vehicles, still with skeletons at the wheel, reduced the trucks' speeds. Skeletons lying on the road were crushed under heavy tires. I supposed the drivers' indifference stemmed from long habit, but I could only think that those bones once belonged to living people just like us. Well, maybe not like us. We were the unlucky ones who had survived because of some freakish genetics!

Just before Ventura, we were attacked by a gang. An old mortar round shredded one truck, but the flyboys made them pay. We left the truck's burned-out husk and bodies where they'd fallen and continued. Neither Becky, who sat beside me, nor I had participated. She couldn't, of course, and I just gritted my teeth and patted my gun, knowing I could do some damage if called upon but not wanting to participate. Shot some pics, though.

Becky had handed me an old digital camera. Hadn't seen one in years. Like everyone else except pro photographers, I'd used my smart phone to take pics…like forever! Had so many memory cards stashed away in my old apartment I'd lost count. 'Course no one would see those images now. Phones didn't work as cameras, primarily because electricity was scarce for charging, so her camera was a good choice, as long as someone had a supply of batteries for it. She did, I guess.

Camera was ideal too, if you had a laptop. No internet, but people still used them, swapping out batteries where there was no power—the government enough electricity for the time being, but maybe didn't think of just using smart phones for cameras because they weren't good for calling anyone. Damn camera was smaller than my smart phone too. I'd remembered it in time to snap the pics. Future air force wanted posters? Or just computer files for known enemies? Didn't care. The attackers snarling faces were recorded for posterity, whatever that might be: enemies of civilization.

I remembered the underwater camera I'd used for crime scenes. Probably still in my apartment with photos from my last dive. Had I taken pics of what I'd found on that boat? Couldn't remember. It seemed like ages ago.

"You didn't even flinch with the grenades," I said to Becky.

She smiled but remained facing forward as our truck weaved around new obstacles. "I only have hearing in my left ear, and that's aided by a hearing aid." She brushed back her short brown hair so I could see. "I turned it off."

Convenient. My recourse for tuning noise out had been Ben's Dewars and other liquor. Never thought I'd envy a woman who had lost her sight and hearing! Decided we were lucky that liquor was so scarce now. Otherwise, I'd become an alcoholic.

"How did you survive?" she said.

"Years of scavenging and looting," I said.

She nodded. "I was lucky. I made it into Santa Maria early on and set up a broadcast from a radio station."

"You were taking a risk."

"Not really. The message was coded. The air force came for me. I was taken to Cheyenne Mountain."

"How's their situation?"

"Depressing. Frustrating. You name it. Their main missions no longer exist. They're almost reduced to the status of an old fort on the American frontier."

"Did they see the attack coming?"

"Yes, but they had no time to react. They could have defended the rest of the country, but not the West Coast. There were a few intercepts at low altitude. We think those missiles' payloads were still dispersed and did damage."

"Madness! How did we let this happen?"

"Your question is about the past. I prefer to look toward the future. I pushed for this satellite launch. After convincing people at the Mountain and Edwards, I flew to Washington to convince the Pentagon. Pentagon personnel, of course. The building is no longer functional."

"With a nice fellow named Hannibal?"

"On the way there from Edwards. Someone else on the way back. Do you know Hannibal?"

"Yes. I betrayed him."

"He was the one you slipped away from at Andrews."

"You knew that?"

"I know a lot about you, Penelope Castro."

I thought for a moment. "You do realize we could die on this mission, right?"

"Dying for something worthwhile is noble. I've been lucky so far. Hopefully my good karma continues."

I thought some more. Was surviving, but without hands, sight, and hearing, good karma? However crazy this bitch was, she was someone to admire. Maybe in the hands of such leaders we could build a new nation, maybe even a new world. But did I want that to happen? A lot of changes would have to occur if we were going to avoid the same disastrous events. And human nature was so hard to change.

∽∽∽

We followed US 101 until we reached Las Cruces where we turned north into Lompoc on Route 1. The day was clear. I could see with my binoculars a rocket sticking up as if to give the world the finger. It must be perched on a launch pad. *When is the last time they'd shot off a rocket from there?*

I also saw a water purification plant far offshore. Wondered where its pipes went. Maybe the Santa Maria area? Coast was agricultural too, but in the old days not as dry as the valley. Maybe the pipes followed 166 into the area around Taft and were used for both thirsty humans and thirsty crops at one time. I realized my knowledge about them, the area, and the base was limited.

Becky was quiet as we made our way through the streets of Lompoc and then entered Vandenberg AFB, no longer home to the 30th Space Wing, in spite of what the sign said. As expected, we passed death and destruction. Two trucks filled with techies and security split off from the main caravan.

"Where are they off to?" I said.

"To confirm the rocket at Complex Six is still functional and prepare it for launch."

"How do you know that rocket will fly?" I said, as we continued.

"We don't. They'll tell us. First, there's the rocket, then the control center at the complex, and finally the satellite. All potential failure points."

"What about personnel? Do we have the expertise?"

"If we don't, no one does. That's another possible point of failure, of course. I'm the weakest link in that group of four, by the way."

"How so? I thought you were our gifted comsat engineer?"

"I was. Someone else has to be my eyes now."

I nodded and then remembered she couldn't see the nod. "Okay. Who's providing the eyes?"

"Other techies. We'll work around my physical limitations. We have to."

As we pulled up to our target building, shots rang out as we took fire from snipers. The driver of our truck received two rounds in the chest.

"Down!" I yelled.

Becky obeyed. I reached across our driver, opened the door, and pushed his body out. I then took the wheel.

Sometimes instincts just kick in. I gunned the truck, taking it right up the steps into the building. "Stay down," I said to Becky as I hit a debris-laden floor and rolled outside the truck along with companions from the back who'd understood what I was doing.

"I think there are four," said one flyboy. "Maybe more upstairs!"

"Two come with me," I said. "The others cover us, and then handle the two down here. We're going up."

The air force leader of the moment nodded, called out a name, and upstairs we went. Piece of cake. The three snipers upstairs were at windows firing on the other trucks. Another was dead already. The remainder didn't have a chance. Silence reigned.

"Guess they offed the ones downstairs," said the second flyboy with an accent straight from the Ozarks. He stood up and kicked a corpse over. The body had a Mohawk, a torso covered with tattoos, jeans, and no shoes. "These are kids. What's going on?"

"Feral animals and feral humans. Meet some lovely citizens of the new Golden State." I collected weapons and motioned them to lead the way downstairs. Common sense had returned to me. I was willing to let pros take over.

∽∾∽∾

Becky was okay. She had a few cuts from flying glass and would have a few bruises. Getting down had saved her. The truck had died for the cause. Its innards under the hood had taken multiple rounds, protecting the scientist.

Our personnel now guarded the building. She had me guide her through dim corridors. She knew where she wanted to go, but needed eyes to help her around obstacles. I didn't have to explain what they were, though. She could hear the rattling and crunching of skeletons' bones.

We passed by a lot of desks for those bureaucratic ghosts. Spotted a dog-eared book on one that piqued my interest: Stephen Hawking's *A Brief History of Time*. Decided to grab it for Ben and tucked it under my belt. Figured the ghost who owned the desk wouldn't mind. Remembered the other book Ben had picked up in the San Fernando Valley, so thought he might like this one too. I remembered trying to read it once—some geeky guy on the carrier had a copy. Likely too elementary for Ben and maybe more of a gift for Sammy, but this was a world where book burners from Bradbury's *Fahrenheit 451* wouldn't have to work too hard—there were few readers anymore.

I considered myself cultured but was never an avid reader. Thought Ben might have been. His eyes would light up with almost any book. I was told once that Hawking's book was a good one. Saw Ken Follett and

Margaret Atwood books too. They were probably from the base library. Good books I'd heard about. Hesitated. Decided to pass them up. I was too busy to read.

We came to a heavy door that could have secured a bank vault. She gave me the code for the keypad, I punched it in, and then her thumb was scanned.

Another reason this woman is essential to our mission!

SOP required her—in this case, me—to punch the code into another keypad once inside within an allotted time. No scan there. I wondered what might happen if I didn't do it in time, but whatever alarm system there was, it was satisfied, and the beeping stopped.

"This a lab?"

"Labs inside a SCIF."

Special Compartmented Information Facility, I thought. We'd had them on US Navy boats.

"There shouldn't be any bodies or debris in here."

"I guess people who took over the base and the gangs we met just now didn't have the right security clearances." Bad joke. Of course, they had no use for a satellite either. "Where to?"

"The satellite is stored in a lab toward the back. We'll need some muscle to help us remove it."

"Where are we taking it?"

"The launch control complex. We need a clean room to unpack it. There's one there."

Geez, couldn't they have just stored it there to begin with? I decided you couldn't second guess the air force's chain of command any more than you could the navy's. "The way to another building won't be easy, you know, even discounting snipers."

"The satellite is shrink-wrapped. Don't worry."

CHAPTER 26

I went back and found four of our guys to help us lift the satellite. It was more bulky than heavy, but I imagined there was a lot of packaging in that shipping container. On the way out, another flyboy stopped us. He held up his com set.

That action made me think about batteries. *What happens when they're gone?* Didn't think anyone was making them. *Also, did the damn satellite need batteries, at least at first?* I thought of those exploding lithium ion ones. *Did age make them explode? Or were they just defective to begin with?* Decided that civilization might come to a grinding halt faster than I'd thought, all for a lack of batteries. There were probably a lot of other essential things ready to expire too. *Most of us are just technological savages who don't know how to build anything.*

"The first group is pinned near the Complex Six launch control facility," the fellow said. "It's not safe to go there. Not yet."

"We'll have to wait," I said to Becky.

"Hopefully not for long. There are things I need to do to prepare the satellite for launch. And we need time to mount it on the rocket."

"Do we need to stay here and guard this facility?" said the flyboy.

"No. It's no longer useful."

"Then I suggest we load the satellite aboard a truck and create a little caravan back to the launch facility." He spoke into the com set. "Where is the brunt of the attack?"

A voice announced the attack was concentrated on their group in the front of the complex.

"There's a back loading dock," said Becky.

"We're heading toward the rear of the complex," the fellow said to the radio's voice. "Once we have the two women inside, we'll work our way round to the front on the outside and help you out."

"Roger that."

Our airman smiled at us. "Ready, ladies?"

"Are the techies already inside the facility?" said Becky.

Our fellow asked the question via his set and received confirmation. *Oh, goody! We're going to another firefight!*

I wondered if being Becky's chaperone would slow me down if things became dicey. It occurred to me that the air force only wanted me to be her bodyguard all along.

Being a diplomatic liaison between Bobby and his group and the flyboys was likely just a subterfuge for my bodyguard assignment.

Talk about a delayed reaction! If I'd had that thought back in the refugee camp, I wouldn't be there putting my life on the line. Now I would have to swallow my suspicions and fears and try to be patriotic. *What a load of crap!*

ೞ

The same four loaded the satellite onto a truck and helped Becky and me onboard. We found wooden benches and strapped down. I didn't think it would be as rough a ride as when I drove up the first building's steps, but no sense taking chances. *Mamacita* always told us to buckle our seatbelts. She wouldn't have ever imagined our present situation, though.

"You handled yourself pretty well in there," said Becky as we bounced along, not enjoying the old truck's stiff springs.

I took the compliment badly, thinking she was just saying, "You did your duty." *Again, what a load of crap!*

The base sat between Santa Maria and Lompoc with launch pads on the coast. Complex Six, our goal, and Complex Eight were on a promontory jutting into the Pacific. For no good reason, I suspected, except that it kept people at viewing sites far enough away. Because most payloads had been military ones, base secrecy had been a permanent paranoia. The location made our ride an adventure—access roads hadn't been maintained in years.

It was an eerie ride with my companion. She was talking to me, but staring at the canvas and ribbing above my head, unseeing. You don't know how much you depend on body language in a conversation until you don't have it—hers was minimal.

"I can't believe you weren't ever in combat," she said, finding a way to continue the compliment.

"Just basic training, and five-plus years as a survivor after the contagion fell from the sky." The latter was an uncomfortable topic for me. "Will the satellite survive all this jostling?"

"It's packed so well it could survive a parachute drop if needs be. You don't leave something like that to chance when you're dealing with instrumentation that costs millions."

"A dollar isn't worth much these days," I said with a laugh. "It's not an assembly line product, I imagine, but a unique one. Who made it?"

There was a thin smile. "There were five. This is the only surviving one. The rest is classified. You have no need to know. I hope you don't mind."

"Yeah, no need to know why I'm putting my life on the line, and for whom."

"You're doing it for the future of mankind."

At last the speech. I was thankful it was short. "Oh, please."

We lapsed into silence, if you could call sounds of the approaching and ongoing gun battle in the distance silence.

℘℘℘

Our truck stopped and reversed up to the building's dock, two others forming a protective shield. I was helping Becky down when there was a whump! and the truck next to us went up in flames.

"Mortar attack! Either take them out or get us inside. Preferably both!" That was me being self-preserving. Okay, I was saving Becky and the satellite too. Saw some of our people fan out. That mortar guy might not have long to live. Our same four friends put the satellite inside first. Becky and I followed, with me holding her hand as guide.

They carried the satellite in and stored it safely in the "clean room"—couldn't imagine it was a "clean room" in the usual sense of solid state circuitry with all the dust and debris around—but once we cleaned soot off and took a look-see, we might still have a functioning satellite. Four techies were already starting that process.

"Two of us will stay at the back entrance to guard

you," said our driver. "Two of us will join the others and go help the ones in front."

"Give 'em hell," I said. Smiled when Becky nodded. She didn't like being shot at any more than anyone else. She turned her attention to directing the techies.

The driver tossed me an AR-15. "You might need it, Penny. As a last resort."

I felt a chill about his thinking I might be the last one standing beside Becky and her techie crew. *Who wants to die for God and country when they no longer exist?* Didn't seem even patriotic Becky was in the mood for that. I fought the urge to join the group that would help our people in front, though. Maybe not for God and country but for brothers in arms. Would have liked to have been there for Ned long ago.

ೞೞೞ

"Do we need a truck again to install the satellite on the rocket?"

Becky nodded.

"They need to clear the launch pad of all attackers," said a techie. "Once we prepare the satellite, it will be exposed. A peaceful little ride to the launch pad is an absolute must."

We would have to wait because the firefight in front of Complex Six's building continued. *What motivates these bastards?* None of them looked like people who might have worked at the base like my brother. *Did they kill or drive away or eat all of that first rebellious group that sent Becky running for her life to Santa Maria? Did my brother's body turn on a spit?*

I heard shattering glass outside the clean room and dashed out. One enemy combatant was trying to enter through a broken window. A burst from my gun added new scarlet tattoos to his bare chest. I went to examine the body. Correction: *her* bare chest. A girl just beyond puberty, her tits not fully developed. I fought down vomit and stuck my head out the window. A fist slammed into my face.

Not so smart, Penny! She has a boyfriend! The blow's force sent me backward. I tripped and fell on my butt. Struggled to my knees. Romeo came through the window, flashing a rusty old bayonet in one hand and a single-shot .22 in the other. He fired the rifle, and I felt a thunk at my waist. *Ben's book! He'll ask about that.* I found the Glock also tucked into my pants and shot him between the eyes.

Couldn't help it. The projectile vomiting seemed like a reverse intestinal purge. *Geez, get hold of yourself!* 'Course, nowhere in basic training do they teach you about the mental anguish generated by killing two pubescent kids who had turned into feral humans. *Maybe their survival mechanism?*

Wiping off the barf with my sleeve, I took up a post at the door to the clean room. No way was I sticking out my head anymore.

CHAPTER 27

That pretty much ended my combat experience at Vandenberg AFB. Soon afterward, things became quiet, Becky and her techies finished their prep, and she and her team moved on to the rocket carrying the satellite.

That launch prep took hours. Made me appreciate that being a rocket scientist called for patience, even at an air force base. Especially when your team of nerds had been reduced to an absolute minimum!

"I think we're ready," Becky said to me upon her return. "Keep your fingers crossed. Will you watch the launch?"

"Isn't it just like the movies? Big countdown in mission control? You doing it?"

"Yes, but I didn't mean watching it from mission control. Security prohibits that. You can just stand outside and watch. It's a better seat than any civilian spectator ever had."

"I'm sure it is. Come to think of it, I think I'll clean up a bit. Is there any water?"

"Try the restrooms just off the entrance. I'd join you if I didn't have work to do. Wish me luck."

"Break a leg." Didn't know if she understood that old

actor's refrain. Didn't much care. Wasn't sure whether I didn't mean it literally.

There was water in the men's room but not the women's. Go figure. So much for equality of sexes in the services. They were still adapting when I was in the navy too. Had a few companions there who were raped and didn't report it.

The COs and XOs were usually macho pricks who had been in the navy for a long time, so it wouldn't have done my companions much good, especially if the rapists were officers.

As I splashed water on my battered face and upper torso in the men's room—it came from the spigot only in a trickle—I felt a little pride that a blind woman and a little New Jersey gal might be saving the nation's ass. Assuming the launch worked and that all Becky said about the satellite doing good was true. *You take what you get.*

What's happened to my brother? He wasn't among the dead terrorists we had fought. *Is he still alive?*

❧❦❧

"Penny, wake up!" Becky's toe was poking me in the side. "We're ready to go."

I'd been exhausted and had fallen asleep. I stood up. "Thanks for not leaving me here."

"We'd never do that," said the flyboy with the Ozark accent. "All for one and one for all."

"Okay. Whatever. I have shotgun."

He looked at his weapon.

"I meant the window seat in a truck."

He nodded. "That can be arranged. We'll be a bit more cramped going back after losing a few trucks. The one you made climb the steps wasn't salvageable either. We'll make out, though."

"Don't you want to hear whether the launch was successful?" said Becky.

"I don't give a rat's ass about any of it. The only thing I care about is that we weren't all killed." I saw Becky's sour expression. Didn't care.

"Thanks in part to you," she continued. "I'll tell you with a sideways comment: Cheyenne Mountain is happy with their new toy."

"Will I be able to watch my old TV reruns anytime soon? I'm thinking The *A-Team* might be fun." *Or maybe too close for comfort?*

"Not likely. Maybe in your lifetime."

I thought of that soap opera so many years ago that had ended with an announcement and a test pattern. "Okay. Whatever. I don't care. Let's mosey back to Edwards, Gomer." That was directed at the flyboy.

"Gomer?"

"Oh, right, he was USMC." Didn't feel like pressing the issue. Nice guy, but if he didn't know what "riding shotgun" meant, explaining the Gomer reference would be wasted. Guessed the air force couldn't be too picky about who were their conscripts. *How does that even work now? Is there a draft?* I punched him softly in the shoulder. "Go reserve that shotgun seat for me."

ഈഈ

Gomer satisfied my request, so Becky suffered the pokes in the privates with the gear shift this time. Fortunately, I'm small and leaned out the window a lot, giving her a bit more space.

"You and Alejandro an item?" she said just after we returned to US 101.

"He might want that, but I'm still a bit ambivalent. Want to form a ménage-à-trois?"

She laughed. It was good to see her relax. "He's a nice man, but I'm more attracted to the colonel."

"Alejandro thinks the boss is nice too, when you get to know him. I'm more ambivalent in that case. He's in the outfit that kidnapped my Ben. Is he paying you any attention?"

"I'm not sure he can move past my disabilities."

"Give him time. Are you with him that much?"

"No. That's another problem. We have different career paths."

Career paths? Does anyone think about career paths anymore? My Becky was a strange woman. "Sometimes a man and a woman can be in diverse activities and still be just as enamored as Romeo and Juliet. Is there chemistry?"

"I think so. He seems so shy."

Landon shy?

"I'll have to return to the Mountain for a bit, as well as Andrews, but I'll try to return to Edwards often. I'll work on him."

"Good for you. Say, you wouldn't want to tell me your real name now, would you? I like Becky, but I'd prefer to call you by your birth name. That shouldn't be classified."

"It only is because too many people associate it with what I do. Originally it wasn't, of course. I had a lot of company." She hesitated. "It's Anna, by the way."

"No last name?"

She frowned. "Maybe someday I can tell you. Thank you for all you've done, by the way. I know you had your doubts. Believe me, I have mine. My home country suffered greatly, but nothing like this contagion, even though it didn't take the direct hit. And FYI: the whole world is a mess right now."

My home country? Was Becky or Anna born a US citi-

zen? Only she or a struggling US government possibly knew. If she wasn't, security had been relaxed considerably. Or she had long ago proved her allegiance to Uncle Sam.

"Oh, I believe you. We would have messed up Mars by now if we could. Say, I wonder if any astronauts or cosmonauts survived. They weren't all on the space station."

"Not that I know of. The ones there died because no one in Russia would be there when they landed."

"You mean they could have returned?"

"Maybe. Just to die on the Russian steppes. Russia's worse off than we are. At least, that's what our imaging from Cheyenne Mountain tells us. Our survivors continue to survive to some extent. Not so much in other places." She jerked a thumb skyward. "Forget about space travel, Penny. The last of it for a while was our launching that satellite."

"You'll eventually need to replace it. Or launch new ones."

"Hopefully it will last long enough that we'll be able to do that."

CHAPTER 28

I lost track of Becky. She had a life among the VIPs who pretended they were fixing and running the country. I thought Becky might have given up on the colonel. I would have.

I was a foot soldier, home from battles, with little left in me for more fights. Didn't see much of Rodriguez either. Tried to convince myself it didn't matter. Gave Ben his book, apologized for its condition. It didn't take much to keep Ben and Sammy happy, but I longed for my happy pills. I was bored and depressed, probably less than other refugees, though.

My family kept me busy, so I didn't have much time for dwelling on the boredom or depression, except at nights. Worked in community gardens—loved doing it, although I wasn't much of a green thumb. Helped Pat Nagi some in her clinic too.

Bonding still occurred in a refugee camp, and there were a lot of needy people who'd seen many awful things before they arrived there, so they needed someone to listen to them and commiserate. Pat, the mayor, and I, plus a few others, provided that solace the best we could. I often cried at night, though. *Who the hell is helping me?*

Thought of killing those two kids at Vandenberg, and

a million other awful things that had occurred in the last few years. *Do I have PTSD? Survivor's remorse? Is this what it is like doing battle and surviving?* My respect for all those who fought and tried to reintegrate into civilian society grew and grew. *Maybe Ned was lucky?*

I still wondered where my brother was. Didn't care whether the SOB was dead or alive, but I wanted to know what had happened to him. *Do I have any real family left? Are Sammy, Ben, and Muttsie my only family now?* I could accept that, but not knowing Bobby's fate was frustrating.

ഇരുന്നു

While the water caravan and comsat launch convinced me that I'd had enough of risking my life for an Uncle Sam who was on his death bed, I still felt adventurous. Wanted the excitement without the danger—join the navy and see the world. In my case, air force, as a damn mercenary. All the time I'd lived in the Golden State, I'd never been to the parks—Yosemite, Sequoia, and Kings Canyon were near, a few others farther north. When I heard there would be an expedition to the Sierras to examine snow packs—it was late April—I volunteered, even though it involved flying in a chopper. Pat Nagi helped with some Dramamine pills that had expired about three years ago.

I learned the air force made such an expedition every spring. If the snow pack didn't improve at all, complete recovery for those valley aquifers would be delayed even more, even though water usage had diminished so much. At least someone was thinking long term. Wouldn't do much good to have a spiffy new comsat if there weren't people around to use it, and people would need water to survive. The monsoons where people had drowned years ago were rare statistical outliers—California was in an even longer drought. There were always the desalination plants, of course. I didn't mention them. I was through with life on or in the water, so I'd prefer to have Mother Nature replenish aquifers if she could manage that. There was always the possibility that the old woman had succumbed to the plague too.

Five of us took off in a beat-up Pave Hawk, but not the same one that had ferried my family and me from CSUN to Edwards. That one was used for recon and combat. Our transport was more expendable and less dependable. Made me uncomfortable to take off in the shaky chopper even with Dramamine.

We flew low enough to follow the river in Kings Canyon—my nerves made me close my eyes at times—but I still saw that the mighty Kings River that had cut that canyon so long ago was just a trickle. The canyon was still king, maybe only second to the Grand Canyon, but the river looked like an ogre's piddle.

We buzzed a few high sierra lakes that had been reduced to ponds too. We determined the mighty sequoias were still standing—in their thousands of years of existence, they were used to fire and droughts.

I wished we'd landed there so I could see some of them up close. We finally landed in Yosemite Valley. I learned it was occupied and not by air force personnel.

I found members of the Yosemite Valley garrison who guarded the air force's fuel depot to be a diverse group of ranchers, farmers, and other misfits from the Big Valley around Fresno, Merced, and Modesto, all ex-military types or weekend warriors and survivors who had found their way into the park.

Others, like forest rangers and staff for park facilities, were there to begin with, but their mortality rates had been the same as everywhere else, just delayed a bit, maybe by those high granite walls. Everyone I saw seemed dedicated, efficient, and happy enough, considering the circumstances.

❧❦

"We're careful about who we let in," said the ex-forest ranger who met our chopper and led us to a community mess hall while others refueled our chopper. "We also keep quiet about what goes on here. First time the air force landed, we took a vote about maintaining the depot for them. The argument that we're all on the same side won out. But we shot down the idea of putting your refugee camp here."

Later, I learned the ex-ranger's name was Oliver Cassidy. Everyone called him Butch. He didn't look at all like Paul Newman in that old classic film, though. He was tall, sinewy, weathered, and bald, and reminded me of a drill instructor I had endured during basic training, a stern but fair taskmaster who I figured only wanted his trainees to survive, which was less important for me because I already knew I wouldn't see any combat. Probably helped me get by after surviving the plague, though.

Butch no longer dressed like a ranger. Couldn't fault him for that. In contrast to his hairless head, he had a full red beard streaked with some gray. A Roman nose made him look a bit like a bird, but binoculars hanging from his neck, green T-shirt advertising Guinness, brown but faded Bermuda shorts, and white sneakers turned gray and with holes in the canvas parts, would make you think "bird watcher" instead. Figured him to be a friend of Gaia's and probably none too happy about what fell from the sky.

"Why's that?" I said, responding to his comment. "There's plenty of space."

"Winters are cold, even without much snow, game gets scarce, and our little truck farms don't produce enough for the people here during the short growing season, let alone newcomers. We barely manage." He laughed. "Our community has a selective immigration policy. We've let in a doctor, two nurses, and an expert from the UC Agricultural Extension Surface, plus a few relatives of people already here."

Our Edwards personnel walking along with us didn't ask any questions. They knew the litany. I wanted to know more, though.

"I bet you have a surplus of water, right?" I pointed to the distant falls.

"In the old days, there'd be so much water in the falls at spring runoff that you couldn't see them in the mist. Now, we don't see much, and, by the end of summer, there's just a trickle most of the time." Cassidy stopped and stomped, raising a cloud of dust. I saw his footprints in the dry grass. "We're in a year-round water-rationing and fire-danger situation here and often lose a good percentage of the crops along the river for lack of water. It's worse in the Big Valley, of course. We've done a real number on the environment, Miss Castro."

"Call me Penny."

"She's ex-navy," said one air force guy, winking at me. "She only understands salt water."

"That's not true. I survived alone for five years growing things and scavenging, unlike certain air force personnel who had a much easier time of it. I had relatives in New Jersey who were truck farmers. It's in my blood."

"Probably some blood from a few undocumented farm laborers too," said a flyboy named Powell, a man from North Carolina who reminded me of that Atlanta bigot I had encountered in that bar so long ago.

Cassidy frowned. "We don't allow that kind of talk

here. And it doesn't make any difference anymore. And it will make less difference in the future, so get past it, friend, or you'll have problems in this valley."

Thank you! I liked Cassidy more already, and Powell had confirmed my initial reaction to him.

જાજ

The leader of our little expedition decided to go on a two-day hike above the tree line to make snow-depth measurements. Of course, that was what we'd come for. I decided to go along, even though I didn't have to do so. There was plenty of slushy snow around from my perspective, making me glad I was wearing sneakers with some tread, but Cassidy and others educated me about the scarcity of precip.

"Where you're sitting used to be buried under twenty-five to forty-five feet of snow this time of year," he said. We'd stopped for a breather. I was sitting on a convenient piece of granite. "We're almost at eight thousand feet now."

I felt the altitude. Made me realize how out of shape I was. "Guess the yeti's white fur isn't good camouflage anymore," I said, still panting a bit.

"In the Sierras, he would be called Sasquatch," he said. He smiled. "Can't say we've seen much of him. Not as many wild animals either. We think a number of species are extinct now."

"I hope endangered ones aren't hunted."

"Hard to tell. And we're all endangered. We're not particular about what we eat anymore. Protein is at a premium around here. There's no hunting just for sport anymore. It's done with bows and arrows and crossbows, and we eat what we kill."

"I saw guns in camp."

"That's for defense," said a listener. "Word's out that Yosemite is a safe haven, so unsavory characters are always showing up to raid the garrison."

"It's easy to defend, though," said Cassidy. "With not many entrances into the valley, only a few sentries are needed. The Merced River doesn't help as much as it used to, though, in forming a natural barrier."

ღღ

When we returned, we had a pool party, both kinds. The camp had a heated pool and the rec center had pool tables. The pool's water was piped in from the Merced River. I felt sure we were depriving drought-stricken people downstream, but Cassidy argued that with snow melt, that wasn't happening. It was a luxury for them, but only in the spring and early summer.

And what luxury! I never wanted to dive again, but swimming in that pool with Yosemite's vistas all around me was heavenly. I even took a full shower beforehand, scrubbing down while trying to ignore all wolf whistles and lewd comments—the shower was outside and only intended as a rinse-off place before and after getting in the pool, before to minimize water use by not polluting it, and after to rinse off chlorine, still used to keep down pesky bacteria. Didn't mind the wolf whistles. All the guys were naked too.

I did about thirty laps. Knew I'd be sore the next day because I was using muscles I hadn't used in a long time. Still, no one could keep up with me, although I suspected my time was about twice what it would have been back in high school.

In spite of Powell, I felt right at home in Yosemite, so much so I was beginning to wonder if I should move my family there. But I didn't much like snow. Growing up in

New Jersey could do that to you. Most people wanted a little snow for the holidays, but otherwise people hated it, except for winter sports fanatics who would drive hours to ski on fresh powder. I did that a few times. Didn't like it. Liked apres-ski's hot toddies, though.

Still, being a truck farmer in Yosemite Valley didn't seem like such a bad future. Something to think about on the way home.

CHAPTER 29

They could brag about their impregnable valley, but Yosemite Valley's defenders hadn't counted on facing tanks and artillery. Just my bad luck to be there for the rude awakening. Next morning, we were stowing our kits back onto the chopper to prepare for our return when Cassidy came running toward us.

"Can we delay you a bit? I need to send a few snipers aloft." He explained the situation.

"You won't stop a tank with snipers," I said.

The chopper's pilot nodded his agreement. "You need anti-tank ordinance."

Cassidy frowned. His shoulders slumped. "We're toast then. They're coming in through the portal via One-Forty. Once they're inside the valley, they can start shelling us with the artillery and tank guns."

"Do we have time to lay a trap?" I asked.

"An hour, max. What are you thinking?"

I asked him a quick question then made my suggestion. The air force personnel and ex-military types liked the idea. What we had were fuel drums—twenty-gallon steel barrels—fuel, and trucks. Most everyone pitched in to fill them with high octane fuel and load them onto two trucks. A caravan of three trucks carrying the fuel drums and volunteers—I was one—drove along the Merced River's canyon road to where a culvert went under it and emptied into the river. The culvert was dry, even with spring runoff, and open in the sense that a steel grill covered it. We pried it off and lowered a dozen barrels into it.

I could see them when standing over the grill that covered it, with kerosene-soaked rags stuck in the top where a hand-pump assembly would be. Similar rags stretched from drum to drum. I hoped the invaders didn't see them until too late.

"Sure you were in the navy?" Cassidy said after we'd finished our prep and inspection.

"Butch, I always admired the Army Corps of Engineers," I said.

"She ain't so smart," said Powell, who was also inspecting our handiwork. "How are we going to explode them?"

"Someone has to hide at each end and light the wicks for the end barrels," I said. "I'm small. So are you." I eyed him. "Are you up to it?"

He shrugged. "Sure, why not? It's a chance to prove you wrong."

"You might have the roles of suicide bombers," said one old ex-military man who had suffered through three tours in Afghanistan and had an empty sleeve to show for it.

"Yeah, where's an arsonist when we need him?" said Powell.

I smiled. Senior Airman Powell would be tested in combat.

⁊⊃⊂⊃

I spent twenty minutes hidden on the river's side of

the culvert and biting my nails until I heard the rumble of tanks. Powell, on the mountain side, might be calmer, but I thought he would have a case of nerves too. The treads made one hell of a racket on the asphalt. The tanks led the trucks pulling artillery guns, and together would have been heard before seen by people back in camp. Stopping tanks dead in their tracks—loved the militaristic pun— would also put up a barrier where others could make short work of the artillery contingent.

There was a tank in each lane of the highway. After querying sentries, we'd estimated that they were going about thirty miles per hour, a bit faster than over open terrain but a leisurely pace for a tank on a highway. Powell and I had agreed to light the wicks of the end drums when the tanks were about thirty yards from the culvert, leaving us a few seconds to seek cover. That was my calculation.

Cassidy had checked it and found any errors tolerable, considering we weren't too precise with either the wicks' lengths or the tanks' speeds.

Worked like a charm, though. Guess the tanks' undercarriages took some damage from rocks, concrete, and shrapnel, but the earth opening beneath them and spewing hellish flames that enveloped the tanks stopped them cold. Helped that the attackers inside were traveling with tops open. Yosemite volunteers, including Cassidy, moved in on the artillery pulled by old army trucks.

I dug myself out from rocks, pieces of concrete, sand, odd pieces of broken asphalt, and gravel and rushed across the highway behind the wall of fire. "Powell?" No answer.

I saw an arm sticking out from another pile of rubble. Went down to it, calculated where his head should be, and started digging. Uncovered him and began to slap his blue face. "Don't bail out on me now, you SOB!"

Began giving him CPR but stopped when he coughed a few times and started laughing.

"Wow! What a rush! A big boom followed by a big, sloppy kiss. Is this frog now a prince?"

I kept pulling off debris created by the explosion. "Don't become too slap happy, you jerk. Breathe. And don't move just yet. You have a piece of the culvert's grate stuck in your shoulder."

"Let's get him to the medics," said Cassidy, who was now standing over us.

"What do we do with the captives?" someone asked.

Cassidy, Powell, and I turned to the group of invaders the Yosemite defenders had rounded up. The captives didn't look too happy, but they couldn't complain much—they'd survived.

"Good question," Cassidy said. "Any suggestions?"

"I'd shoot'em all," said one companion.

"Think they'll return if we just kick them out of the valley?" I said to Cassidy.

"I wouldn't try it if I were them," he said.

"Then I'd give them the heave-ho. They can walk back to wherever they came from."

He smiled and nodded.

৩৩৩

"I should have planned that better," I said after taking a sip of Wild Turkey Butch Cassidy had been saving for a special occasion. We were back at camp in his cabin, one used by park tourists ages ago. I'd used his primitive shower facilities and was resigned to my hairdo resembling an irate porcupine. "The mountain on Powell's side contained the explosive wave there. Mine just dispersed down into and along the river."

Cassidy held up a hand. "Most of it went as we wanted. Don't overthink it. It worked, so everyone's happy. That was quick thinking in an impossible situation. You deserve a medal."

I decided it was time to change the subject. "Where did those guys come from? They looked better organized than the average cannibalistic marauders I've known. And I assume driving a tank takes some skills or they'd have had Google make them self-driving long ago."

"We took four prisoners. They're ex-national guard like some of us here. Maybe they'd even tried to join us but we didn't let them in. They're tightlipped, but we'll work on them. We want to know if there are more of the same. We might not be so lucky next time."

"I saw two bulldozers bigger than tanks when we left on that little hike to measure snow depths. Use them to block entrance roads. You can always unblock the roads later if you need to exit for some reason."

He nodded. "That's a good idea. Maybe we should have allowed them to put the refugee camp here." He smiled. "Or convince you to stay on. We need people with ideas."

"I have a family. Believe it or not, I'm on vacation, and I thought this just would be a sightseeing trip. A ride to see national parks."

"Some vacation," said Powell, knocking on the door jamb with his left fist. His right arm was in a sling. "Permission to come on the bridge, captain?"

My turn to smile. "If you have your sea legs, flyboy."

He plopped into an empty camp chair and crossed his legs. "I want to thank you, Penny. I now understand how you survived five years without any help."

"You didn't do too bad yourself, but you're a lousy kisser. Better work on that. Just not with me."

PART 5

Water for a New Life

"Thousands have lived without love,
not one without water."
~ W. H. Auden

CHAPTER 30

While returning to Edwards, I'd decided that venturing away from the refugee camp on dangerous expeditions wasn't the best thing for me or my family. I'd seen enough of what was left of California and the country. The refugee camp was boring, but at least it was safe, I was surrounded by people who gave me comfort—and I could give some back. There was the issue of having more space, though, so I wasn't one hundred percent sure. Nothing was ever definite because situations changed.

About three months into the return to that life of boring subsistence, though, I was asked to join a discussion inside the base. Three big security goons looked like they weren't about to take no for an answer. *What the hell? They're feeding us, right?* Then I thought they might have something planned for me for springing Ben. Kind of neat that he was right there under their noses all that time, but I didn't want to break up my family. Didn't expect donuts and coffee courtesy of the government. Figured the worst, in fact, in spite of all the help I'd given to the air force.

I had some positive thoughts too. Maybe they wanted to give me an award for helping to save their damn satellite? Or my contributions at Yosemite? Couldn't believe it was for the trip for water in the tanker trucks. All that seemed long ago. Was sure I didn't want any rewards either. I wanted to minimize my contact with authorities because they always seemed to put me in dangerous situations, beginning with those five-plus years of surviving after the skies fell in. Yosemite was supposed to be an easy excursion, after all.

The room I was taken to was the same one where I'd met Becky. I was offered a can of coke, a pleasant surprise. *Prisoner's last meal?* I was noting all the sugar content listed on the label—it wasn't diet. Tasted syrupy because I hadn't had anything sweet like that since the stale donuts in Missouri on the way to Andrews and cookies from old vending machines on the return. Would have liked coffee, but knew water was always at a premium and good coffee even scarcer. The three musketeers filed out, leaving me alone with my room-temp coke.

There was an intriguing satellite pic on the wall. I wondered if Becky's satellite took it. *Is it also a spy satellite?* Guessed a satellite could be programmed for com and surveillance with the proper onboard equipment, a multifunctional platform for both civilians and military. Becky and her group of techies had spent long enough prepping the damn bird for launch.

I stood up and examined it. Looked at the date. Not recent. About a year after the shit hit the fan. Recognized Tiananmen Square in Beijing. *Cheyenne Mountain's old artwork?* There was a huge pile of clothes, mostly military uniforms. Naked people were barbecuing other naked people.

I shuddered. There was a caption who said, "Justice is served?" *Black humor?* Was that intel? Had it been the Chinese or North Koreans? Both had a habit of saber rattling. Maybe it had been Russia? Any of them could reach the West Coast of the US with their missiles; the Russians could even do it from Moscow. I tried to remember who our real enemies were back then, the most evil ones likely to be the guilty assholes.

I decided it didn't matter anymore. Sat back down to wait.

⌘⌘⌘

Colonel Landon entered the room with a folder and took a seat opposite me. I studied him a bit, thinking of my discussion in the truck with Becky. His haughty little mustache and aloof manner didn't do it for me. He didn't even look good in uniform. That turned on some women. I didn't know what Becky saw in the guy. Hmm. *She doesn't see anything in him.* I smiled. *Maybe a blind woman looks into the inner soul and sees good qualities in a man?*

One TV rerun we all liked to watch on the carrier was *Hogan's Heroes.* Landon reminded me of Colonel Klink—more in his being a pompous little ass who wasn't much taller than me but walked around like he had a broom handle up his butt. Was always polishing his specs too, although I think Klink had a monocle. Wondered who was doing his eye exams and making his glasses now. Hadn't seen glasses for a while, although Ben used reading glasses that were just magnifying lenses. Meant that Landon wasn't a pilot, just a bureaucrat.

Landon reached over for a handshake. I stared at the hand. To his credit, it was calloused. Maybe he wasn't just a paper-pusher. Score one positive quality for old Becky. "You're a survivor, Ms. Castro," he said, withdrawing the hand. "We admire your grit and determination."

"That and a can of beer would be reward enough," I said with a smile. "I prefer ice cold, not room temperature. Neither shaken nor stirred. And, because you want something from me, maybe I could receive that in return for what I can give you. Hell, I'll even become your mistress if you find me some good whiskey." *Becky might frown on that, though.*

He laughed. *Better when he's not so damn serious.* "I'm happy to see you haven't lost your sense of humor, considering all you've been through. How's your little family?" I shrugged. He continued. "A while back, just before he went to Andrews, Ben told us Sammy's father was the main course for a beach gang. That had to be tough for the kid. How is Ben, by the way?"

"You'll never find him."

Landon smiled. "We know he's with you and Sammy. Washington decided his memory loss was real. I told them that even before they took him. No way a man can suffer an injury like that and keep his wits about him. Sometimes higher-ups cave to logic and reason, even if it takes a while."

I nodded. So this wasn't about my punishment for springing old Ben. No rewards or medals mentioned, either. *What's it about?* I was sure Landon didn't just want to chat.

I looked around. "Thought this would be some kind of seminar about how to survive the air force's hospitality. Where is everyone?"

"Just you, Penny. You and me. I want to discuss how you and I can save the world—SoCal at least."

"What a load of crap! It's over. We're in a post-apocalyptic nightmare now, bozo. Live with it. Recognize the futility. I can't do anything to help you. Not anymore. Maybe Ben could if he had a mind left."

"Ben put in his time," Landon said. "He deserves a

quiet retirement. Your first clue should have been that he speaks Russian, by the way. Funny he didn't lose that ability."

I glared at the colonel. *Maybe this is about springing Ben after all? Or maybe they want to experiment with Ben's brain?* "I've been working with him, but he can't remember much of his past. Is he Russian? Give me something to tell him. He'd appreciate that."

"His grandparents were. Changed their surname when they came to the US. Raised him because he lost both parents in a car accident. He worked at Cornell. We don't know if there's anything left there. It's too risky to check, even for us. We don't patrol much north of Edwards anymore either, except for trips for water." He did a little drumbeat on the table with his fingers. "Back to Cornell. The New York City area was hit hard. Millions dead and the few survivors spilled into the burbs, even upstate, looting and pillaging. But anyone could guess that. All urban areas suffered as the plague headed east. We imagine his old grandparents in a retirement community didn't survive."

"My mother didn't either. She's buried in South Jersey."

"Yes, that was a nice little piece of subterfuge. Like I said, you've shown grit and determination. You can help us, even though Ben can't."

Down to business. New shit will hit the fan. I was preparing to duck. "Why should I?"

"Because you've served your country and served it well. You showed your patriotism getting that satellite launched, for example."

"Hmm. You wanted me there in case I could talk sense into the people who almost killed Becky, including my brother. I did it to find my brother. He wasn't there." All a lie, of course. I still didn't know why I'd done it. It wasn't patriotism. I paused to choose my words carefully. "Or maybe just to be Anna's bodyguard." Enjoyed his frown when I said Becky's real name. *Security!* "I figure my country was at least partly responsible for what happened. What did happen, by the way?"

"Classified. You've likely guessed most of it, though. We suffered a surprise attack."

"Are you guys still playing Pentagon games after all these years? Was the satellite part of that? Give me a break! Or can't Pentagon wonks admit their mistakes?"

He sighed. "I guessed this would not go well. Everyone blames us, and there's probably some just cause for that. But diplomacy only goes so far when you're dealing with fanatics. Those overseas, Penny. Not you."

I shrugged. "I'll give you that. But I'm not helping you. Just let me return to camp and enjoy what life I have left with Ben and Sammy."

"Just one question then: what do you know about desalination plants?"

"Ours are big and, when new, they were supposed to forever end California's water problem, which they didn't accomplish, although they probably helped. Oh, and you can see them from all over the LA area. We saw one smoking once. Right after that was when I saw your helicopter for the first time."

"The smoking platform you saw was destroyed by feuding factions." He took an aerial photo from the folder and shoved it toward me. "Look like a desalination plant?"

CHAPTER 31

I ignored the *TOP SECRET* label. This pic wasn't from Cheyenne Mountain. It had been taken from a recon helicopter, probably one from Edwards. Palm trees and farmland were incongruous companions for piles of debris and what might be a village that tried to hide under a canopy of solar panels. "No, it looks like Heaven and Hell as conjoined twins."

"Ignore milling combatants and conflagrations. Look more closely."

I studied the pic some more. "It's huge. Not the original design, I'm sure. Has it been expanded? Better said, who expanded it? The solar panel array is only about a third of the whole platform now."

"Each platform has been expanded into something as close to an oasis as you'll find anymore. Dirt and fertilizer have been brought in from somewhere. Some crops were always being grown, but now there are a lot more. This seemed like a cross between a Brazilian *favela* and Shangri-La when our helicopter was attacked and we shot back. We're pretty sure things there are back to normal now." He smiled and winked. "Does that pique your curiosity?"

"A bunch of farmers became creative. So what? Farmers are always creative."

"We want those oases. We want their water back for SoCal. That's what!"

For the first time, I saw anger and determination in his eyes. I nodded. "Makes sense," I said in a soft voice. With so few people now, one functioning platform could help a lot and allow more time for aquifers to recover, assuming they could. "You'd still have to ration, though."

"I don't think so. The population here on the West Coast has been reduced significantly. We don't know why certain persons survived—we're interesting if only for that reason—but that doesn't matter. Those oases would help us along a path toward normalcy for that small population at least."

I was nodding, having already beaten him to those thoughts. *So just do it, bozo!* Handed the TOP SECRET pic back to the colonel. "Fly troops there and take over the damn desalination platforms then. Seems simple enough to plan. I can't contribute much to that effort, and, like I said, I won't."

"First, we don't have the personnel nor the choppers to carry them. We'd have to use boats and be sitting ducks for those who are controlling the platforms. Second, we still think that a Normandy-style invasion might work if we had some divers sneak in at night and plant a few well-placed bombs. And develop some useful intel first, of course, before we do that."

"Given all your restrictions on personnel and equipment, that plan sounds reasonable," I said. "Maybe something like a SWAT team would even be better than the Normandy-style invasion." Then it hit me! "You don't have any divers, do you?"

"Bingo. That's how you can help. The plan is to take platform by platform. Your SWAT team idea is a bit different from what I was thinking, but I like it."

"I'm no SEAL. Hell, I was never even in combat."

"But you did good work for the police and you survived after the plague. Rodriguez said you guys had an arsenal with you when he picked you up. You and Ben killed four marauders on the way back from Andrews. You helped us on that trip for water, at Vandenberg, and Yosemite. All that tells me you can participate in combat if you put your mind to it."

So he knew about the zombies who tried to rape me and wanted to put Ben and me on barbecue spits. Wondered if this asshole knew when I first had my period. I sighed. Big Brother was still at work and maybe had even an easier time doing it because 350 million people had been reduced to…how many?

"Let me talk it over with Sammy and Ben," I said. "I'd like Sammy to have a chance for a better life. He's been through a lot. But I don't want to leave him alone in this world. I need him and Ben too. I reaffirmed that conclusion in Yosemite, something that was supposed to be a scenic vacation."

"Understood. Tomorrow, same time?"

I nodded.

এ৩এ৩

Rodriguez ushered me back to the camp.

"He's one of the good guys," he said en route.

"Who? Landon?"

Rodriguez nodded. I had my doubts. Didn't know the SOB that well either. Becky thought highly of him, though.

"That might be, but he's still willing to send good men and women to die in battle."

"Just one woman who can also teach us to dive."

"And where would I do that?"

"San Diego Naval Station. We own it now by default."

I considered what that meant. Should have known old navy divers, many of them friends, were now dead, because I was the only diver they could find. Thought about all those old friends and colleagues dying a horrible death. Fires for revenge were rekindled. They'd been smoldering all the time, of course. But it was hard to blame anyone on the platforms for the plague. What fell from the sky was indiscriminate. Everybody on those platforms was a lucky survivor like me, people who had some kind of natural immunity to the contagion. Some genotype those brilliant Asian scientists hadn't covered in their nefarious bioweapon's design.

"There were no survivors?"

"Not one. A few inland like you, but no military. Not too many even know how to fly a plane or sail a boat anymore. From what I'm told, sailing is easier than scuba diving, though."

How could we let this happen? I realized the question was irrelevant now. It always had been. Fires for revenge changed to smoldering cinders once again.

"Depends on what you have left to sail," I said.

"Depends on where you're at. In Seattle and Norfolk we have two subs. The one in Seattle is Chinese; the one at Norfolk is Russian."

"How did we obtain those?"

"What I'll say is classified because I know what you're thinking. A visiting admiral from Norfolk who wanted to try to resurrect San Diego told Landon about the subs. Their crews were seeking asylum because they were afraid to return to their bases. They'd gone silent."

"Why don't you use the Chinese one to attack the platforms?"

"Because they dumped their missiles and other good

stuff, including personal firearms. Those Chinese weapons are about seventy kilometers deep in the Mariana Trench, for example."

"So our sailing fleet is reduced to almost nothing. What do we have?"

"A few ships in the harbor we don't know how to resurrect. And a lot of those rubber landing crafts with silent outboards SEALs often used. Not sailboats, I guess."

"No, they're not. A real sailboat would be a lot quieter, but that's two things to teach you, and the navy wouldn't have many sailboats around. They're used by beach gangs, though, because they don't need gas. What about fuel, by the way?"

"Like everything else that's manufactured or refined, it's scarce, but Uncle Sam has enough to get the job done. I wouldn't worry about that."

"No, my worry is about Ben and Sammy. They're the only real family I've ever had, discounting my worthless brother."

He frowned and held open the tent flap. I invited him in, but he excused himself. I saw him walking away, shaking his head and muttering. *Did I say something to offend him?* Later I learned what it was.

Went inside to talk to my boys and Muttsie.

ᥱᘺᥱᘺ

My boys said that whatever my decision, they were okay with it. I'd figured they'd say that. I was still mulling over pros and cons when my name was called. outside the tent. Smiled. It was Harold "Hannibal" Hooper. I wanted to hug him and apologize, but he was with a stranger, a dumpy man in a wrinkled suit.

"Mr. Winston here is from DC, Penny, and he wants to talk to you."

Not my idea of the best reunion with Hannibal as my attention turned to Winston. He looked like a bureaucrat. Another pair of glasses, these with thick lenses that made his eyes look like a bug-eyed ET's. *What does he want with me?* All sorts of alarm bells were sounding in my head.

Winston, a ghoulish person with blanched skin, was already turning red in the sun. I guessed he didn't crawl from under his rock that much. Maybe he'd spent years in some bunker in the Washington area, wondering when it was safe to exit and count the dead. I disliked him even before he spoke because I felt sure that he was almost as responsible for our situation as anyone who had fired those missiles at us.

It never made sense. It used to be that astronauts and cosmonauts in the International Space Station would comment, upon looking down at the blue home world, that we were all on spaceship Earth together and should learn to get along. Now they were all dead, and almost blind moles like this troll were still alive and likely thinking contrary thoughts to the astronauts.

I almost turned around to leave him standing while I returned to my tent.

"What about?"

Winston clasped his hands behind his back like a priest about to launch into a fire-and-brimstone sermon condemning all parishioners to hell for having sex on Sunday morning. Even looked like one a bit—Friar Tuck with pop-bottle glasses.

"I was sent to convince you to help us with the desalination plant project."

Project? I thought we were planning an invasion. "Hmm. I guess I should be flattered, but all the way from DC to see little ole me?"

"I have other business here as well, so don't flatter

yourself, Ms. Castro. We're trying to put the country back on its feet again. I hope that by now you understand that."

"Are you saying it's my patriotic duty to have a role in the invasion?" I said in a voice loud enough so that the gathering group of refugees could hear.

"Something like that," he said with a smile. "I understand you're ex-navy and an accomplished diver."

"Something like that," I said. "Listen, Washington sent the wrong guy to convince me, unless you're also carrying an apology from the government for their role in creating this godawful disaster."

"We were caught by surprise," he said with another smile, a bit more forced this time. "I can't talk about details for security reasons."

I could see the crowd getting restless. "I bet that cloak of security hides a whole lot of terrible sins. It often does."

"Think what you like, but they attacked first, not us."

"Who's 'they'?"

"I'm not at liberty—"

"—to discuss details. I know. We'll probably never know why the world went to hell." I approached him and poked my index finger into his fat little belly. "I'll do what the colonel wants, Mr. Winston, but I'm not doing it for your sorry ass. Are you capable of understanding that?"

There was scattered applause from the crowd and a few bravos. He nodded and offered a handshake. I stared at his hand. Felt like spitting on it. Now some jeers. His face became redder, and it wasn't from the sun.

He shrugged, turned, and headed for the jeep.

"Sorry about that, Penny," Hannibal said.

I hugged him now. "I'm the one who's sorry. I deceived you. Do me a favor, though. Find a way to drop that SOB into a crevice on the way back without hurting yourself." That was all a whisper in his ear, of course.

He squeezed me back and found my ear. "Can't do that. It's flat terrain around here. Maybe on the flight back? An ejection at forty kilofeet into the Grand Canyon?"

Knew he wouldn't do that either, but the thought he might was somehow comforting.

 భాయా

Once I'd made a decision, I decided I needed to give Ben something to do. Knew Olga was badgering him a bit and didn't want him to worry about me either. Because Landon had spilled the beans that they knew about Ben, we'd already stopped hiding him. We'd learned some physics together—relearned in his case—and in the process I saw him become more the teacher than the student.

So I suggested he offer free courses to the refugees and air force personnel.

"I don't expect any success with that," he said. "We were motivated to learn. They're probably not. Maybe too busy too."

Refugees? I doubted it. Didn't know about the base personnel. "It would have to be on a volunteer basis," I said, "so you'd expect volunteers to be motivated."

"There won't be any volunteers."

Epiphany! "What about teaching them Russian?"

"They won't see the need for it."

"Yeah, it might be a dead language like Latin now, but so what. I'll suggest it to Landon. Bet he'll make sure there'll be volunteers. Who knows? We might be training future ambassadors if there are any Russians left. Call it preventative medicine. Who knows? Maybe Putin or someone worse is still in charge over there, and we'll have to meet him some day."

So it came to pass that Professor Benjamin Thomas started to teach a select group of "volunteers" Russian. It was a mixed group of the more nerdy types. Ben said they were fascinated by the Cyrillic alphabet. Go figure. And Ben wrote the first and only new Russian language textbook. I imagined there might be some old ones at that Reagan library, maybe even some old letters from Gorbachev to Ronnie. But that Russian course made Edwards a cultural oasis in the California desert.

It was time to revisit a real one. We began to plan an invasion.

CHAPTER 32

One morning two weeks later, a chopper dumped the colonel, six flyboys, and me at the naval station. Rodriguez was one volunteer among the air force personnel. I didn't count the colonel as a volunteer. It was his plan, after all, so he was management—a wannabe DDE directing the Normandy invasion? For my sake, I hoped he had as much luck as DDE. Thought people on the platform wouldn't be as stupid as the Nazis, though. The allies had fooled them completely.

I thought we'd fly to San Diego just offshore and then swing eastward to land at the base. Instead, the pilot left the sea route farther north at Encinitas and flew along I-5 to exit 13B, where he followed Harbor Drive, as if he were driving a van delivering supplies to the base. Seemed strange. Learned later he did it for me. Thought it would make me feel better, I guess, being over land, but seeing the I-5 pretty much in the same shape as the 405 depressed me instead. Saw what once had been the nude beach at La Jolla off to our right. Zero nude sunbathers that day, and I saw a few bleached bones not covered by sand flashing in the sun just behind the helicopter's shadow. Bleak was the appropriate word.

There were navy ships anchored offshore, like Rodriguez had said—two cruisers and a destroyer. Their minimal crews' ghosts on board were likely still there guarding these remains of the American fleet. The sailors on shore leave were probably all dead too. The mighty navy that had survived two world wars and was in a lot of other shit after that was now buried in the past.

Missing were aircraft carriers and submarines. Not too odd. They'd likely all have been on patrol and now floated on high seas like the *Flying Dutchman*, but the cruisers and destroyers usually participated in a battle group as protection for carriers, so it was a bit strange.

Maybe some survivors had stolen an aircraft carrier and gone looking for revenge? Supposed some others had survived the plague and now controlled a sub. What were they all going to do? Launch missiles at the contagion's source or even DC? Did they even know who'd been the source? Wouldn't change anything much. Apocalypse-squared is still apocalypse. Might save human beings a lot of trouble too—just put us all out of our misery…please!

With those happy thoughts, I started putting our plan into action.

☙☙

Although I was more familiar with other ports, I had liked San Diego. It was a navy town, like Norfolk. It also had featured enough population diversity that I didn't feel everybody was looking at me like I was some kind of exotic animal. And the weather was almost always top notch, so I could display my bod on the beaches a bit and just look exotic.

Once I'd accompanied Kathy, my BFF from ordinance, for a long weekend on leave where I received a taste of that hedonistic San Diego lifestyle. Her parents were rich and lived in a mansion, complete with tennis courts and large pool. Both parents were type-A, the father some financial guru who traveled all over the country, and the mother a lawyer. Friday and Monday we bathed in the nude and sipped tropical drinks brought to us by a jolly old Hispanic maid who was amused by our shenanigans.

"How'd you ever opt for the navy when you could have this kind of life?" I said to Kathy.

She sat and hugged herself. "I had to get away from them."

"From your parents?"

"You didn't receive enough attention from your parents. I was drowning in it. On and on about making something out of my life, finding a rich husband with a rich family, and popping out beautiful grandchildren. Although my mother received her partnership by working long hours, she was a throwback. For her, women's lib meant not having to work and enjoying the good life."

"So, why didn't she?"

"Because my father would have lorded it over her that he was the one making all the money. Guess he hadn't counted on her having a career equal to or better than his. I was an only child, and Berta practically raised me. Private schools, sweet-sixteen ball, the works. Boring, boring."

"Berta's the one bringing us drinks?" Kathy nodded. "I like her," I said. "She's my kind of person. So are you. Guess you survived a troubled childhood too, just the extreme opposite of mine. Why return here now?"

"We're in San Diego, my adopted hometown since my father moved us here. It would look odd not to come here. It's like being in a fancy hotel, as far as I'm concerned."

"Except that it's free."

"It comes with a tax. At dinner tonight they'll likely start berating me again about how I'm wasting my life."

"I can understand how parents might wonder what their kid will do once she leaves the navy."

"It's more than that. Like I said, I should either become a breeder or somebody important—their definition of importance, which involves making tons of money and having lots of power over people."

"You should do what you want to do. You have the wherewithal to do that."

"I wanted to be an artist. Both my parents said that was a waste of time and only the lucky amount to anything."

"Nothing like a little pep talk from Mom and Dad," I said. "Let's change the subject. Do you like the guy on the top or the bottom?"

She giggled. "I'm a second-story girl. Why should men have all the fun?"

I thought about that. "I see your point." I clinked her glass. "Rid'em, cowgirl!"

Not long after that, she was transferred from the carrier to a destroyer. Now she was probably dead along with ninety percent of the world's population. I'll forever remember her as a friend who helped me get through dark days after losing Ned.

༄

Civilians used to take a series of classes to learn how to dive. The first lesson anyone should learn was how to be smart. Even experienced divers became lost in sea caves and wrecks, were tangled in something, or forgot to check their equipment. One little screw-up could get you killed.

The underwater environment wasn't a natural one for

human beings. Your subconscious knew that even though you could sometimes trick your conscience into forgetting it. My fear of water caused me to have more respect for the ocean than a lot of newbies who had no such fear, became careless, and paid the price.

I'd never taught any kind of class. Okay, I'd taught Ned a few things—let's call that the one-on-one Socrates method. Teaching a bunch of flyboys, all men, who could lose focus with one glance at my boobs—I was in a bikini where the top had some support built in—that taxed Professor Penny's meager abilities as a teacher and her patience. Had to admire all those teachers who could handle a class of thirty-five to forty-five students—herding a bunch of kids where only a small percentage gave a damn must have been trying. I'd been a student without motivation. I'd done well enough, but would have done better with a better attitude.

Reluctant student, reluctant teacher—that was me. I'd promised myself to never dive again, remember? I controlled my fear of the water. It was harder to control my loathing of it. When you made a dive and surfaced to see a world gone mad, it was like a reverse baptism—something the Devil might have thought up to torture my soul. I was something like a DIY psychologist, though, and calculated that my loathing for the water was a by-product of seeing dead bodies on the sheriff's dive boat and shore. The water was guilty by association, as if that made any difference—or sense.

So I tucked my loathing and repugnance for dead bodies into the same dark corner of my mind as my fear of water and Ned's loss. The critical question was always there, of course: *Do I have enough barriers built around that corner so my demons can't escape?* Figured the answer to that was more like experimental psychology, me being the lab rat in Skinner's maze.

ↄ◌ↄ

All six air force volunteers became or were good, strong swimmers. That helped. A few had done some snorkeling, mostly as kids. That helped too. I started them with snorkeling first just so they could all become used to breathing with something in their mouths and using flippers. Wet suits were required. The Pacific waters were still cold. Seemed colder than normal, in fact.

There was also muck in the water. Reminded me of my first dive for a body in a pond. The muck extended out from shore twenty miles or so. Remembered the waves being higher, too, so figured the thicker soup damped some wave action.

I'd have to discuss the physics of that with Ben. Depended on whether he'd arrived at wave motion yet in his physics retraining.

I remembered the crap on cars' engine blocks, so I warned the others not to gulp any water. Everyone now had every kind of shot base docs could brew up, but no one had convinced me that they had one for the plague that had rained down. I was pretty sure they didn't have that, not even for that interim president back at Andrews. Mayor Ballesteros's fear that the government only wanted refugees around to serve as guinea pigs was ever present in my mind.

The chopper had flown in medical staff after us and some serious security after that. The former checked our health every morning. The latter made sure all the danger was limited to virus and microbes, not other human beings. San Diego was as dangerous as any other abandoned big city. Colonel Landon oversaw it all as part of his management role.

"Diving looked easier on TV," Rodriguez said one evening while we all ate our MREs.

"On TV, you can do a DNA test in an hour," said a medic.

"Or fly to Mars to grow potatoes," I said. "Scuba diving was a hobby for many people, but it isn't easy. It requires skill and experience. And we have secondhand equipment."

"I thought you checked all of it," Rodriguez said.

"I did. Checked compressors too. But even the gasoline for them is old." I gestured to a pile of junk off in a corner. "Cracked hoses, bad gauges, oxidized fittings—we're in business only because of the law of large numbers—thanks to the Pentagon's overstocking, you can find something that works. But we're working at the tails of risk distributions."

"I have no idea what that means."

"It means we found enough functioning items in all that old equipment for our purposes. Thank the navy for over-supplying and redundancy. I'm being conservative about equipment selection, but we still might have some failures. That's why we have the buddy system. It's unlikely you and your partner will suffer an equipment failure at the same time."

"But you don't have a buddy," said the medic.

"I'm aware of that," I said with a frown.

CHAPTER 33

While I was teaching the group to scuba dive, I received a quick course on desalination plants taught by Dave Richards, an engineer Hannibal flew in from DC just after Winston when they were certain I'd do my "patriotic duty." Unlike the bureaucrat, I liked Richards, who seemed to be a born optimist. As a surviving scientist, he had reason to be optimistic about his employment. I figured my job as a diving instructor was a one-time deal—I wouldn't have it any other way. Other incursions could be made by the group I was training.

"First, a bit of history," he said. "In 2015, there were more than eighteen thousand desalination plants in one hundred fifty different countries that had a combined annual capacity of thirty-one-point-six trillion liters of water."

I had no problem with the concept of liter—you could still find big bottles of Coke, but they were far beyond their expiration dates, of course.

"Sounds like a lot, but it was only one percent of worldwide freshwater use."

"Overall water usage is a lot less now," I said, pulling down the corners of my mouth. Preferred to say that to saying the demand is lower. "Maybe a lot less than thirty trillion."

"Because we don't have a reliable census, even in the US, we have no idea what our needs are, but you're probably aware that needs are considerable around here if you count growing food among our priorities."

"Why weren't there more plants? The California drought was already humming along in 2015, even though they received a small respite in later years."

Richards nodded. "Good question. The answer is cost. The general technique of reverse osmosis was okay, but the polyamide filters commonly in use then—that's a type of polymer—degraded quickly when exposed to chlorine, so two steps were required: remove chlorine before desalination and then add it back later, because potable water requires chlorine as a disinfectant."

"Was that process energy efficient?" I said.

"With modern pumps that use solar energy and plant configurations that use outbound waste water to help pressurize incoming water, the membrane technology was the weak point in the process."

"And manufacturing it in quantities," I said. "You need thousands of filter tubes stuffed with rolled-up membrane sheets."

He smiled. I liked the smile. "Sounds like you know a bit about this," he said.

"Not the latest developments. But let me jump ahead." He nodded. "What can you tell me about our target platforms?" I asked.

"Your reconnaissance will have to fill in details, but, generally speaking, a modern desalination platform is a multilevel structure. The top level is always comprised of solar panels. The lowest level might be fish farms. In between you'd maybe have vegetable and fruit farms—something like what we used to call truck farms—maybe with some small livestock, no sheep or cattle. I'm not sure what you'll encounter, but aerial reconnaissance indicates large additions were made to the farming area."

"Perhaps even more visible because no one makes solar panels anymore?"

"Yes, something like that is hard to come by. Even the Pentagon depends on surplus now for the most part. Another reason is that we think each platform is self-sufficient: They've cut themselves off from the mainland."

"Which tells us they have the means to defend themselves."

"No guessing about that. Our choppers have been fired upon."

My preparation might have been better if I'd been in some combat while in the navy. Didn't think my previous experiences counted for much in this case.

☙❧

The buddy system worked, especially for beginning divers. I taught it and insisted on it. We still almost lost one flyboy, Sam Smith—at least he wasn't named Joe—when his buddy became ill one day. Smith was getting a bit too cocky and insisted on going down alone on a training dive where he had to recover an old air tank I was using as a surrogate body. Call it a quiz for the students in my little course.

I knew something was wrong when fifteen minutes passed and he didn't surface. I went in after him. He wasn't anywhere near the tank. I treaded water and looked around. The murky water didn't help me spot him.

There were always currents, and they often changed directions. The ones that day were strong and flowing out to sea, almost an extended riptide. I hadn't wanted to swim in that—there was a front blowing in—but the team had insisted. Everyone wanted to begin the prep.

Spotted Smith in eighty-foot deep water about four feet from the bottom doubled over like he was a cheerleader trying to make the letter A. *Cramps?* The good news was that he still had his mouthpiece; bubbles showed he was still breathing and his equipment was still working. The bad news? Not knowing what had happened, it made sense to bring him to the surface.

Damn fool came to and fought me, though. Made me think there was something wrong with the air mix. Mine seemed okay, but Smith had filled his tanks last. Either there was something wrong with that mix or he had a bad case of indigestion. Aneurism? Heart attack? Diving could trigger all sorts of weird things that didn't appear on physical exams.

I grabbed one of my weights and KO'd him with a little head tap. That likely wasn't advisable, but I was desperate. Bastard was stronger than me and had been grabbing for my hose. I'd seen panic in his eyes.

We surfaced. Rodriguez helped me haul him into the boat. Removed his equipment. When I saw he was breathing more normally, I slapped him awake.

"What the hell happened?" I said.

Smith looked confused at first as he glanced around at the others in our little group. "Don't know. I just felt weird and lost it, I guess. Thanks, Penny."

"Yeah. We don't need more of that happening." I turned to another group member. "Don't get his tank mixed up with the others. We need to test that air."

I discovered the mix wasn't regulation. All the tanks' contents were a little off, but progressively thinner in oxygen than mine, the first, to Smith's, the last. He'd been breathing air like that found atop Mt. Everest. Too much nitrogen too. Nitrogen narcosis plus asphyxia—not a good combo. I'd minimized the former with three decompression stops on the way up. Never learned how that compressor failed—I'd checked it almost every time we went for dives. It was old, of course.

We brought a substitute compressor online, and the problem disappeared, but I added more lessons on how divers could detect bad air and what to do about it.

જીન્જી

We worked hard, the "professor" as much as students. There were equipment drills, invasion mockups, and endless diving, including fighting underwater, teaching my fellows where divers were most vulnerable in offensive and defensive maneuvers. I channeled my basic training drill instructor a bit, but my course was an advanced one for water combat. I also met with the colonel enough times that he understood what our advantages and disadvantages were—I wanted him to have realistic expectations because most bureaucrats didn't.

I'd never given much thought about battle tactics while scuba diving, but Ned had described a lot of them to me. That information helped me prepare our commando force. Couldn't say we'd be as good as SEALs in that regard, but we would achieve a good approximation.

Of course, it would be unexpected challenges that could kill us. Murphy's Law applied to battle situations just like everything else. You tried to plan for contingencies, to the point your trainees were bored out of their minds, but there was always something to bite you in the butt.

Once we were on the platform, a different kind of battle would ensue, so we also trained to be a SWAT. Didn't know anyone outside SEALs that owned both skill sets, and wished I had Ned to teach us fine points, but Rodriguez did a great job. Sometimes we took dips to soothe bruises and wash off sweat after sessions of target practice—limited—ammo was at a premium—martial arts, and dashes and laps.

I felt my body getting back into shape, though. Next time I made love to Rodriguez, I'd be a tigress to his tiger. Now I was often too tired to even think about it. Came to appreciate the training Ned had gone through.

"We're doing maybe ten percent of that," Rodriguez said one time we had collapsed on the beach in exhaustion. "Except for the various skills needed for the events, a SEAL has the strength and stamina to be a decathlon winner. I knew a few. Smart guys too."

I remembered Ned telling me I should learn calculus because it'd help me drive a car. Didn't understand that, but guessed he knew the subject.

"A group of SEALs is the ultimate SWAT team—the best of the best."

I thought maybe Stephen Hawking was pretty good too, but knew what Rodriguez meant. The best at what they do. My team wasn't too shabby, though. Maybe the best of what was left?

We had some fun too. Our football games, four against three sometimes, my taking the role of ref other times, were welcome diversions. An old red, white, and blue American diversion. Rodriguez, who'd played some high school ball, wasn't a bad QB, meaning he could pass and run the option, so he was always picked first. I was picked last if I played. My strength was taking a pitchout on the option and running like hell. Had plenty of practice at the latter in the five-plus years before I arrived at the refugee camp.

Had to give the colonel credit—sometimes he joined the games. He was as good a passer as Rodriguez, so he went early when choosing teams. Funny how games in prep for a serious op help mold *esprit de corps.* Here we were, survivors of one sort or another from diverse backgrounds, yet we worked together to achieve a common goal.

By the end of my little diving course and all the SWAT training, I was thinking they might be ready to kick some butt. Wasn't so sure about myself.

CHAPTER 34

My final exam wasn't easy for my students. We took four dinghies to within half a mile from one destroyer. I had no idea about what we'd find onboard, but figured it would be bad enough to test psych reactions too. My pupils weren't SEALs and hadn't seen a lot of bad action because Uncle Sam's Air Force had protected them from it. None of them had accompanied me to Vandenberg either. While we weren't going into a shooting situation on the destroyer, my exam would tell me a lot about whether I could trust them in a combat situation. Always the nagging question of whether I could trust myself, of course. Thought I could control the latter, but how others reacted was a different challenge.

"We can all rappel up and down walls," Smith said, studying the destroyer. "That's basic training. But that wall isn't vertical."

I eyed the few degrees slope from the sea up and out to the deck. Smiled. Smith had seen the difficulty. They wouldn't have support from the ship's hull. "Let's see whether you can reach the deck and what you do once onboard," I said. "And let's say I want to know what's on these ghost ships, so a complete recon is necessary."

"Do you think it's seaworthy?" said Rodriguez. He winked at Smith. "She's trying to make sailors of us."

"Our brief reconnaissance might tell us it is, it hasn't sunk yet, and the recon could be useful intel for future ops up and down the coasts. Maybe I want to blow gangs to kingdom come with the big guns, assuming artillery shells are still available."

"That's not a bad idea," said Smith. "Might be an alternative way for taking the platforms too. Ever mention that to the colonel?"

"I might. I'll say it came from you, though. Don't want him to think I've gone over to the dark side. We don't know who the people are on those platforms."

"I'll mention it," said Rodriguez. "You stay out of it."

"Because the colonel might be a misogynist?"

"Because he still considers you a civilian."

"You don't?"

"Hell no," said Smith. "You're one of us, Penny."

I liked that. Didn't know if it was justified. Smith and the others might be better prepared than I was, not to mention more energetic and motivated.

The swim through mucky port waters was all done at thirty-foot depth. We popped up and treaded water while rappelling cables were shot skyward. It took a while before they were all well secured. I looked at my waterproof watch. Didn't expect the platform's deck to be that high, but that delay was something to think about.

Rappelling up the destroyer's side wasn't any different from basic training exercises, as Smith had said. The incline just meant it was all arm and leg strength, though. We attached flippers and masks to our dive belts and ascended. I thought of ninjas climbing the walls of a medieval Japanese castle. Didn't expect any shogun on top, though, or a Tom Cruise to help us with evil ninjas.

We split up and explored around and in the ship. Because it was anchored and most crew were given shore leave, there weren't many dead sailors onboard. I should say skeletons. The air was just as dry onboard as it was on the coast. It was a bit weird to see skeletons dressed in navy fatigues. I found the XO's skeleton with his spiffier duds. No sign of the captain. He must have given himself shore leave too. Or the XO had his and it was the captain's turn.

In my part of the recon I came upon one skeleton that made me lose my breakfast. Recognized the peculiar golden chain with the golden crucifix attached. To be sure, I plucked off the nametag: Ensign O'Leary. Knew it was Kathy O'Leary, my old BFF from ordinance. Fortunately no one was around when my sobs echoed around that hold.

For most of my time in the navy, I'd been on a carrier, so the destroyer seemed small. But it was big enough that no one saw me bawling. Even the smaller ship seemed empty, although it had become a mausoleum for a bunch of sailors. It was that for Kathy.

I brushed away tears and pocketed the necklace and nametag. Something to remember her by when I had more time to grieve.

We all met in the galley and reported our findings. I was the last one there. I didn't mention Kathy. No one there had known her. There was probably no one alive who had known her besides me. That made me feel lonely, but I was keeping my feelings private.

"I'll also suggest to the colonel that we loot the ship," said Rodriguez. "There are plenty of supplies here that we could use."

"Any idea why that wasn't done before?" I said.

"And I'm wondering why local beach gangs didn't do it," said Smith. "Most of them have boats."

"They're maybe a suspicious lot," I said. "But USAF

missed a bet here. Looks to me like the government, whatever remains of it, just abandoned San Diego. Moreover, I can't believe that some sailors didn't survive. There weren't many survivors in general—the percentage must be small—but you'd expect a few."

"Likely eaten by beach gangs," said Smith. "Or joined them."

"Yeah, I think we dropped the ball," said Rodriguez. "There could have been some sailors here who needed our help. We were all comfy in our bunkers and didn't think about them."

"How long was that?" I said.

"About six months. Orders from above. While we waited for what was dispersed to thin out, we were going stir crazy."

"Why would you take the chance and even come out?"

"More orders from the Pentagon. They said it was okay."

"And you believed them?"

"Our superiors did," said Smith. "Some caught the plague and died. Moot point now. We can't carry back any of these goodies. A half-mile is too far for hauling any load."

"Especially underwater," I said.

"We have to do that again?" said Rodriguez.

"You bet. It's easier than surface swimming. And safer. Sea state's high today."

I'm just a pushover—I gave everyone a passing grade. Rodriguez told the colonel about Smith's idea for turning destroyer guns on the platforms and collecting goodies from the destroyer and other ships. The colonel admitted Smith's idea might be useful for future ops, but he wanted to keep it simple for now. I think he had more confidence than I did in the air force SEALs, but that was okay by me, as long as it didn't get me killed.

CHAPTER 35

In the evenings after our sumptuous MRE repasts, Colonel Landon and I continued to study and debate potential tactics. Thanks to some TOP SECRET blueprints, I had a good idea about what was under desalination platforms besides murky, toxic water—at least what was there when they were built. I wanted to be sure, though. Richards had implied a reconnaissance run was needed. I agreed. We decided to do it at night.

Landon had offered some argument about how I was the leader so I shouldn't put myself at risk. In other words, he preferred to send someone else for the recon. I countered that argument by pointing out that they still weren't pro divers and that I had more of a chance to react safely if I encountered surprises. Blueprints or not, those aerial recon photos had showed me that expecting no surprises wasn't an advisable plan of action. Besides, someone had taken over those platforms by force, which meant that they might offer some deadly surprises. He gave in. Maybe my female charms? Or the realization I could clobber him and make him say uncle?

Swimming in inky, murky waters wasn't my favorite thing, considering all those demons corralled in that dark corner of my mind, but it wasn't as hard as it sounded. I had often looked for bodies underwater at night in my years as a diver for the sheriff's department. Dead bodies couldn't attack me, but whoever now "owned" the platform could—big difference! But snooping around a platform for ways onto it still seemed easy enough because the bad guys weren't expecting underwater reconnaissance.

We'd salvaged a whole bunch of those USN rubber boats with super quiet motors and already used some of them in our fake attack against the destroyer. I now had our security forces paint over all navy lettering—white, orange, or yellow on black letters were too visible. Paint was faded, but it had been luminous once, implying they were never designed for clandestine ops. We packed up one and took off for NAS Point Magu. I always thought its mascot should be that little blind cartoon guy, but the Pentagon never exhibited much humor unless it was the case of underlings faking laughs at a general's or admiral's jokes.

I'd seen during the destroyer test that Sam Smith also knew a lot about boats. From the Point, which was between Leo Carrillo State Park and Oxnard, he took me to within a mile of the desalination platform near one of the Channel Islands, where he cut that near silent motor, and we coasted to a halt in quiet seas.

"After I'm in the water, backtrack to two miles and hold station," I said. "Return here in an hour and turn on your pinger."

He nodded. Upon my return, I would hear the underwater pinger with my little battery-powered sonar unit if I were within a hundred yards or so of the boat. No one else would…or so I hoped.

"Be careful," he said softly.

I wanted him to give me a hug for good luck, but that seemed a bit unprofessional. Nodded and went backward into dark waters, sank to about twenty-foot depth, and headed in the platform's direction.

ↄ৩৫৩

Swimming underwater at night was something like swimming in old printer's ink. You might as well be swimming in some pool in a cave. I'd done that once, but I was able to use a light. A pilot would appreciate the difficulty of heading for that platform—I was dependent on the GPS unit strapped to my wrist and aerial recon coordinates—guessed enough sats still worked, although I had to surface to receive signals because salt water and radios don't mix well. At times I could swear I was swimming vertically, not horizontally, though. Eerie.

While ocean covered a good portion of the Earth's surface and our ancestors crawled from it to begin our life on land, human beings didn't belong in the underwater environment. A scuba diver was like an astronaut on a spacewalk, especially at night. A deep-sea diver in a pressurized suit, even more so. One old movie I'd seen on the carrier haunted me still. *The Abyss* even affected Ned because it involved US Navy SEALs. The only sci-fi movie that's scared me more was *Alien*—I identified with the main character.

In that inkiness, I could imagine ghosts, not ETs, swimming with me, not threatening but keeping me company. Good ghosts. George and Angela, my other sheriff's department buddies, Kathy and other navy salts—all protecting me from bad ghosts. Or did feral humans who wanted to eat people make bad ghosts? I'd killed a few, and, if they were around, they'd be trying to drown me.

I cursed Bobby as my hydrophobia returned. I'd made it that far by pushing that fear away into that dark corner of my mind. Now it came back. Cursed myself too. I'd promised myself to never dive again. Now Landon had me doing his wet work for him. Didn't enjoy that espionage pun as much as I'd expected, so cursed Landon for that too. Almost lost it when the current grabbed me.

I became caught in it, but soon realized it wasn't an ocean current—it was the near riptide-strength intake where seawater was sucked into the purification plant. *Talk about bad luck!* Because pipes to land weren't functioning anymore, they couldn't need to process a lot of seawater, so it was just bad timing.

Maybe they only did it at night? That was a new datum that might affect our plans. They still wouldn't be doing it all night, though. Even with all the additional area added for crops, one platform couldn't use a whole night's worth of fresh water. Even if the new tenants had spas and took showers three times per day, they couldn't use a whole night of water. And they wouldn't be sending it to the mainland either, otherwise I wouldn't be there.

'Course there might be multiple functioning intakes. The platform was huge, and the old blueprints showed several intakes. My only escape was to bust a gut swimming perpendicular to that current as if it were a riptide current and hope I didn't become caught in a discharge current that carried me away from the platform. Figured that wouldn't be as strong, though. After all, purified water stayed onboard the platform now—I'd just be in salt-saturated waste water and debris at lower pressure. After storage tanks were filled, the whole system would probably shut down.

Were other surprises waiting? Likely not. How many mods could bad guys make to a platform, given present circumstances? It wasn't like a pipeline company was at their beck and call.

I soon discovered I was wrong about mods because of the many homemade additions to the platform I found.

Another detail I was wrong about: There was a diver working on some kind of debris trap on another intake valve, and he saw me. A big, strong guy! Like a shark going after a clown fish.

I didn't have a light, so he must have seen my shadow or my bubbles. The resulting chase showed why male and female swimmers didn't race each other in swim meets, not that I was in prime condition to even compete. He caught up with me.

Fighting underwater isn't easy. That guy should have taught that section of my course. A karate chop's power was weakened by water viscosity, though. That saved me from his first aggressive move after grabbing on to my ankle and pulling me toward him. Instead of breaking my neck, it only gave me a sore forearm. That hampered my agility in the water.

But he was no longer holding on to me. I was a slower swimmer, but I had faster reflexes. A big body was often at a disadvantage in close quarters. It was this wannabe SEAL's downfall. I grabbed his air hose with my left hand, circled him from behind while he tried to find it, and pinned him. Took him about six minutes to drown, even though I helped that along with my chokehold on him.

I hauled him back where he'd been working and faked an accident. Easy enough to do. Cracked his face mask with one of my weights—the same one I'd clobbered Smith with—and left the hose dangling along with the new trap.

I was thinking now I should have guessed the platform had some divers, even just to check things out underneath every once and a while. Another detail overlooked in our planning sessions. I cursed my lack of foresight. Considered myself lucky too. The guy was a brute. Only presence of mind and a bit of luck had saved me. Although adequate, he hadn't been all that used to fighting underwater—his initial weapon was surprise. I'd had some training at underwater combat, thanks to Uncle Sam's Navy, although I was a bit rusty—never any call for it when I worked for the sheriff's department. And Ned's descriptions of his training had come in handy too.

I continued my recon mission. My ghosts and hydrophobia were gone for the time being. Didn't miss them at all.

CHAPTER 36

While the photo recon coordinates seemed spot on, the original blueprints we had of the platform were dated—many recent mods weren't on them. It was much larger than what the blueprint showed, just like I'd seen on that TOP SECRET aerial photo, or maybe more. I managed to scramble aboard amidst a tangled mess that looked like a mangrove swamp of old pipes and piles of sand, sludge, mud, weeds, and various crop residues. *What do you call a landfill when it's in the middle of the ocean?*

Somehow they had created *El Rancho Grande* floating off the California coast. Advantage: I had plenty of cover as I moved in zig-zag fashion toward the platform's center in the stifling heat still present under the shade of solar panels. Disadvantage: It wasn't easy terrain to move through—my time was running out. The delay with the platform's brutish diver hadn't helped my schedule. Recon was best done in a speedy fashion—speedy in, speedy out. In my defense, I hadn't had a lot of experience. Ned had talked about generalities a lot. "No wasted motions," he'd say. "Memorize everything your eyes see but don't overthink it."

Ned had likely used a cellphone camera, but I took a

lot of pics using a digital camera Landon had provided. Probably filled most of a memory card. If I had to perform recon, I wasn't going to be sloppy about it, and I didn't trust my memory. Knew our group could use the intel too if only to complement those blueprints and flyover pics. One of Landon's tasks was to keep all intel organized on a base laptop. Those files could mean the difference between life and death for me and my pupils when our invasion became a reality.

I reached the center, circled the little village, enjoyed aromas of home cooking, found a dairy barn with foul odors that killed the good aromas—so they had bigger livestock now!—and made my way back. *Have the platform's original techs and engineers become farmers?* Sure seemed that way. I considered how we might take the place over. Couldn't see it being an easy gig, and I didn't pretend to be a great military strategist like DDE— I was still thinking of Landon's Normandy comment, doubted he could compare with Eisenhower in strategic savvy either.

I swam like hell on the return trip. Didn't make the rendezvous on time, but dependable Smith had given me some leeway. Plopped onto the black rubber bottom of the dinghy with a thud as he headed toward the distant shore. In my exhaustion, I managed to ponder about how we'd need to refine our strategies. I'd have to allow that there might be divers. I'd also seen kids in that village. Remembered my Sammy. Didn't want our guns anywhere near those kids. No way. I don't buy that collateral damage shtick.

I knew that many military ops ran the risk of collateral damage, a Pentagon or spy business term for damage to hospitals, for example, and innocent civilians. Our enemies hadn't paid much attention to that moral issue when they hit us with the plague. I could argue that they had paid for that, though. This was a different situation. Now seven of us could be doing bad things to innocent civilians, many of them children.

While it was probable that there were bad guys on that platform—I'd just killed a close approximation in self-defense—I was one hundred percent certain that no kid on that platform was a bad guy. Even if their parents were, I'd always had a hard time justifying any attacks on kids when their parents were stupid or violent. Bad people often created more bad people in their offspring, of course, when they turned into adults—I once read about kids in the Nazi Youth Corps—but they had been indoctrinated with evil.

I also thought about people having kids. *That's a good sign! Maybe human beings have a future on this planet?* I was snoozing by the time we reached safe harbor at Point Magu station and Smith woke me. Rodriguez piloted us back to the deserted San Diego navy base in the fishing boat we'd co-opted.

I crawled into bed about four in the morning. At six, Landon entered the barracks and bellowed at me. I sat upright and grabbed the top sheet. No privacy allowed in this man's army! Or air farce.

"We need your recon intel," he said.

"Gee, it would be nice if you let me pee first. And get dressed."

He smiled. "Fifteen minutes, Castro. Smith said you didn't tell him much except you had to kill someone. You okay?"

"Yes. I could have used a few more Z's. I was too exhausted to tell anyone much. So was Smith, but I don't know why." I glared at the colonel. "Now get the hell out of here. I'll be there."

I was—in twenty-five. I was a civilian now, and a volunteer. Wasn't going to let the bastard stomp all over me like some raw recruit. And knew he couldn't do anything about my tardiness. The motherfucker needed me!

∽∾∽

"You look terrible," said Rodriguez.

"Not surprising. I fcel terrible. Let's get on with this." I turned toward the colonel. "Throw away your plans. I'm not killing any kids."

"What? Who asked you to do that?" He looked at Rodriguez as if to accuse him.

"Don't blame me, sir," Rodriguez said. "I'm here regretting comments about a woman's looks."

Landon smiled. "I'd think that Penny has a right to look terrible. She was working most of the night, unlike some other people who were sleeping. Let's back up."

'Course Rodriguez hadn't been sleeping unless he snoozed on that fishing boat.

Landon turned to me. "Why do we have to change plans? What did you find?"

I explained. He began to flip an old coin. I found it annoying, as if my fate were left to chance.

"I see what you mean. But SoCal, to survive, needs that water. And not just from that one platform. Any idea how they obtained the necessary soil and other stuff?"

"Other material is likely guano. I expect that the nearest Channel Island's a wee bit smaller, and anything else is probably just the equivalent of a garbage heap becoming a floating landfill."

"How big a group are we talking about?"

"About forty hovels, each not holding more than a small family. You do the math."

Landon nodded. "Say husband, wife, and two-point-five kids. Maybe one hundred eighty people, and forty possible combatants, or thereabouts, discounting women and kids."

"You passed third grade math," I said. He didn't need all the mental gymnastics. At one man per hovel, you get the forty. More importantly, if his calculation was correct, there were about one hundred kids. "You might be too high with the two-point-five, but there are enough kids that your Normandy-style invasion isn't possible."

"Hard for seven of us to take over that size of a group," said Rodriguez.

"Depends on how well armed they are," said the colonel, "and how well trained."

"Guy I had to kill seemed to have some training. How recent I don't know. Once aboard, it could be a one hell of a firefight."

"The seven of you have more training," said Landon.

"Six," I said. "Leave me out of it. With bullets flying around, you'll have young kids as collateral damage. I want no part of that."

"Okay, help us put our other Rambos on the platform and don't participate from then on," he said.

That switched on the old sailor's lingo. "Fuck you! That's still being part of it." I was satisfied to see the crimson rising from his neck to his face. "I'm a volunteer, remember? I'm resigning from this team right now."

Rodriguez looked at the colonel and then at me. "If you participate, there will be fewer chances any kid will die," he said.

I now directed my wrath at him. "Okay, give me a gun, Rodriguez, and I'll shoot anyone who goes near a kid! Including you. Do you think I'm that naïve?"

The colonel squirmed in his chair. "We have to do this, Penny," he said in a voice that was almost a whisper. "Greatest good for the greatest number, and all that."

"That's just another way of rationalizing collateral

damage," I said. "And didn't you see those old movies *Star Trek Two* and *Three*? Military's been using that argument since prehistoric times, killing a lot of good people in the process, and that guy with pointy ears wasn't so damn smart because he bought into it."

He thought a moment. "Okay, then. Come up with an alternative plan."

"Alternative to what? Not my job, and I don't see you even had a viable one to begin with, considering the number of people now on that platform. And I can't see any way to invade those platforms without putting children in danger."

"We'll find one," said Rodriguez.

CHAPTER 37

I knew water for SoCal was a big thing. The base trucked in water from the San Joaquin Valley's artesian wells, every trip putting the air force fellows in serious danger—of course, they had neglected to mention that to little ol' me when I went along for the ride. People died on those trips. I knew that from personal experience. Didn't want any more experiences like that.

The aquifer in the Big Valley was in good shape in spite of the drought. Over a span of years, a meager snowpack in the Sierra still replenished it, and people were no longer using it for agriculture. *There are hardly any people! That might change.*

And it would be at dangerous levels for a long time and much better for survivors to start those pipelines functioning. That was common sense. Killing kids wasn't worth it, though. Not from my perspective.

I was back at the refugee camp when Rodriguez came to visit. He entered the tent. Sammy jumped up and saluted. Rodriguez roughed Sammy's mop of red hair and shook Ben's hand.

"Want some coffee?" I said. "Real coffee? Top Secret intel: We have a bit left in our meager stores. Don't advertise it, flyboy."

"No, you keep it and drink it. I don't want to be reminded about what I'm missing." He plopped into a camp chair that had managed to survive, given our heavy use. I thought it had been on the edge with me. It screamed surrender with his compact bulk. "I came to discuss a plan." I put my fingers in my ears. He stood up and pulled them out. "Hear me out, please."

I thought a moment. "Okay. Sammy, why don't you go see if those nice little boys and girls are playing slow pitch. You're not getting much exercise since we stopped being nomads."

"Aw, Penny, I want to listen to the plan. What's it for?"

"I'll tell you a bit about it after I talk to Rodriguez." He left with Ben. I sat in his chair, the other chair. "Okay, *pendejo*, let's hope you're not wasting my time."

He made his spiel. I liked the plan. I could have my cake and eat it too. Sort of. It was a drama in two acts. In the first, I was Pied Piper. I'd dress as a clown and attract all the children. In the second act, the air force's SEALs would attack and take over the platform. We would have to convince Landon it would work because our plan was more complicated than his. Plan B usually is. But his Plan A was already dead and buried from my point of view.

෴

"Where are we getting a clown costume for Penny?" said Colonel Landon.

"Base infirmary. There are costumes there. Medical personnel often put them on to cheer up sick kids." Rodriguez smiled at me. "Get sick kids laughing and they'll forget they're sick, at least for a time."

"Works for me too," I said. "'Course, the kids on that platform aren't physically sick, although there might be some mental cases among them because their parents might be violent psychotics in dire need of straitjackets. I hope that's the case, and not sane people just trying to survive and take care of their families." I paused a moment to recalibrate. "I don't have much practice being funny ever since we were hit with the plague. Who will make me laugh?"

Rodriguez snapped his fingers. "We'll make you into a sad clown. How 'bout that?"

"I'd have to be sadder than those kids to make them smile. We don't know what their lives are like."

"Kids are always more positive than their parents."

"Tell that to the kids who are war survivors. And you didn't have my childhood. My mother rode a broomstick when she wasn't beating me with it. I'll give it a theoretical and politically correct psych name that's outdated: overly zealous adult supervision. My father wasn't around for a long time, so she took it out on us. You'd be surprised how many unhappy kids were fodder for military recruiters." I thought of my BFF Kathy again. Parents' wealth is irrelevant.

He held up his hands. "I surrender. Colonel, it's your turn."

Landon shrugged. "She's right, but so what? The mental state of those people on the platform isn't the problem. Even if they're cannibals and eat their children, taking command of that platform is something we must do." He waved his hand in dismissal. "Fine tune that plan. We have to try it because it's the only one we have. I'm not into killing kids either."

So Plan B for the op went ahead as planned by Rodriguez. What occurred wasn't covered by the plan. It usually wasn't. Shit happened. Murphy's Law was more important than Newton's Universal Law of Gravitation and Einstein's Special Theory of Relativity. The Pentagon had never learned that. Same with politicos. Probably never would.

CHAPTER 38

I repeated my recon swim, knowing now where the huge water intake was so I could avoid it. Sea state was even calmer so I stayed a bit nearer the surface. My bubbles wouldn't be seen by any platform observer— no moon, although some phosphorescence on wave tops this time made me feel that the swim was from *A Midsummer Night's Dream* with Titania lighting the way. Didn't have that on the first swim to the platform, so this one was easy—until I drew nearer to my destination.

Some fish slept, but there was enough action that I wished I had a harpoon gun, especially when a few small sharks started to nose around the strange black fish in their domain. They seemed to be congregated around the platform. *Had they dumped remains from cleaning a slaughtered animal?* Generally sharks were more frightened of you than you of them, but they made me nervous. Always did. Even little ones could bite a sizeable chunk of meat from you. Nothing personal. Like a lion with an antelope. The great circle of life, but I didn't like being on the prey side of the predator-prey shtick.

The bottom wasn't in sight in the inky, murky waters. Seemed murkier this time. Hit a few chunks of stuff. *Raw sewage? Shark chum? How far does patriotism go?*

No diver from the platform this time to greet me. I scrambled onto it and disappeared between piles of junk. Struggled from the wet suit. The clown's outfit in the waterproof bag I'd strapped on behind my scuba tanks was still dry. Spent almost a half hour, preparing for my role.

That involved applying my war paint. While I'd practiced back at camp, I had a bigger mirror and a lot more light. I still managed to look like a sad little female clown. My natural curls were already in disarray. Clothes were easy, although a bit too floppy. Decided I'd much rather be cheering up sick kids back on base. At least there wouldn't be bullets flying around back there. Was sure they would be on the platform before the night was through. Thought my highest priority was making sure no kid on that platform would be hurt. That was a lot of responsibility. Even preferred to fight tanks in Yosemite to this op. Or get a com satellite launched. Risking my own hide seemed a lot more appealing than risking a kid's. I thought of Sammy. Would I see him again?

Penny the Clown walked into the little village, trying not to trip over her big clown shoes. I was thinking all the while: *Is this the craziest thing you've ever done in your entire life?*

Probably should have added *and most dangerous.* Seven against how many? But that was for the future. Now it was just me and my unskilled lying. Maybe I could fool kids, but what about adults? I had to convince them at least that I was alone and therefore harmless. Thought a moment and crossed myself. Couldn't hurt and it might help.

The little mirror I had used to prepare for my role hadn't shown how ridiculous I looked, only my face, but as I walked my imagination created a mental picture. Because I'm small, I'd once jumped from a large cake at a bachelorette party. My appearance had to be in that category. The bride-to-be was approaching the cake with a knife, so I jumped the gun. I was the only one to say "Surprise!" I was in pasties and a G-string with a sash that said, "Malcolm, take me I'm yours!" Not one of my prouder moments. I remembered it clearly. Stuck in the cake, I wasn't drinking; all the others were. I could have used a stiff one right then.

☙☙

It was between nine-thirty and ten p.m. Bigger kids were still awake, and they awoke the little kids. Word spread like wildfire.

About fifty of them followed me to an open area and congregated around me, and so did some smiling parents until the platform's security detail made an appearance, wiping away the happy smiles—knuckle-dragging party poopers, huge security types who were no longer night-club bouncers only because there weren't any functioning nightclubs.

They made Rodriguez and his flyboy friends look like small cherubs. Someone without a sense of humor must not have liked the idea of my performing.

Goons came for me. I decided to play it cool. Held out my arms.

In rusty old handcuffs and stripped to my skivvies— my only clothing under that stupid clown suit—they took me toward the platform's center. I was ushered into a room with a table. One head honcho was sitting there.

"Sit down!" I was going to make him say please— knew I could turn him inside out in about thirty sec-onds—but figured the goons were just outside the room. I sat. *Might as well hear what the SOB has to say.* "Who are you?"

"You first. I don't know you or what you do here. I

expect new men in my life to introduce themselves. Be courteous."

He smiled. It was a psychotic smile that could freeze your soul. A Hitler or Mussolini's smile of insane evil. I decided to nickname him *Führer*. Seemed appropriate.

His tonsure seemed to make his pointy head seem pointier. It was also a small head set on a corpulent body. Reminded me a bit of a Conehead from reruns of an old TV show on the carrier. Maybe SNL? He was dressed in a cheap suit with a wrinkled shirt and tie that only came down to two inches above his waste. A true misfit. *How'd you become the dictator here, mister?*

Of course, I knew the answer. He'd taken over by getting rid of anyone who stood in his way, just like Hitler and all the other despots the human race has been plagued with throughout history. He was the kind of guy who would unleash the contagion upon the world—a paranoid narcissist with no concern about others, only wealth and power. He had his little fiefdom, and he intended to keep it.

Maybe I'll have a surprise for you, asshole. Just give me a chance!

"I'm Josef Braun. Now it's your turn."

Wow, Penny, maybe he's even German! But I knew many nice Germans and people with German ancestry. *This man is not nice!*

"Call me Penny the Sad Clown. Fun for the kids. I came here to make a few bucks."

"We don't use money. You're from the mainland."

"You don't know that."

"You're not from here. We maintain lists of the people who live on platforms. There's no Penny on any of them."

"Maybe because my real name is Penelope. But you don't have a right to be here either, do you? You're a squatter. You don't own the place. The government does. Or the California Water Authority, to be precise."

"I'm the mayor. And I'm the government now."

I wanted to wipe the smirk from his fascist face. Restrained myself.

"And we own this place. We run our operation like a kibbutz."

Sure, go ahead and insult Jews! "Caboose, kibosh, kibbutz—you took the place over after the sky fell in. That means you're from the mainland too. Politicians, not even sleazy ones like you, didn't work on the platforms. They'd have been too far away from their bloviating speeches, press conferences, schmoozing with the idle rich, and three-martini lunches. How many engineers and techs did you clods have to kill?" Figured I'd pay for that spiel.

He shrugged. "Desperate times call for desperate measures."

"Parroting trite sayings doesn't work with me. Any engineers and techs left?"

"Enough to keep the place running. We don't need to run at full capacity anymore."

"I know that. You cut the water off to SoCal."

"And you came here from the goodness of your heart to amuse our children?"

"Some parents seemed to like the idea of the show too, even though I had just started it. Guess you and your thugs don't have a sense of humor. There's always some asshole who hates to see kids have fun. Or hates clowns. Have some kind of hang-up about clowns, Mr. Mayor?" I pointed to the closet. "Other monsters might be in there. Beware!"

He ignored the last barbs. "I'll concede I had some people protesting your capture." His fist pounded the table top. "But I won't have mainlanders meddling in our lives! I have a responsibility to my people. We have to keep you savages away from here."

I shrugged. "So, let me go back. I'll tell all the people who hate your guts that you canceled my performance. They'll see you scum don't give a rat's ass about their children and will overrun the platform. Mayor on a spit. Doesn't sound appetizing, but what the hell?"

He thought a moment. "I'll allow the performance if you tell me how you arrived here."

"*Star Trek* transporter beam from the Amazon jungle," I said. He frowned. Before he could berate me for insolence, I waved a hand around. "How many tons of dirt were needed for the expansion? Oh, that's right, you're not an engineer, so you can't answer that question."

"Oh, but I can." He quoted a number of tons.

I couldn't get my head around that number. He quoted a number for tons of seagull guano too. They'd flourished on the island. On the mainland, they were eaten, so they avoided feral humans now. Darwin at work. Hell, I avoided feral humans too, and here I was among them. A cleverer tribe maybe.

"All from the island. We've stopped for the time being because we're self-sustaining now."

I wondered how they still kept it all afloat. Next time I was underwater, I had to check that, preferably in the daytime. Maybe added oil drums? Guessed even thugs could become inventive. "Good for you. Mainland people are dying of thirst, though. You're hogging the water. Thirst or starvation. That's what you've condemned them to."

Again the fist. "Not our problem!"

That ended the discussion. I thought I'd be roasted for dinner, but I was thrown into a small, dark room while they decided what barbecue sauce to use. Maybe they'd give me a taste test?

I remembered with fondness some foody trips taken from Norfolk. Southern barbecue was a meat-lover's delight and a vegetarian's nightmare. Most offered a taste test, but I just sampled everything and paid the price later. The indigestion was more likely from the wild mix of meats and sausages and sauces—but oh!—was it such a treat when I was eating it. Couldn't imagine sampling my own flesh. Almost dry-heaved because my stomach was already in a knot. Cursed this mayor for giving me those thoughts.

⌘⌘

Later that evening I had a visitor—a chaplain, the Reverend Timothy Moss. I hadn't seen one in ages—not any religious person, for that matter, unless I counted the skeletons at Mission San Fernando. The only things distinguishing him from other males on the platform were long sideburns and a clerical collar. The rest of him looked as shabby as Ben Hur had when I met him; at least the Reverend wasn't naked.

"The work of God just doesn't pay well anymore?" I said before he even spoke. "I don't have anything to offer. And I'm not buying what you're selling."

Moss smiled. "Oh, but you should. The children asked me to talk to the mayor. He's given permission for one performance if you swear to God you'll be on your best behavior. Because I'm his representative—"

I smiled. "Best behavior" was always relative, and I interpreted it loosely, especially when it came to that asshole of a mayor. Some nice parents must have bowed to their children's pressure.

"I'll need my costume returned."

He nodded. "Of course. Do you so swear?"

Hmm. That was a hard one to answer, considering my

dilemma. "What's in it for me?" I said. "I came here thinking I could make some money, or at least barter for some things that would be useful to me on the mainland."

"What would you like?"

"How about some fresh fruits and vegetables and any protein you have dried or salted. I have a family to feed."

"What kind of family?"

"A boy and an old man." I didn't mention Rodriguez who was waiting nearby with five others in those rubber boats. Smith, who ferried me in, was waiting with them. Figured extended families didn't count for the reverend.

"You seem like a good person, Penny Castro. I'll have the mayor arrange something. Do you expect us to give you a dinghy too?"

Oops! Mentally cringed at that. "I guess you didn't find it," I said. "It's a big platform." He hadn't said anything about discovering hidden scuba equipment, so I'd keep that ace up my sleeve for a while. Figured he wouldn't bother to have security look for a fictional dinghy either, but, at the same time, he couldn't imagine I'd swum in all the way from Point Magu. "That just shows you I'm not asking for much."

He nodded with a smile.

"We're only three people. We don't need a whole lot."

"What do you do for water?" he said.

"Too heavy to carry around, *padre.* We make do with catching dew runoff and storing rain water. Like I said, we're only three." I waved at the large half-gallon bottle of water and glasses on the small table in my prison cell. "Probably more water all at once than I've seen in many years." Wasn't about to mention Yosemite and the Merced River. Didn't want him to know I could afford tourism in California.

"I'm sorry we cut it off. We need it for our own use."

"So I'll just charge you with second degree murder or

manslaughter and hope you burn in hell. Maybe genocide as well. You likely didn't plan to kill anyone specific." I smiled at his squirming. Decided to soften the guilt a bit. "You're pretty wasteful here. Nothing like a real kibbutz."

He brightened. "You've been to the Holy Land?"

I shrugged. *Why not? My past is irrelevant here.* "Years ago. Before the world went mad. I was in the navy on leave. Spent a few days in one. Nice people. Good food and wine. They have farming in arid conditions down to a science."

I didn't say I'd used some of those techniques in my own gardens, but I had—what I could remember. They seemed to work too, although the Golden State was more arid now than I could remember Israel being. He was more interested in holy shrines. I did the best I could to remember my short visit. Talked about the Wailing Wall and Mount of Olives and a few other places I managed to remember. His questions helped stimulate those memories.

I wondered what the Middle East was like now. Israel was like an oasis in a region of chaos. Of course, it had caused some of the chaos, especially in the West Bank and Gaza Strip. Centuries of hatred between Semite tribes were hard to overcome. History hadn't treated the region well either. An artificial creation of nations and their boundaries after World War Two had poured salt on festering wounds. At least with colonial powers, though, there had been peace in the region. Didn't know right from wrong there, but figured it no longer mattered.

After the magical mystery tour of the Holy Land, the clergyman left and a mayor's thug brought me my clown suit. The small transmitter, an adapted pager that some VIP no longer needed because he was dead, was still sewn into the waist and undiscovered. Was I going to hit the button to call my SWAT buddies? Only if there weren't many adults around the children and just a few goons. I could handle a couple on my own and keep the children safe, but a mixed audience was something altogether different.

CHAPTER 39

Even at the late hour, the kids and the preacher were there for my performance as well as the three goons who had led me to my meeting with the mayor. He wasn't present. I was lucky. Three knuckle-dragging hulks I could handle. I figured old Timothy Moss wouldn't cause me any problems—he didn't want kids to be hurt either.

I remembered clowning around for my family when I was a kid, putting on something akin to a circus act similar to what I'd seen in a traveling circus. Those were good times—there were few in my childhood.

Circuses were pretty much a part of our past even before the sky fell in. Once you got rid of lions, tigers, and elephants, what did you have for enjoyment? Clowns pie-throwing at SPCA or PETA members? I knew the latter had meant well, but they had killed my childhood dream of becoming the female Toby Tyler. Denied thousands of children the small pleasure of experiencing a real circus too. Maybe they should have used robots or holograms of animals? Worked in films. Might be hard to pull that off in three rings—or even one. Even Ringling Brothers had folded. Were their animals now running wild on conservation land with no humans to care for them? I could imagine Bengal tigers slinking through grasslands in southern states looking for prey. For feral humans?

I adapted my childhood show to get the kids laughing. Went through some Disney tunes, including that Mary Poppins super-song—had to mumble the words a lot because I couldn't remember all the lyrics from the movie. Some songs I hadn't sung since I was the platform kids' age. They were fun songs too, but my childhood wasn't a lot of fun. Hoped I was doing right by Sammy and Ben. Added Ben to that list because he often acted a lot like a child.

Halfway through, I pressed the button on the device hidden in the costume's lining. At the end, I sat cross-legged and sang "Edelweiss" from *Sound of Music*. Some kids joined in. They probably had no clue what an *edelweiss* was. I was sure they no longer existed, like a lot of other flowers. Weeds were about the only flowering plants now, their sickly flowers found on some hills that sometimes trapped rain from ocean breezes moving inland. 'Course Maria von Trapp née Rainier was Austrian, and so were edelweiss flowers. Maybe wildflowers still existed on the slopes of the Alps? One could only hope.

From the corner of my eye, I saw six silent and crouching forms about fifty meters away, slinking toward the village at the platform's center. The air force SEALs had landed. The twenty-first century Normandy mini-invasion had begun. I hoped this D-Day went well for the allies too.

I stood up and bowed to the kids. They applauded and looked happy. Even the preacher applauded and looked happy. I glared at the thugs who were my guards. They didn't crack a smile.

"Guess you can take me back to my cell now, fellows."

It was appalling what men knew about anatomy. Many

were narcissistic pricks who didn't know anything about women's plumbing or our erogenous zones. Some didn't even know what a prostate was until they or a relative came down with prostate cancer. About the only body part they worried about most of the time was the size of their penises and maintaining their erections. The nature of the beast, I guess.

In spite of their ignorance, men admired women for their bodies. A brainy lady intimidated them, although some could get by that if the bod was attractive. Men were also reluctant to talk about all this. There were some advances made in western society, but the world had plenty of societies where women were still considered property, couldn't vote, and often couldn't be seen without male accompaniment. *That's not tradition; that's stupidity. Those women should have staged a revolution!*

Evolution also gave men many advantages—they could pee standing up, they avoided the pains of giving birth, and they didn't have to suffer through PMS every month. Of course, their plumbing could be disadvantageous too: hit 'em in the balls and they were in agony, and a catheter or gall stone could be a painful experience. It was interesting that evolution followed these paths.

Which was the weaker sex? Dunno. Men tend to be stronger—they were warriors and hunters in prehistoric times—but they could be sissies when it came to pain. And I could just about deck any hulking man on a one-on-one situation because I was quicker and full of surprises. I supposed if they ganged up on me, their brute strength would have won the day. Too bad they were so cute and cuddly—otherwise women wouldn't need men at all!

The three stooges nodded and approached me. I kicked off my clown shoes and became lethal. Two of them would have been easier, but I managed. *Número Uno* received a kick in the *huevos*—scrambled eggs for him, so he might be singing like a canary for a while. *Número Dos* received a fist in the throat that broke his larynx and left him suffocating. Too bad. I wasn't calling for EMTs. And *Número Tres* pulled a gun, so I threw a low fullback's block that might have broken at least one ankle after his bullet tore through my loose clown outfit. Put a chokehold on him, and he went limp too. But *Número Uno* was still writhing on the boardwalk, so I put him out of his misery with another kick, this time to the head. Did it with the heel, of course—it's the toughest part of the foot. Missed my old sneakers—I'm from New Jersey, so I still called them that—but you made do with what you had.

I didn't know if they were all dead. Didn't much care with the adrenaline rush and my pissed-off state at my lot in life.

"Stay with the kids!" I said to Moss. Saw the stain in his groin and smiled. *Yes, preacher, women can be violent too. Don't piss me off!*

I hoped that the kids would be safe enough with the preacher. His paleness was exacerbated by the harsh spotlight that had been turned on me when I began to perform. He looked like he was still struggling to control his bladder, but he nodded.

I moved toward the platform's center to help the rest of the team.

∽∾∽∾

Until then, my only weapons were my hands and feet. That soon changed. I found a platform dweller with a third eye and figured he no longer needed his Glock. It had a laser sight and extra clips. *Glock? Where the hell did he get that? Maybe an ex-cop? NRA biggie?*

Years of training took over as I checked the gun's condition and then moved forward, safety off.

Even divers in the sheriff's department needed to qualify with small arms and physical combat. A sheriff in California was in charge of policing an entire county, and those were often the size of some New England states. By the time the contagion fell from the sky, many small SoCal municipalities could no longer afford to invest in local police, so they let the local sheriff's department handle everything. Wasn't ideal because we were always short of personnel—eternal problem: fat bureaucrats cutting budgets so they could have more pay and hire more fat bureaucrats.

Add that training for local law enforcement to self-defense learned in basic training and you can understand how I could do some damage, especially after our commando drills in San Diego, which had been intense. I was never a good shot, though, but I shot out the spotlight with only two tries.

Our main problem on the platform soon became what to do with those who surrendered. Many did. Most platform dwellers had no desire to fight when facing a well-trained and lethal SWAT team. Some were already worried and asking about their kids. Couldn't blame anxious parents and relatives for that. As far as they were concerned, we were terrorists. And some might have been through it all before back in the day when the current owners took over the platform.

Two injured from our team stayed to keep an eye on those POWs. Because our force no longer had surprise on its side, I joined the rest to launch an attack against the mayor and the remaining thugs protecting him. He had about ten, but I'd already taken out three of them. Rodriguez yelled that some techies were with the mayor too. *Can we save those and eliminate the mayor and his thugs?* Didn't know if we had techies who could run the plant. *Maybe Dave Richards?* And we needed to pump water through those pipes again. *More work for divers to connect them?*

One of our team was taken out, and there were some more close calls. I took a bullet in the shoulder and Sam Smith took another one in the leg. I ripped off strips from my costume to create a makeshift tourniquet for him. City hall was turned into Swiss cheese before the remaining thugs surrendered.

Where are the mayor and techies?

Rodriguez found the VIP in his little office. He'd put a gun barrel into his mouth and pulled the trigger, creating a mess. Cleanup would be non-trivial. I found Rodriguez standing over the body. Remembered he'd never met the SOB.

I put my arm around Rodriguez's broad shoulders. "He was probably expecting the same treatment they gave others. I think a lot of engineers and techs were their victims when they overran this platform."

Rodriguez nodded. "It's still a hell of a way to die. Speaking of which, where are they?"

Wasn't difficult to imagine what I'd do if I were a techie gone to the Dark Side wanting revenge for being invaded. "I think they'll blow up the platform."

I had nightmarish thoughts about saving children who might not know how to swim from drowning. Or, bloody bodies being chum for those sharks I'd seen on the way in. Those thoughts affected me more than the mayor's scattered brains.

☙❧

Rodriguez and I dashed off to where all the equipment that made the platform into a desalination plant was housed. *C-4? Nitro? HMX? How big a bang were they planning?*

I had a healthy respect for explosives of any kind. A bit, plus shrapnel, could rip human bodies into shreds. We had an entire platform of potential shrapnel. Once read a little book by Vonnegut—"little" meaning that it well matched my attention span—titled *A Man without A Country*. In addition to the title describing a lot about how I felt, I managed to remember something from it, something about shrapnel being invented by an Englishman of the same name, and asking if we all didn't wish we could have something named after us.

Perfect irony, of course.

Problem was, shrapnel could be anything. Years ago two terrorist bros had put screws and nails in pressure cookers and set them off at the Boston Marathon. That started a whole chain of terrorist attacks in the US and Europe that used everyday stuff, even semis and delivery trucks. Messy, lethal, and terrifying. And all launched against innocent people. That was the difference between us and them. Sometimes we caused civilian casualties; civilian casualties were the terrorists' main goal. And the SOBs had killed my Ned. I was certain about that.

We both remembered where the little control room was located on the blueprint. From there, one or two people who had some technical knowledge could control the process of turning seawater into potable liquid. Finding the techies there would have been too easy, of course. They were elsewhere among all the pipes and pumps and chemical and water tanks beneath the canopy of solar panels. And not all together either.

Again, I considered what I would do: Spread out, plant charges, and radio a leader that my explosives were ready to detonate. Any terrorist worth his salt would know how to do that. Techs would too, in theory, especially if trained for that eventuality, but would they go through with it, knowing they'd likely disappear into the deep to be fish food along with everyone else on the platform? Their actions originated in a misguided dedication to the mayor, their cause, and psychotic thirst for revenge. Or, was it the kid on the playground with the football syndrome?—*if I don't like the way you play, I'm taking my football and going home.* Here, we were talking about life and death, of course.

We began a game of cats and mice, only the mice had the advantage of knowing the playing field and having bigger claws. I heard one reporting in on a walkie-talkie. Was used to flyboys using them, but it showed the platform defenders were prepared…and stingy. The gentle farming folk probably didn't even have flashlights.

I motioned to Rodriguez to take that mouse out. *Will Alex think to disconnect wires?* Minimizing the area damaged by an explosion might be a good idea, even if we managed to do no more. I peered into the gray under the solar panels that formed the ceiling of the maze of pipes and valves. Crept through that high-tech jungle, feeling a bit like that *Predator* guy hunting Arnold. Guessed Arnold had been playing video games in a nursing home when the plague hit, but I wondered what happened to the last governor of California. *Is there any state government left? Anywhere in the US?* Never thought about it before. I'd been too busy surviving. They likely had been busy with that too, if not dead.

I spotted another who was reporting in. Didn't want to interrupt him because that would cue the jerk at the detonator. *Let the reporter be. Are there other stringers?* I moved on.

I saw the guy with the detonator. He was more sideways to me but looking in Rodriguez's direction. I circled a bit and snuck up behind him. Was five feet away when

some shreds from my clown suit left over from making
Smith's tourniquet caught on a valve, making my signal-
ing device drop to the ground. The sound of hardened
plastic on metal echoed around the maze of pipes and fix-
tures.

He turned toward me, detonator raised.

"Stop! You don't want to die that way." The diffuse
red dot from my laser sighting was right on the bridge of
his nose, but a pink residual glow—faulty lens?—lit his
face. "Bobby?"

My brother's fingers hovered over the detonator. "We
can both live here in peace, Penny. The government can't
have this platform."

"What's left of the government wants water for survivors in SoCal."

"They're responsible for this mess. How can you believe they're sincere? Politicians don't care about ordi-
nary people."

I guess he didn't count the Hitler-like mayor in that
group. "The few who are left aren't so arrogant," I said.
"Do you think I would be helping them if I wasn't sure
they wanted to help us? Besides, we outnumber them, so
we can hold them to that."

"I don't think so."

His eyes told me he was going to press the detonator.
My bullet dropped him in his tracks. I sank to my knees
and bawled. *Damn, damn, damn!* I had just killed my last
living relative.

Rodriguez joined me and put a comforting hand on my
shoulder. His hand tightened when he heard who the victim was. He made no comment about that. What could he
say?

"We'd better disconnect things. Karl has explosives
experience."

My years of training and that night's battle lust evaporated at that moment, being replaced by plain old Penny's love for Sammy and Ben. Rodriguez and the rest seemed capable enough to carry on, so I left, replaced Karl, who was guarding prisoners, and sent him limping off to help Rodriguez and company.

❧❧❧

"You planned this all along!"

I turned and eyed Reverend Moss. No longer pale, he looked like he was trying to call down a lightning bolt from God to strike me dead. I hoped he didn't have that much leverage, although after killing Bobby, maybe I deserved it.

"I will not let my people die of thirst and starvation," I said.

"And what will you say if that's the fate we all will now share?"

"That I did my best." I saw the three thugs I'd killed—I'd confirmed that—and thought of my brother again, turned, and heaved. Shreds of cloth from the flowing clown suit made good rags to wipe away vomit. I noticed the blood from the shoulder wound then. Turned back to the preacher. "You think you were doing God's work here, Timothy? You weren't. You couldn't. There is no God. Even if there were a God, human beings don't deserve him." I waved my arms like a crazy woman, Glock still in hand. "Maybe not you, but the people here on this platform were hypocrites. And somehow my brother was swallowed up by your insanity. You were living the good and safe life—food, water, shelter, and even pretending you're basking in God's holy grace—while the rest of the world is in need and going to hell."

"That's—that's harsh," Moss said.

"The truth often is. Get over it. Things will change,

beginning right now. Your platform is only our first target. We're bringing water back to SoCal, whether you
like it or not, old man."

CHAPTER 40

The USAF tank trucks now carried water obtained from the pipeline Sammy and I had discovered. About equidistant from Edwards to the San Joaquin Valley but a lot safer, so more trips per week were possible, but our refugee camp and Edwards were still in water-rationing mode. Some platform parents and kids had integrated into the refugee camp too, so the number of refugees was larger. Others had stayed on the platform. Air force security now guarded the platform as well as the base and camp. Spread us pretty thin, but the colonel was planning an assault on another platform, and some of the platform's farmers had volunteered to help in the task.

"Don't think the clown act will work this time," Rodriguez said as we sat on camp chairs in front of our tents, watching the sunset.

Gaia seemed to ignore our plight and just kept on doing her thing, in this case providing beautiful sunsets in the west. We couldn't see the ocean, but we used our imaginations. I'd hung up my fins for good this time.

"Not unless the colonel does it," I said. "He's the best clown around, you know."

"Cut the guy some slack, Penny."

"I don't have to. He's not my superior officer. And he's probably a closet fascist."

He shrugged and thought a moment as I tried to decide how many anemic clouds on the horizon were needed to make that great sunset. *Gaia would know. She's a small planet in a big Universe. I'm just a speck of stardust.*

Evenings were special, extra-special if Rodriguez was off-duty. We'd talked to Moss about a wedding ceremony. He shared his time between camp and platform now. Couldn't say we were friends with the reverend yet, but I'll admit the man worked hard to save his flock from eternal damnation—it was enough to be damned in the here and now. He'd agreed to officiate at the wedding. While Mayor Ballesteros and Colonel Landon were qualified, the traditional religious ceremony seemed a nice idea. I had to remember to ask Moss what religion he represented, though. Didn't much care, but I didn't want to be caught by surprise with unknown mumbo-jumbo.

I felt a little guilty about using the airman's emotional attachment to discover more about Ben and Sammy's histories. There wasn't much more on Ben that wasn't classified, but Sammy's parents were interesting. They had met in Africa. The pair of do-gooders had fallen in love there. Their lives together could have been one real happy, sappy romance novel, except that their tragedy was so real no fiction writer could have invented it. Rodriguez's research into databases via a crumbling Pentagon intranet, maintained for the most part by Cheyenne Mountain servers, was a bit illegal, but it satisfied my curiosity. Sammy came from good stock, and the world needed more people like his parents.

We tended to avoid the topic of my brother. Bobby and others who died joined the growing number of graves near the camp, from young children dying of malnutrition and childhood diseases there were no longer any vaccines for, to combatants, not only from the platform invasion but those killed on truck trips to the San Joaquin Valley and other patrols and ops like Vandenberg.

❦

I was working on Rodriguez to leave the air force and maybe head into the Big Valley to do some farming. I had no future as a scuba diver and didn't want one with the air force or anywhere else. And I liked growing things, especially good, healthy food. He promised to think about it.

Maybe he didn't want to be a farmer. On the other hand, he had no future in the air force either. They couldn't keep things going for much longer without factories to supply them and other support structures. You could only go so far with surplus. There were some factories that could still function, I supposed, but no one to run them. The air force's planes would soon all be grounded for lack of parts and fuel. Amazing they had lasted this long. Air force personnel would also blow away with the hot, dusty winds as pilots soon realized there would soon be nothing to fly nor food on base to eat.

People had few choices. Every refugee in the camp was thinking about leaving soon. A few had gone to the platform, but space was limited there. There might be more available soon if the colonel had any success. Others had headed off for the Big Valley already, prepared to fight for their land and make a go of it. We all thought of ourselves as pioneers.

Water availability would determine where people would go. Without water, nothing grows, not even human beings. Some refugees, especially those from the platform, wanted to rid the beaches of marauding gangs. I figured there was no hurry to do that. They would end up

killing each other eventually. Until then, those who wanted to fish needed protection. The air force couldn't provide it, so the people had to arm themselves for that too.
Maybe sheriffs would return to keep the peace. Old West
Redux?

ↃↄↃↄ

While the captured platform and future ones might
help solve the water problem, we had a welcome surprise
a bit later that sent air force personnel scurrying off to
San Diego again. I wasn't involved, but Rodriguez filled
me in on the details. An aircraft carrier had come limping
in. How that skeleton crew—the live ones—had managed
that minor miracle said all kinds of good things about
Uncle Sam's Navy. Made me proud.

The sailors and AFB brass had a brilliant idea for solv-
ing the power problem. I'm no engineer, but I thought it
might work if a lot of engineering ingenuity was applied
to the problem too. The idea was to bring the ship's nuclear reactor onshore and use it.

I made one suggestion that Rodriguez passed on to the
VIPs running the show: anchor the ship and construct
power conduits from it to the shore. It would be a floating
power station.

Last I heard they were still debating about how to use
that reactor. I had always been a fan of power reactors,
seeing them as a compromise between fossil fuels and
clean energy sources. Reactors aren't clean—they produce radioactive waste that must be disposed of—but
they produce a lot more energy than green sources. I
couldn't see a lot of windmills and dams being construct-
ed anytime soon, and solar panel technology was impossible to sustain without solar panels.

Could they solve the engineering problems? The first

requirement was personnel. Were they any nuclear engineers left alive? Didn't know. They'd been an endangered species before the world went to hell because environmental activists didn't like nuclear power plants. I supposed there weren't many activists left. *It's a crazy world.*

CHAPTER 41

The kids on the platform had started me thinking about babies. Could I have one? Helping Doc Nagi deliver a baby left me doubtful about whether I should even try.

A pregnant woman in the refugee camp was still a rarity, but Lisa Polk decided to follow the time-honored tradition of giving birth at the most inopportune time. Her water broke right outside our tents, she turned pale, and I caught her before she hit the ground.

"Find Doc Nagi," I called to Sammy who had seen the whole episode three tents away and come running. He spun and headed the other way.

Pat Nagi came sprinting with Sammy in the lead. She caught her breath, kneeled, and made a quick diagnosis. "Are you having contractions?" she said to Lisa.

"Not yet."

Pat smiled. "Too early then. They'll come. Sammy, Penny, help me put her on a cot."

Sammy took one look at all the liquid. "Not on mine."

"We'll put her on mine," I said. "I can always find another cot."

With that, we began the baby watch. Pat left to make other rounds—she had become the old-fashioned type of doctor who made house visits more than attending people in her own tent—and I was left alone to take care of Lisa, with Sammy as messenger in case Pat was needed. She said to fetch her when contractions were five minutes apart and lasting one. I thought that might be a while.

It was, but at the end, eighteen hours later, in the wee hours, the progression of the countdown to launch seemed hectic. I sent Sammy off to fetch Pat and busied Alex and Ben with readying boiling water, soap, rags, towels, and anything else I could think of, including a pair of Sammy's pajamas I calculated could fit Lisa. Being prepared was a good thing. Sammy found Pat dealing with two other emergencies. The kid's head was showing by the time she arrived, and Lisa was screaming loud enough to wake the entire camp.

She gave birth to a healthy baby boy. He seemed to be bundle of concentrated energy and only slowed when he was sucking on Lisa's tits. *Men!* Couldn't say the same for Lisa. It was her first. She was saying, "Never again!"

Old Penny was a basket case too. Like I said, the experience left me thinking that Alex and I shouldn't try to have kids. Maybe we'd remain ZINKs—zero income, no kids. 'Course I already had Ben and Sammy, and Alex sometimes acted like a big kid too.

ↁↈↁ

So Doc Nagi and I solidified our BFF status, but it took a hit. The colonel had been working on her, and she caved. A fledgling research effort had started to determine why a few persons had survived the plague when they'd been exposed even on day one. The argument used to convince her was that a vaccine (if viral) or treatment (if microbial) had to be developed to prevent future outbreaks among a growing population of people without immunity, especially kids. Made sense on the surface, but they had to work hard to convince her, and she had to work hard to convince me.

I had three good objections: One: I didn't want to be a guinea pig. Two: I suspected that scientists somewhere were designing a variant of the contagion that would kill everyone the next time. And three: laboratories that could develop a cure were gone. The NIH, CDC, and major university research centers no longer existed. The whole exercise was a waste of time from a practical viewpoint. Or was there some lab squirreled away some place where a government team was continuing research efforts?

The colonel's interest was evidence for the existence of a lab somewhere, so the decision on whether I was right about number three had to be postponed—the proposal was made by the government, whatever was left of it, after all. My other doubts related to number one were dismissed by Nagi and base doctors because we would be members of a group, the larger the better to perform statistical analyses. Number two was dismissed as my paranoia. They just repeated the SOS, though, about preventing future outbreaks, which Nagi thought was a good argument. What decided me was that she would participate in the test too. If the guinea pigs became lemmings, we'd go off the cliff together.

Sammy, Ben, Nagi, and I appeared with a group of refugees. The number of "volunteers" wasn't great, so that statistical argument made less sense. But I guessed even just a handful of people could allow doctors to spot something common that might be the smoking gun that would prevent our attackers from completing their evil mission. The whole process of poking, prodding, and taking samples didn't take long either, but it allowed me to see that the base's medical infrastructure was pathetic. Fancy diagnostic machines in use ten years ago sat idle—

in general, there were no parts to fix them nor technicians to repair and run them nor enough electricity to power them. Hoped that secret lab was better equipped.

One negative about no longer having much modern medical equipment and supplies: you didn't have a little stick to test and see if you're pregnant. After morning sickness and a bit of a bump, Pat Nagi made the diagnosis after listening with a stethoscope.

Pat tried to alieve my doubts about my pregnancy. She was a good friend. Alex and my boys helped too. Penny was going to be a *mamacita.* Hoped I could do better than my mom.

Life went on. We soon had a name: Roberto if it's a boy; Roberta if a girl. Alejandro, Sammy, Ben, and I would call the baby Bobby or Bobbie, of course.

∽∾∽

We finally made it to the Big Valley, that part called the San Joaquin Valley. The air force was nice enough to transport those families that wanted to homestead. Ours rode in a chopper. I was surprised they used that fuel, but maybe they thought getting us out of the refugee camp would save all kinds of money. Or maybe they were just goodhearted?

The valley was hot. The ride wasn't bad because the chopper was moving fast enough to create a breeze inside the crowded vessel.

Upon landing, we found ourselves with no breeze and 118-degree heat. Could we just be in a heat wave, or would the entire Southwest be like this until the season changed.

Kids didn't seem to mind it. For them it was all an adventure.

I wasn't sure how Alex felt about it, but I was happy

to get away from the air force. I didn't need any more adventures in my life. I wasn't even depressed anymore.

EPILOGUE

Two Years Later:

Young Bobby was acquiring some immunization by playing in dirt and dust with some wooden toys Alex and Ben had made for him. I watched the three men working in the blazing sun trying to make the old artesian well functional and felt guilty. I was pregnant again. Alex had promised to take me to Pat Nagi when the baby was due. Not sure I trusted anyone else.

In a quiet moment together, old Ben had admitted he'd recovered some of his "skills," as he called them. He told me to keep that quiet, though, because he didn't want anything to do with any government programs for retaliation. From hints and discussions with Alex, Sam Smith, and other air force personnel just before we'd left the refugee camp, no one living was certain who the culprits were. Maybe that was a good thing?

I figured the whole plan had backfired on them, so who cared anymore? Somebody did, though—otherwise, why make us go through all those tests? My paranoia speaking again. We'd never received any results. I suspected that despicable characters like Winston were planning something. Couldn't imagine him as the pure sci-

ence type, and the government types, what little remained, likely had to occupy themselves with something
nefarious to be content.

❧❦❧

"Do you know what this place was called?" Sammy
said, joining me for a breather. He waved his hand to in-
dicate the entire area around what we all now called
Nuestro Ranchito.

We had found an old farmhouse sitting on many acres
in the low foothills. Nearby local roads eventually led to
a main highway that goes to Kings Canyon and Sequoia
National Parks.

The house had been in bad shape, one side scarred by
a past fire. We'd repaired that and the expansive front
porch and made the inside livable.

Like farmers and ranchers of old, we worked hard
from dawn to dusk while there was light and huddled together at night in a living room with crates and homemade cushions for furnishings. Candles had replaced
flashlights. We all had beds on the second floor, meaning
creaky springs and thin old mattresses on simple frames.
We found Alex and my double in the master bedroom
when we arrived. Alex and Ben found four singles in
nearby houses. Little Bobby slept in a large crate that had
become his crib.

A country kitchen filled with old pots and pans, stain-
less steel cutlery, and chipped dishes was serviceable.
There was no running water for showers, sinks, or toilets,
though. For the latter, we used an outhouse/shed combo
out back.

Pioneer days! We had years of work ahead of us, but
we were happy—a family forging a future for ourselves.

I lowered my rifle—I was on guard—and decided to

spoil his fun. "Ben says it was called Lemon Cove," I said. "Lemons were bitter fruits from trees that needed irrigation to grow. Remember when we found that powder and mixed it with water? That's how lemons with sugar tasted."

He nodded. "Maybe we can grow lemons again?"

I glanced at our pathetic vegetable garden and the many rows of shriveled skeletons of dead trees beyond. "Yeah, maybe Ben can help us find a way to do that just as soon as he and Alex finish bringing that artesian well online again."

Sammy smiled. We had a lot of projects like that planned. It would take years, but *Nuestro Ranchito* would take shape. Our lives had forever changed. I squinted up at the sun. *Maybe changing for the better?* Gaia was smiling at us again. *She's given us another chance.* I liked that.

☧☧☧

After dinner, the fellows surprised me by singing "Happy Birthday."

I wiped away a few tears. "Who found out it was my birthday?"

"'Remembered' is the right word," said Rodriguez, "not the date, but to check it on our so-called marriage certificate." He had filled out my section with Timothy Moss using the same military records one of his men had accessed that first day I'd met them.

We never had a cake, but there was dessert—a flat, thick, cornmeal tortilla covered with canned peaches and brown sugar.

"Thought of using matches for candles, but they burn too fast. Sorry about that."

Probably good to save the matches and candles. I gave

him a big kiss and hug. "Good thing. We wouldn't want to burn down all the new construction." I then gave hugs and smooches to Ben and Sammy. "This took some planning, guys. Can't figure out how you did it without my knowing."

"Easy," said Ben. "When you're standing guard with Bobby, we're off whispering. Bobby makes enough noise to provide cover."

"Think of imaginary candles," said Sammy, "make some wishes, and blow them out."

With an uncertain future and another baby on the way, the only goal that came to mind was having a safe and boring future for my little family. I'd had enough adventures for a lifetime.

I thought of the people I'd lost—Ned, George, Angela, Marge, Sheriff Hancock, Kathy, Bobby, and many others—mental ghosts now fading among survival memories. Sure, the future was an unknown, but the known past had to be put aside to make room for it.

There were no gifts. What do you give a woman who has nothing—and everything!

❧❧❧

That night Alex and I took our usual walk. We often strolled among those dead lemon trees late at night when the boys were all asleep. Bobby slept a lot, of course, but Ben and Sammy put in their hours too because everyone worked hard.

It was our time alone. We'd walk into the ghostly orchard with rifles slung over our shoulders until we found a nice spot to gaze at moon or stars. Years ago the night sky wouldn't have been as clear because the valley was always in a perpetual haze from manmade pollution, especially when they were crop dusting.

He put his hand on my tummy. "Another sleeping boy?"

"Maybe a girl? Who knows? What do you want?"

"I'm fine with either one. We need to go see Pat for a checkup, you know."

"I'm fine, now that the morning sickness has passed. You worry too much."

"Someone has to. Say, what's that?" He pointed to the sky.

"Looks big, whatever it is. Maybe ETs are landing to save our asses."

"No, something big is burning up in the atmosphere."

We later learned that we'd seen the International Space Station's end, a crematorium for three astronauts and two cosmonauts' bodies.

Was it an omen for the end of humanity? Were we the last humans? Time would tell.

Note from Steve

You have just finished reading *The Last Humans*. I hope you enjoyed Penny's adventures. I know you have many reading choices, so I'm humbled and thankful you have chosen my book. If you can find the time, please write a review for Amazon that tells other readers and me what you liked and disliked about this novel—only a few lines are needed and you will be doing a great service for the reading public.

Here are some other thrillers and sci-fi books of mine you might like:

Clones and Mutants Trilogy…
Full Medical
Evil Agenda
No Amber Waves of Grain

Chaos Chronicles Trilogy…
Survivors of the Chaos
Sing a Samba Galactica
Come Dance a Cumbia…with Stars in Your Hand!
Now all three books are available as a bundle in The Chaos Chronicles Trilogy Collection

Others…
Soldiers of God
More than Human: The Mensa Contagion
Rogue Planet
Pasodobles in a Quantum Stringscape
Fantastic Encores!
The Secret Lab (YA sci-fi mystery under the pen name A. B. Carolan)

The Secret of the Urns (YA sci-fi mystery under the pen name A. B. Carolan)

I also write mysteries. Don't miss *Rembrandt's Angel* and its coming sequel, *Son of Thunder* (Penmore Press), and my Chen and Castilblanco detective series (Carrick Publishing).

Descriptions of all my books can be found on my website http://stevenmmoore.com, where you'll also find free PDFs you can download. You can also visit me on Facebook, https://www.facebook.com/authorStevenMMoore, or my author pages on Amazon and Smashwords, and my Twitter handle is: @StevenMMoore4.

Around the world and to the stars! In libris libertas…

Notes, Disclaimers, and Acknowledgments

For four decades, the Soviet Union's threat seemed all too real. In grade school, we had drills where we hid under our little desks. (I had to stand in the corner once when I called the teacher an idiot for thinking that such drills would protect us from a Soviet missile attack. Now I realize he probably didn't believe that but had to follow orders.) Even before the Cuban missile crisis, I was reading dystopian and post-apocalyptic thrillers and sci-fi. I remember book titles like *Brave New World*, *Fahrenheit 451*, *1984*, *No Blade of Grass*, *Not This August*, and many others. Their negative tone matched my moods and the times. Nowadays we have a resurgence of interest in such stories.

Dystopia is just the antithesis of utopia. I find it less interesting compared to post-apocalyptic. After the apocalypse, what about the survivors, if there are any? I'm not new to these subgenres of sci-fi. While one could argue that my novels *Survivors of the Chaos* and *More than Human: The Mensa Contagion* are both dystopian and post-apocalyptic, the apocalypse occurring in books preceding that first novel on one of my fictional timelines—in particular, in *Soldiers of God*—and the dystopia in the first part of that first novel. *More than Human*'s first part portrays the apocalypse and, in this case, the post-apocalyptic period isn't negative when Human 2.0 appears. In a previous thriller, *Rogue Planet*, there are also dystopian elements. In *The Last Humans*, I focus on the survivors of an apocalypse and their desperation and loneliness; the result is a post-apocalyptic thriller that only has a wee bit of science and very little sci-fi.

When I was pounding stakes and carrying equipment for a civil engineer in 120-degree summer heat in the Bakersfield, California area to earn money for college, it often occurred to me that the agribusinesses in the Big Valley would disappear without water. Maybe prescient thoughts induced by lack of salt as my sweat was sucked off by that unforgiving environment? Our main projects were to grade large fields to make the most of irrigation, but without water those fields would become dry desert and never revert back to the tule swamps from which they came. Some of that scenario came to pass not long ago as California struggled with its drought. Starting in 2016, heavier snow packs and monsoons provided a temporary respite, but there is no doubt that the threat of drought remains. *El Niño* is a fickle child; that respite is a statistical outlier in the state's desert-like history.

In this novel, I've imagined exacerbating circumstances that occur when there is no one left to turn irrigation pumps on. Every living thing needs water. That those circumstances are created here by a biological attack on the West Coast is only one possible catalyst we can imagine. The nexus between us and the planet can erode in many ways, some of them quick, others slow. Are we over-farming SoCal? Will water tables recover and stay that way? I don't know the answers to these questions, but I do know somebody should try to find them.

There will be water shortages in the future as climate change marches inexorably on. One possible partial answer can be found in desalination plants like those considered in this novel. The briefing Penny received about them was modeled after an article in *Science News*. That article, "Quenching Society's Thirst" (8/20/2016 issue, p. 22), is an up-to-date presentation of issues involved and possible future development of necessary technologies. Without water there is no life.

I've added a few near-futuristic wrinkles, of course, to match the novel's post-apocalyptic nature, although they don't make it sci-fi. Considering that much of California would be a desert without irrigation, the idea of those oases sprinkled around the Sahara came to mind. Fighting over such enclaves isn't new in sci-fi—one of my novels, *No Amber Waves of Grain*, was already inspired in part by John Christopher's *No Blade of Grass*, which uses that theme. The inspiration here is even stronger. We've inherited our territorial impulses from our simian ancestors; in times of stress, they're bound to come to the fore—that's human nature. That the desalination plants become the oases is a new twist on this old theme.

I've been a bit ambiguous about the perpetrators and the means they used to attack the US. Obviously it wasn't a nuclear attack, but I wanted to portray how a biological attack can be just as disastrous and have unforeseen international consequences. Old World War One agents like mustard gas or modern ones like sarin gas are passé when one considers the unlimited lethal designs possible with DNA manipulation. It seems that we've developed a successful Ebola vaccine just recently, but a killing bioweapon worse than Ebola might be on the near horizon. Here the plague is airborne and the attack on the West Coast of the US still affects the remainder of the country and the world, including the country or countries that unleashed the attack. It isn't clear that there would be any survivors at all, but then we wouldn't have Penny's adventures, would we?

Penny's adventures are written in first person. This was both a challenge and an advantage. The challenge is obvious: I'm not a woman. However, many of my characters are strong, smart women, and I've written a trilogy about one in first person before, "The Mary Jo Melendez Mysteries." (Penny Castro bears some resemblance to that novel's protagonist, Mary Jo Melendez, but they aren't interchangeable, and Penny is better prepared.) I've also known and admired some strong, smart women and count myself lucky in having that experience (see below).

The advantage is that some things must remain unknown to the reader because they're not known to Penny, although she often makes conjectures—the nature of the contagion and the perpetrators of the attack on the US, for example. That adds a bit of mystery to this post-apocalyptic thriller.

I was born in California's Big Valley, so it was quite a trip down memory lane for me to revisit some of my old haunts. The Golden State has a lot going for it—it would be the seventh or eighth most important nation in the world if it ever separated from the US. That also has advantages and disadvantages. The increasing population has long been a strain on infrastructure and facilities, not to mention real estate demands, so much so that many people move north, making the West Coast (including Vancouver, British Columbia) a rapidly developing region of the world. California has Silicon Valley (featured in Mary Jo's second novel), and the Washington area has Boeing and Microsoft. Add to this mix some of the most awesome vistas in the world and you'll know why I often feel homesick. Yet I still could imagine a post-apocalyptic tale. That's not hard to do for many spots in the world these days. As Penny says, time will tell whether such tales remain fiction or become fact.

The poem at the beginning is an old one of mine, of course, not Ben's. It's amazing what you can find in old boxes in the basement (too many moves). But I didn't mind giving Ben credit.

No book is published without a good team providing expert help for the author. I would like to thank all my beta-readers and editors who helped me prepare the manuscript for submission, in particular Carol Shetler and Scott Beallis. Black Opal Books' excellent staff has been exemplary in their help too: Acquisitions Editor Lauri Wellington, Senior Editor Faith C., and Cover Artist Jack Jackson. Amanda Kerr of Bookbuzz.net provided her usual effective book launch marketing.

Last but not least, I want to acknowledge the great support and understanding of my wife and best friend. There are many reasons why I've been able to write so many books. She's the most important one by far. Her patience and love over many years has been a solid foundation for my creativity, whether in scientific research or fiction writing, as well as many other things in our long, rewarding life together.

Steve Moore
Montclair, NJ
February 2019

About the Author

Steven M. Moore writes sci-fi, mysteries, and thrillers, short stories, blog articles, and book and movie reviews. He has written many novels—two for young adults under the pen name A. B. Carolan—and his list of works includes four series. He also has three short story collections. His stories reflect his keen interest in the diversity of human nature he has observed in his different abodes across the US and in South America as well as in his Latin and European travels for work and pleasure. His interests include music, physics, mathematics, forensics, genetics, robotics, and scientific ethics. He also has an active blog where he now focuses on reading, writing, and the publishing business with articles of interest to readers and writers alike. He and his wife now live just outside New York City. For more details, visit him at his website http://stevenmmoore.com.

www.ingramcontent.com/pod-product-compliance
Lightning Source LLC
Chambersburg PA
CBHW060228100726

47907CB00003B/557